THE WICKED & THE DEAD

MELISSA MARR

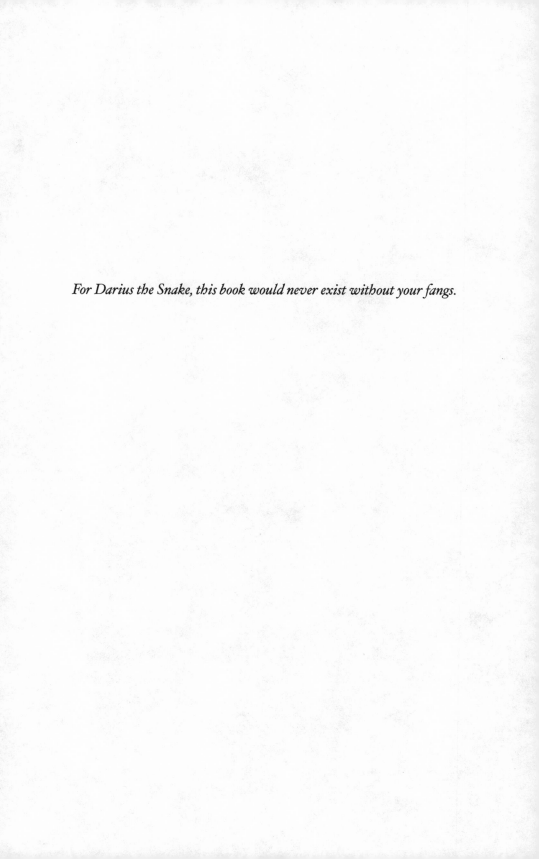

For Darius the Snake, this book would never exist without your fangs.

QUALITY CONTROL:

This work has been professionally edited and proofread. However, if you encounter any typos or formatting issues, please contact assist@melissa-marr.com so it can be corrected.

Chapter One

AUTUMN IN THE SOUTH WAS STILL BOTH HUMID AND HOT. NEW Orleans was always a wet city. Wet air. Wet drizzle. Beer soaked streets. *Other* things spilling out from behind trash bins. Sometimes, the heavy air and frequent rain was just this side of too much.

Most nights, there was nowhere else I'd rather be. We were a city risen from the ashes, over and over. Plagues, floods, monsters. New Orleans didn't stop, didn't give up, and I was proud of that. Tonight, though, I watched the fog roll out like a cheap film effect, and a good book in front of a warm fire sounded far better than work. The nonstop rain this month would wash away evidence of the things that happened in New Orleans' darkened corners, but I could prevent bloodshed. It was more or less what I did. Sometimes, I spilled a bit of blood, but if we weighed it all out, I was fairly sure I was one of the good guys.

More curves and sass than actual *guys*, but the point held. White hat. Dingy around the edges. I blame my persistent nagging guilt.

A *thump* on the other side of the wall made me pause.

Could I hurl myself over the wall into Cypress Grove Cemetery? It wasn't the *worst* idea ever—or even this month—which said more about my life than I'd like to admit.

I listened for more sounds. *Nothing*. No scrabbling. No growling.

I needed to be on the other side of the wall where tombs were lined up like miniature houses. The tree branches I'd used last time were gone, probably trimmed by someone who saw their potential. Now, there was no graceful way to hurl myself over the ten-foot wall.

Every cemetery in the nation now had taller walls and plenty of newly-opened space for the dead. Cemeteries had become "stage one" of the verification of death process. Honestly, I guess graves were better than cold storage at the morgue. The lack of heartbeat made it impossible to know if the corpses would walk again, and those of us who advocated for beheading all corpses were deemed callous.

I wasn't sure I was callous for wanting the dead to stay dead. I knew what they were capable of before the world at large did.

At least I was prepared. A moment or so later, I shoved a metal spike into the wall, cutting my palm in the process.

"Shit. Damn. Monkey balls."

A ripple of light flashed around me the moment my blood dripped to the soil. At least the light was magic, not the police or a tourist with a camera. While the laws were ever-changing, B&E was still illegal. And I was breaking into a cemetery where I might need to carry out a contracted beheading. *That* was illegal, too.

It simply wasn't a photo-ready moment—although with my long dyed-blue hair and nearly translucent skin, I was far too photogenic. I won't say I look like I've been drained of both blood and color, but I will admit that next to a lot of the folks in my city, I look like I've been bleached.

I fumbled with my gloves, trapping my blood inside the thick leather before I resumed shoving climbing cams into gaps in the wall. Normally, cams held the ropes that climbers use. Tonight, they'd be like tiny foot supports. If I were human, this wouldn't work out well.

I'm not.

Mostly, I'd say I am a witch, but that is the polite truth. I am more like witch-with-hard-to-explain-extras. That smidge of blood I'd spilled was enough to send out "wakey, wakey" messages to whatever corpses were listening, but the last time I'd had to bleed for them to rest again, I'd needed to shed more than a cup of blood.

I concentrated on not sending out a second magic flare and continued to insert the cams.

Rest. Stay. I felt silly thinking messages to the dead, but better silly than planning for excess bleeding.

At least this job *should* be an easy one. My task was to find out if Alice Navarro was again-walking or if she was securely in her vault. I hoped for the latter. Most people hired me to ease their dearly departed back in the "departed" category, but the Navarro family was the other sort. They missed her, and sometimes grief makes people do things that are on the wrong side of rational.

My pistol had tranquilizer rounds tonight. If Navarro was awake, I'd need to tranq her. If she wasn't, I could call it a night—unless there were other again-walkers. That's where the beheading came in. Straight-forward. Despite the cold and wet, I still hoped for the best. All things considered, I really was an optimist at heart.

At the top of the wall, I swung my leg over the stylish spikes cemented there and dropped into the wet grass. I was braced for it, but when I landed, it wasn't dew or rain that made me land on my ass.

An older man, judging by the tufts of grey hair on the bloodied body, in a security guard uniform had bled out on the ground. Something—most likely an again-walker—had gnawed on the security guard's face. Who had made the decision to have a living man with no special skills stand inside the walls of a cemetery? Now, he was dead.

I whispered a quick prayer before surveying my surroundings. Once I located the *draugr*, I could call in the location of the dead man. First, though, I had to find the face-gnawer who killed him. Since my magic was erratic, I didn't want to send a voluntary pulse out to find my prey. That would wake the truly dead, and there were plenty of them here to wake.

Several rows into the cemetery, I found Alice Navarro's undisturbed grave. No upheaval. No turned soil. Mrs. Navarro was well and truly dead. My clients had their answer—but now, I had a mystery. Which cemetery resident had killed the security guard?

A sound drew my attention. A thin hooded figure, masked like they were off to an early carnival party, stared back at me. They didn't move like they were dead. Too slow. Too human. And *draugar* weren't big on masks.

"Hey!" My voice seemed too loud. "You. What are you . . ."

The figure ran, and several other voices suddenly rang out. Young voices. Teens inside the cemetery.

"Shit cookies!" I ran after the masked person. Who in the name of all reason would be in among the graves at night? I ran through the rows of graves, looking for evidence of waking as I went.

"Bitch!"

The masked figure was climbing over the wall with a ladder, the chain sort you use in home fire-emergencies. Two teens tried to grab the person. One kid was kneeling, hand gripping his shoulder in obvious pain.

And there, several feet away, was Marie and Edward Chevalier's grave. The soil was disturbed, as if a pack of excited dogs had been digging. The person in the mask was not the dead one in the nearby grave. There *was* a recently dead *draugr*.

And kids.

I glanced back at the teens.

A masked stranger, a dead security guard, a *draugr,* and kids. This was a terrible combination.

The masked person dropped something and pulled a gun. The kids backed away quickly, and the masked person glanced at me before scrambling the rest of the way over the wall—all while awkwardly holding a gun.

"Are you okay?" I asked the kids, even as my gaze was scanning for the *draugr*.

"She stabbed Gerry," the girl said, pointing at the kid on the ground.

The tallest of the teens grabbed the thing the intruder dropped and held it up. A syringe.

"She?" I asked.

"Lady chest," the tall one explained. "When I ran into her, I felt her—"

"Got it." I nodded, glad the intruder with the needle was gone, but a quick glance at the stone by the disturbed grave told me that a fresh body had been planted there two days ago. That was the likely cause of the security guard's missing face. I read the dates on the stone: Edward was not yet dead. Marie was.

I was seeking Marie Chevalier.

"Marie?" I whispered loudly as the kids talked among themselves. The last thing I needed right now was a *draugr* arriving to gnaw on the three dumb kids. "Oh, Miss Marie? Where are you?"

Marie wouldn't answer, even if she had been a polite Southern lady. *Draugr* were like big infants for the first decade and change: they ate, yelled, and stumbled around.

"There's a real one?" the girl asked.

I glanced at the kids. I was calling out a thing that would *eat* them if they had been alone with it, and they seemed excited. Best case was a drooling open-mouthed lurch in my direction. Worst case was they all died.

"Go home," I said.

Instead they trailed behind me as I walked around, looking for Marie. I passed by the front gate—which was now standing wide open.

"Did you do that?" The lock had been removed. The pieces were on the ground. Cut through. Marie was not in the cemetery.

Shaking heads. "No, man. The ladder the bitch used was ours."

Intruder. With a needle. Possibly also the person who left the gate open? Had someone wanted Marie Chevalier released? Or was that a coincidence? Either way, a face-gnawer was loose somewhere in the city, one of the who-knows-how-many *draugar* that hid here or in the nearby suburbs or small towns.

I pushed the gates closed and called it in to the police. "Broken gate at Cypress Grove. Cut in pieces."

"Miss Crowe," the woman on dispatch replied. "Are you injured?"

"No. The *lock* was cut. Bunch of kids here." I shot them a look. "Said it wasn't them."

"I will send a car," she said. A longer than normal pause. "Why are *you* there, Miss Crowe?"

I smothered a sigh. It complicated my life that so many of the cops recognized me, that dispatch did, that the ER folks at the hospital did. It wasn't like New Orleans was *that* small.

"Do you log my number?" I asked. "Or is it my voice?"

Another sigh. Another pause. She ignored my questions. "Details?"

"I was checking on a grave here. It's intact, but the cemetery gate's busted," I explained.

"I noted that," she said mildly. "Are the kids alive?"

"Yeah. A person in a mask tried to inject one of them, and a guard inside is missing a lot of his face. No *draugr* here now, but the grave of Marie and Edward Chevalier is broken out. I'm guessing it was her that killed the guard."

The calm tone was gone. "There's a car about two blocks

away. You and the children—"

"I'm good." I interrupted. "Marie's long gone, I guess. I'll be sure the kids are secure, but—"

"Miss Crowe! You don't know if she's still there or nearby. You need to be relocated to safety, too."

"Honest to Pete, you all need to worry a lot less about me," I said.

She made a noise that reminded me of my mother. Mama Lauren could fit a whole lecture in one of those "uh-huh" noises of hers. The woman on dispatch tonight came near to matching my mother.

"Someone *cut* the lock," I told dispatch. "What we need to know is why. And who. And if there are other opened cemeteries." I paused. "And who tried to inject the kid."

I looked at them. They were in a small huddle. One of them dropped and stomped the needle. I winced. That was going to make investigating a lot harder.

Not my problem, I reminded myself. I was a hired killer, not a cop, not a detective, not a nanny.

"Kid probably ought to get a tox screen and tetanus shot," I muttered.

Dispatch made an agreeing noise, and said, "Please try not to 'find' more trouble tonight, Miss Crowe."

I made no promises.

When I disconnected, I looked at the kids. "Gerry, right?"

The kid in the middle nodded. White boy. Looking almost as pale as me currently. I was guessing he was terrified.

"Let me see your arm."

He pulled his shirt off. It looked like the skin was torn.

"Do not scream," I said. My eyes shifted into larger versions of a snake's eyes. I knew what it looked like, and maybe a part of me was okay with letting them see because nobody would believe them if they did tell. They were kids, and while a lot had changed in the world, people still doubted kids when they talked.

More practically, though, as my eyes changed I could see in a way humans couldn't.

Green. Glowing like a cheap neon light. The syringe had venom. *Draugr* venom. It wasn't inside the skin. The syringe was either jammed or the kid jerked away.

"Water?"

One of the kids pulled a bottle from his bag, and I washed the wound. "Don't touch the fucking syringe." I pointed at it. "Who stomped on it? Hold your boot up."

I rinsed that, too. Venom wasn't the sort of thing anyone wanted on their skin unless they wanted acid-burn.

"Venom," I said. "That was venom in the needle. You could've died. And"—I pointed behind me—"there was a *draugr* here. Guy got his face chewed off."

They were listening, seeming to at least. I wasn't their family, though. I was a blue-haired woman with some weapons and weird eyes. The best I could do was hand them over to the police and hope they weren't stupid enough to end up in danger again tomorrow.

New Orleans had more than Marie hiding in the shadows. *Draugr* were fast, strong, and difficult to kill. If not for their need to feed on the living like mindless beasts the first few decades after resurrection, I might accept them as the next evolutionary step. But I wasn't a fan of anything—mindless or sentient—that stole blood and life.

Marie might have been an angel in life, but right now she was a killer.

In my city.

If I found the person or people who decided to release Marie —or the woman with the syringe--I'd call the police. I tried to avoid killing the living. But if I found Marie, or others like her, I wasn't calling dispatch. When it came to venomous killers, I tended to be more of a behead first, ask later kind of woman.

Chapter Two

As far as I knew, I was the only person in all of New Orleans who offered *draugr* services. Ours was one of the proclaimed havens for the again-walkers. We rebuilt after losing ground to a series of hurricanes and fires about eighteen years ago. For us, rebuilding required tourists, so New Orleans had decided to embrace the dead, which was unheard of for a smaller city, but we weren't just *any* city. We had a history with the dead and with magic.

Elsewhere in the world, only the large cities had been so accepting of *draugr*. New York and London. Prague. Berlin. Lima. Moscow. Manila. Sydney. Rome. Cape Town. Tokyo. Vancouver. The reveal of the *draugr* spanned continents, cultures, and races. Admittedly, conservatives claimed the larger cities only accepted them as a ploy to thin their populations, but I figured it was simply impossible to ferret the *draugr* out in such vast cities. Why start a losing war?

Despite the romanticized attitudes of some people, *draugr* were not the sparkling angsty vampires of popular fiction. They weren't crypt-napping, bat-transforming, cape-wearing creatures of the classic stories either. They were creatures out of mostly forgotten Icelandic folklore. Modern people, injected with a venom that had peculiar bio-magical traits, woke and eventually carried on as if they were alive.

It was the decade-plus gap between waking and clarity that was the main issue.

The youngest ones had no ability to control their hunger—or their venom. Whatever rules defined the *draugr*, they had a fail-safe: venom from a creature under a century old was unable to infect the living. Enough venom from any of the older *draugr* and a person woke up after death.

I stopped them when they did so. It was my *raison d'être*. And I was damn good at it. I was vague on the right terminology, but the meat of it was that magically reassembled corpses would push their way out of their tombs and follow me like a ghastly second-line parade. All the foot-shuffling, but none of the jazz.

These days, though, I mostly just killed *draugr*.

"Alive," I texted to Eli. I've rejected his help the past few months, but we have a peculiar friendship. He was—for reasons I had no desire to know—living in this world, although he had more than enough fae blood to cross over to *their* world any day he chose. Instead, he stayed in New Orleans.

"Headed to Karl's," I sent in a group text to my other three closest friends.

That text was more of a formality than anything. Most nights, I met my very human friend Sera at her work if she was finishing when it was already dark. We'd been friends for years, and despite her insistence that she was perfectly fine, it took only a few minutes out of my week. I'd spend almost as long worrying, anyhow.

The walk was almost four miles, so after a quick scan to be sure it was safe, I let myself *flow*. I was careful not to do it around my friends—or most people. Seeing a living person move like a *draugr* would raise questions I preferred not to address.

Tonight, I covered a couple miles in mere moments.

I slowed before I reached the dense tourist section that was the French Quarter, but the streets were mostly empty at this hour. Curtains were drawn. A few cars passed. The government of New Orleans bought cars and hired drivers, as well as built walls to protect our beautiful cemeteries—and by extension, both the tourists and locals.

I walked along Lafitte, heading toward the French Quarter.

My phone buzzed. Eli texted, "Injured?"

"No," I texted back. I paused and added, "Thanks."

Before the fateful day when the world discovered that not every dead thing was a cause for mourning, tourists were still strolling day and night. They dropped their dollars at strip clubs and restaurants and marveled at Mardi Gras. A century or so before all that, they came in droves to visit the city with the first ever legal red-light district. My city was and had been all about tourism for almost as long as we were here. Ours was a bold cry: Come, come to our swamp, and leave your money with us.

These days, tourism is more of a daylight activity or restricted to the patrolled zones. Fifteen years ago, after the first international news incident from our city—"Handsome Young German Ripped Apart on Bourbon Street"—the wise souls with marketing minds reconsidered their approach to drawing tourist dollars. We were and are still dead-friendly, but the city added even more taxes to pay for increased police to patrol the still-flourishing tourist area and played up the "vampire" aspect as if *draugr* were the same thing.

They aren't. *Draugr* are reptilian, cold-blooded, and venom-spewing.

But the allure of immortality was strong—as long as you didn't think about years of drooling, biting, growling existence or an eternity with the urge to tear throats out. I didn't get it, but death tourists came to New Orleans hoping to see a *draugr* either for the fantasy of eternity or the titillation of being close to a predator. They roamed close to the perimeter of the patrolled areas in hopes of spying something grisly—safely seen through the lenses of their over-priced cameras.

Tonight, I was far too aware of the blood on my trousers to want to get near the tourists. Even now, the group I'd been trailing was moving around obstacles almost as one entity. They were almost to the French Quarter, the section of my fair city that was so heavily patrolled that tourists could still feel secure in the dark. Post-Reveal, the Quarter had become a tight clutch of stores, bars, and restaurants. Busking musicians worked every intersection. Neon and crowds filled every space so there was no chance of shadows that could hold fanged surprises.

I'd reached the well-patrolled greenspace of Louis Armstrong Park, so I sped up and passed the tourists. They were safely in sight of the patrols, and I was late to meet Sera.

"She's armed," one said in that shocked way as I passed.

Of course I was armed. Necromancy was terribly alluring to things that had been—and honestly, still were—dead. Night or day, I felt far more at ease with weapons in reach. I'd walk naked in the city before I'd go unarmed. Long before the rest of the world knew that the night held surprises with sharp fangs, I was watching in the shadows.

As I walked, I slid between another tour group and a double-parked car to avoid ending up in a photo. The first "blue-haired ghost" image to go viral was enough lesson for a lifetime. I wasn't a ghost. I was a witch with oddly pale skin.

Several street patrol officers standing on corners met my gaze as I passed, and I gave a small nod each time. Our silent conversations, inquiries on if there were any *draugr* nearby, were reason enough to escort a few tourist groups. I wasn't really guarding the tourists, just traveling in the same direction. I wasn't even actively looking for trouble. If I happened to get to behead a *draugr* along the way to the patrolled zone, it was just a cherry on my evening.

Better me than one of the officers who wasn't innately equipped for combat.

My phone buzzed. Eli texted, "I'm available if you want me."

I smiled, despite my better judgment. There were plenty of things I might want from Eli, a few of which made regular appearances in my dreams. But I also knew what Eli wanted—and needed—out of life, and I could never give it to him.

I shoved my phone in my jacket pocket and sent out a pulse of magic, feeling for *draugr.* They registered as blanks in the canvas, spaces where there was no life, but somehow motion. At best, I usually could scan a couple blocks. Considering the speed at which they moved, that offered a blink of warning. Not always enough, even for me. It was still more than humans got.

I felt nothing, so I darted around the line trying to get into Karl's Cajun Coffee. I waited for Sera to notice me. The line extended far enough that I knew she wouldn't be ready for a good fifteen minutes. It was her shop, and she never left when her staff was this deep in the weeds. Like Karl, the original owner, she was devoted to both her staff and the brand's recognition.

I went to the tiny staff bathroom, changed out of my bloodied trousers and into the back-up pair I'd stored there. I kept a change of clothes at my friends' homes, as well as Sera's coffee shop. My job made that a necessity. The blood would probably come out of these just fine, so I bagged them and went back out to the shop.

"Behind you," I murmured several times as I went behind the counter and poured myself a cup of black coffee.

Grumbles from the line faded when I slid into a recently emptied chair and put my sheathed sword on the table in front of me. I wasn't threatening anyone, but I didn't feel like listening to their bitching. I took my "payment" for protecting Sera in endless cups of quality coffee. It was the only way Sera tolerated my overprotectiveness.

So, I sat and watched her charm the wary and weary with the

sort of grace I'd never have. Sera was a striking mix of curves and bold features. Average height. A voice like warm honey. If I was anywhere near her type, I suspected that the one night we'd spent together in college would've become a habit, but as she politely pointed out back then, she was looking for love, and I was looking for sex. That detail hadn't changed.

Since that night, five years ago, I no longer slept with friends because the risk of ruining a friendship had been made crystal clear to me then. I couldn't risk losing someone precious to me again. Honestly, over the years since, it hadn't even been a complicated choice—until Eli. He was about as subtle as a rock to the head.

I re-read Eli's texts while I sipped delicious chicory coffee and waited on Sera to decide she could leave guilt-free.

A buzz of incoming messages pulled me away from considering bad decisions. Another job offer? That was the third one this month. Typically, I averaged only one a month. Sometimes, I had two. Three was unheard of, and three within the first ten days was worrying. I hated to do it, but maybe I should give in and get back-up. I opened my text log with Eli and considered what to say.

"You okay, Gen?" Sera was beside me, coat and bag in hand. Usually, I was on my feet before she was there.

"Sorry." I held my phone up. "Work stuff."

She gave me the pinched look that she always did about my job, but she nodded. I didn't miss the look she shot at the trash bag next to me. She handed me a more subtle canvas grocery bag, where I shoved my trash bag of bloody trousers.

"I'm okay," I assured her.

We were silent as we left Karl's together. Knowing the little she did about what I did, she was obviously worrying. It was what she did.

Carefully, I offered, "I fell. They were just dirty."

"A fight?"

"No." I smiled, and then, trying to sound lighter, I added, "Fell after going over a wall."

As I escorted her to the safety of her car, I wished I hadn't mentioned work. It was hard to explain to her why I did what I did for pay. Sure, removals paid well, but most people stayed clear of the kind of danger I hurtled myself into monthly. Sera, like the rest of my friends, didn't know I was uniquely qualified to do this job. If I told her about the masked woman with the syringe or the kids in the graveyard, that would take her worry from its usual level to lecture-land.

"You know, Jesse could use help at the bookstore," she said as she opened her car door.

"What about you?" I teased, trying to shift to anything but lectures or anxiety. "Need a barista?"

Sera sighed in that put-upon way of hers. The last time I tried to help her, serving coffee and pastries to customers, she'd come near to punching me. Often. Sera wasn't violent, but I was apparently lousy at customer service.

"Honestly? If you were serious, I'd cope, Gen. I don't like you risking yourself. There are options. Just think about—"

"Darling, I love all of you guys, but we would hate each other if we mixed business and friendship."

Another sigh. "You're being careful, though, right? I mean it, Geneviève! I don't know why you take these *murdering* jobs, but . . . I worry."

I melted just a little. All three of my very human close friends —Sera, Christy, and Jesse—worried about me. Christy coped by stopping to watch me train sometimes. Jesse nagged and lectured. Sera fussed and plotted to convince me to choose a safer path.

"*Draugr* are already dead," I reminded her softly.

"Obviously not or you wouldn't be out acting like some ancient warrior with a damned sword," she muttered.

I squeezed Sera's hand. "I'll do better. Don't worry."

Sera nodded, closed her door, and drove away while I watched.

She and I were both businesswomen, even if she would really prefer my business was just about anything else. We are what we are, though, and what I am is good at killing. That didn't mean I should be careless, though.

It was time to face Eli.

Chapter Three

Rather than send another text, I headed straight to Eli's bar. If I couldn't handle seeing him one-on-one, we sure as fuck weren't doing a job together. I'd refuse the job if I had to.

I made my way to the edge of the Marigny which had more or less merged with the quarter. The area between the tourist heavy French Quarter and Frenchmen Street used to be prime biting— or mugging—territory. Now, that space was filled with shops, so the safe area extended to the bars on Frenchmen Street. The whole quarter, the edge of the CBD, and the edge of the Marigny were all included in the area where the police were present. Once you were in the patrolled zone, you were safe.

Getting in or out of patrolled zones required a car—or the willingness to risk a biter.

New Orleans, and most *draugr*-friendly cities, had adjusted to a new reality that meant no more unregulated car services. In New Orleans, if you wanted to get to the patrolled pockets in the Garden District, the Marigny, or Treme, you used the city app to summon a car. The city police would also give lifts if they could, moonlighting as drivers for tips. Driving was a lucrative job, and the drivers' unions had the power to influence laws in many cities.

During the day, the streetcars were safe, but at night, you paid or you risked your life. Some people still had cars of their own, but owning a car meant walking from building to parking. Only the desperate, the foolish, the poor, or the tourists walked at night.

"Crowe." The doorman greeted me as I reached the oddly named Bill's Tavern. He glanced around, expecting either trouble or my friends. When he saw neither, he frowned and said, "Boss didn't mention any biters hanging around."

See? Everyone knew what my job was. "I'm just stopping in to see Eli."

The doorman's expression went carefully blank. Months ago, the tension between Eli and me had twisted into a fight that most of the staff overheard—and remembered. I couldn't blame the doorman for the wariness in his expression. I'd given Eli plenty of space the past few months.

All the doorman said was "Go on in."

"You good on rounds?" I asked, trying to remind him I wasn't all bad.

The doorman frowned. "Boss takes care of us, Crowe. You'd have to ask him if supply is low."

I nodded. Eli bought stock of my special *draugr* bullets, despite the cost. He was much like Sera about his employees. Sometimes, with him, I thought it was cultural. He treated them like he was their liege-lord.

And he tried to protect me.

Over the last year, I'd realized that Eli's request for my help at Bill's Tavern was a ruse. Eli was strong. I'd seen him throw a rampaging *draugr* into a fence with enough force to shatter stone and bend rebar. Eli was trying to take care of me. He'd probably been doing it far before I noticed. Either way, I still killed monsters there and drank for free.

But, tonight, I wasn't there to drink.

I walked in, scanning for the fae man who plagued my dreams. He stood behind the polished wooden bar, low bar lights casting a glow over him that highlighted his ethereal beauty. No human was as striking as even the least of the fae. Even the horrifying ones had a strange charm that was undeniably memorable, a trait that was fae-beautiful even if it violated mortal standards for beauty. Eli was far from horrifying. His glamour tamped down some of his beauty, but either it didn't quite work on witches—or maybe that was my *other* blood.

Eli motioned for a bartender, and in a matter of moments, he was around the bar and in front of me. "Geneviève?"

"Eli."

"Are you injured?" He stared at me, as if he could find the source of the few splatters of blood on my jacket.

"It's not my blood." I met his gaze and added, "I fell on a wet corpse."

"Only you, petit four. Only you." He shook his head and motioned to his already-crowded bar as if it were a castle, and he was a king. "Come in. Drink with me."

Something about a faery inviting me to drink had me repressing a shiver. "I thought you were working."

Eli shrugged in a way that only a man like him could pull off: elegant, careless, and utterly telling all at once. That half-shrug of his was often to avoid discussions—usually for my benefit. "Vodka? Gin? Whisky?" he asked.

"Tequila?"

His answering smile made me remind myself not to flirt. Dealing with someone as fae as Eli had taught me the beauty of nuance. Of course, that led to me over-analyzing everything he did or said for subtle clues and declarations. It made me feel like a fool, but the more I analyzed, the more I realized that I *had* to do so with him.

"We got on well over tequila," he said, offering me the bluntness that he'd been practicing for me, just as I learned to read his subtlety.

I offered him one of his half-shrugs.

Eli laughed joyously. "Tequila it is, cupcake."

I went to an empty corner table and watched him. His features were sharp, more cut glass than Roman statue. His mouth made me think of a courtesan's lips, full and luscious, and somehow vaguely cherry-stained. The worst of it was the energy woven into his very fiber. As a witch, it called to me, whispering promises of magic I could have for my own. If I stared at his hair, strands too dark to be merely black, I could see stars, eternity, a universe I wanted desperately to touch. His skin was no better. I knew from punching him once that electricity to rival my own magic slid through his veins, and the only way I touched him now voluntarily was with more than one layer of material between us.

I swallowed my own surge of desire as he joined me at the table. A part of me wanted to intrude on his mind as I could with the dead. I could, theoretically, do that with living beings, too, but the few times I'd succeeded were sheer accident and left me with a blinding headache.

When I'd tried to intentionally read the mind of another person—Jesse and Sera both—I'd left them with a raging headache. That made honing my telepathy skills near impossible. Still, I caught stray thoughts, and with Eli, they were always about me or us.

I shoved the instinct to try to read him away, too. If I wanted to know what he was thinking, I'd simply ask. Truth be told, I knew he'd answer. The problem was my hesitation in letting him know I had questions.

He'd brought two chilled glasses, each with only a couple cubes of ice, and an unopened bottle of Casa Dragones Joven. I paused when I saw that.

"The whole bottle? What's the occasion?" I asked cautiously.

He poured, not glancing at me. "Us."

"How so?" I accepted my chilled glass of expensive, delicious tequila.

"You're here after a job. Alone. Tired. Blood on you." He stared at me, not yet drinking. "This means you would like my help."

"What if I just wanted a drink with a friend?"

"Then you would've gone to see Jesse or perhaps Christy," he said lightly. "Am I wrong? Is there something *else* I could do to please you, bonbon? Or are you here to resume our partnership? I'll say yes either way."

I lifted my glass. "To partnership."

"To partnership," he echoed, laughter barely hidden in his voice. Even if I'd hidden my desire, he still knew it existed.

We drank in silence for a moment. Honestly, such tequila deserved at least that much respect. Around us, the bar filled with a crush of people—more than a few darting admiring glances at Eli. I couldn't decide if I was feeling protective or possessive, but I sent out a jolt of accidental magic toward the room.

He refilled our glasses. "Should I ask what that was?"

"No."

He nodded. This was one of the many reasons I liked having Eli around—despite his need to repeatedly call me by some sort of dessert. In fact, I enjoyed his company enough that I pointedly hadn't asked why he did so. I was happier not knowing. Realizing how much meaning he layered into the mundane, sometimes I simply chose to wear my ignorance like a well-loved dressing-coat.

"So, Geneviève, what would you ask of me?"

"The job seems like a simple enter, behead, and exit." I leaned back and watched him.

"Stealth?"

"Lafayette Number One," I said.

Eli grinned. Sometimes, I thought he took too much glee in

helping me, and it made me wonder about his past. But I wasn't asking too many questions these days. Every job left me a little closer to exhausted, more than it should.

But as quickly as his amusement had arrived, it was gone. "You know I'll do my best. You have my word."

"I trust you," I reminded him. "You're a good fighter, too."

Despite the tension that had grown between us, Eli had never let me down. Honestly, that was part of the problem. He was everything I could want—if I wanted someone to keep.

"I am honored," he said with a dip of his head. His voice was rough, and that spoke volumes, too. Eli said no more; he simply finished his drink and stared at me.

I wondered again if there were nuances in our conversation that I'd missed. It wasn't like I could find a how-to book on navigating a complicated, sexually-charged friendship with a faery. And while Eli didn't broadcast his heritage, his fae nature was obvious.

When asked, Eli admitted to having "some fae." Calling him half-fae was like calling me "a little bit witch." Whatever his heritage, he managed to look like he ought to be in every glossy magazine, selling anything, promising everything. Instead, he was making promises to come out into the dark and protect me as we broke into a cemetery and beheaded drooling face-gnawers.

After a few more quiet moments, I refilled our glasses again. "Why do I always feel like I'm saying more than I realize?"

"Because, my lovely peach pie, you are a clever creature," he said mildly.

I shook my head. "That's not comforting, you know?"

Eli laughed and stood. "You will tell me when you need me?"

I wasn't dense enough to answer that remark, so I said, "I'll tell you when we're doing the job." I paused. "There was a weird thing earlier."

"In New Orleans? How would you notice?"

"Fair." I smiled. His love of our shared city was what we'd first bonded over. "Masked person. Possibly female. Attempted to inject *venom* into a kid."

"Unsuccessfully?"

"Yeah." I thought about the kids. When I was their age, I had the sense not to go looking for again-walkers and the skill to do it anyhow. "They were lucky tonight. . . but if you hear anything . . .?"

"Of course. I'll call you immediately." He took my hand and pulled me to my feet. "Shall I drive you home? Or are you going hunting?"

"As tempting as both ideas are, I'm going to call a car." I gave him a wry smile. "I think I need a minute alone to clear my head."

"If you must."

"I must," I stressed.

"Until we next meet, Geneviève." He nodded once, made a gesture to one of his omnipresent staff members, and then told me, "The driver will be out front momentarily."

"I can call a car," I objected.

He scowled. "And I can have you driven home."

It was going to be a *thing* if I continued to object, so I said, "I appreciate it."

"Of course."

For a moment, we stood there, not retreating, not advancing. Maybe it was relief that he'd acquiesced to my request for help or happiness that he'd be back at my side. Maybe it was simply joy that he was in my life when I was feeling so out of sorts. Regardless of the reason, I leaned closer and gave a light kiss in the air over either cheek.

"I'm joyous that we are back to this point," Eli said in a voice that seemed more appropriate for bedroom promises. "When you are ready to proceed further, I'm here."

No amount of logic could negate the images stirred by his

words in that tone. I swallowed and attempted to appear unaffected, but I didn't speak. I couldn't trust myself to say anything remotely blasé at that moment. The darkness in his gaze made it quite clear that I was fooling no one.

Sometimes, I hated the way he could make me tumble toward lust. Other times, I wanted to kiss him into submission.

Chapter Four

"This is a terrible plan, Geneviève," Eli stressed as we stood outside the locked cemetery a week later. "Even you must realize that."

I stared at the fence in front of us, sparing a glance for the ever-darkening sky. The moon wasn't winking at me yet, but sunlight was fast escaping. I'd met the widow. I'd made arrangements. It really ought to be simple.

"You always think my plans are terrible," I muttered.

"Would you like to see my scar from the debacle at St. Anne's, bonbon?" Eli reached down as if to unfasten his trousers.

"Only if you want to add a new scar, cupcake." I'd seen the wound when it was fresh. A *draugr* had tried to go for Eli's femoral artery. I lopped its head off while it was mid-bite, and the weight of the head tore a bigger hole. I still felt vaguely guilty about it. "Maybe you should head back. Being around me will lead to more scars sooner or later."

Eli laughed in a way that seemed at odds with where we were. "I am here with you, Geneviève, instead of safely ensconced in my tavern or home. Does that not imply a willingness to bleed for you? I would accept many scars to be near to you if that is the cost I must pay."

"That's sounding close to a vow, Eli," I warned as I walked along the fence, hoping I'd somehow missed the groundskeeper completing his rounds. "I don't want a vow."

"No vow, frosting," Eli said lightly. "Just raw truth. I have faith in your skill."

"Same," I admitted.

He gave me a smile. "But?"

"I'm exhausted, and we're behind schedule. And Marie Chevalier, the one that ate the security guard's face, vanished. I'm honestly not sure what to expect."

"And so, I am here to assist you," he said. "And, Geneviève, I have *dressed* for this outing. I even shopped for new trousers." He gestured to his black trousers, coat, and boots. He'd skipped a scarf. No elegant jewelry adorned his hands or wrists. "What do you think?"

I rolled my eyes as if looking at him was a chore. "You clean up well enough."

He flashed me a smile that meant he heard the things I refused to admit. "Only for you."

Tonight, he was wearing a black knit cap to hide the glimmers that were visible in his hair when my magic was in play. A part of me wanted to ask why my magic disrupted his glamour, but the rest of me remembered that asking about his secrets would mean sharing my own.

We stopped in front of the still-locked gate.

"Do you want a boost, gingerbread? Or shall we pick the lock?"

I shot him a surly look. "I paid for the gate to be unlocked."

"I see." Eli pointedly glanced at the very obviously locked gate. "Money well spent."

"At least it was a write-off as a business expense. Good for taxes."

"When did you start paying taxes?"

I shrugged and scanned the area. The sun was dropping, vanishing seemingly faster and faster by the heartbeat, as we stood in front of a wrought iron, silver-tipped fence. The groundskeeper was either late or gone. Give a man enough money to let you inside to kill a few dead people, and he had enough money to get out of town instead. I couldn't say I truly blamed him. New Orleans was a difficult place to live, and the life expectancy at graveyards was lower than in most jobs.

Still. . . the soft tinkle of a grave bell from the middle of the shadowed graveyard was proof that the family was probably right. I was there to check if my client's late husband, Alvin Chaddock, was awake.

If it wasn't him, someone else was awake.

Either way I needed to get in, do my job, and get out without detection. It was that or deal with the consequences of Chaddock's return. The dead man getting away meant no check, a potentially messy hunt, and awkward police station visits. No one wanted that.

The grave bell was jangling faster.

"Over?" Eli asked.

I studied the *actual* problem at hand: minor B&E. There weren't any better options. "Over."

I could hear my quarry inside the fence, and unfortunately, the delay in entry meant that I would have to deal with the security cameras, too. Lafayette Cemetery had invested in cameras that recorded everything after dark, as if nothing bad could happen during the daylight. The video was likely already recording the sounds of the corpse that verified that he'd made plans for an unhealthy afterlife.

"Ready when you are, butterdrop." Eli pulled on a pair of

thick lined gloves. Iron burned his kind—and touching me had other complications.

"Always ready," I said, because the reality was that ready or not, the dead would come, and what I was made me uniquely able to stand against the dead, whether I wanted to or not.

Destiny—even one created by your parents—was an inflexible jackass.

Chapter Five

THE SOFT TINKLE OF THE GRAVE BELL WAS QUICKLY BECOMING obnoxious as the deceased cracked the lock on their vault.

I circled the fence, looking for the best entry point. I wanted to avoid spending too much time walking through the graves, since the last thing I needed was an army of dead bodies animated to do my bidding.

"Here," I told Eli as I admitted to myself that the only way *in* was over.

After a quick boost from Eli, I hoisted myself up by grabbing the wrought iron just under the sharp points on top of the fence.

Eli, despite the metal being poisonous to him, practically vaulted over the fence. I had a leg over, and he was on the ground grinning. He reached up and grabbed my legs, so I slid into his arms.

Without so much as a smoldering glance, Eli lowered me to the ground and stepped away. "I hear it."

My sword was in hand before I could think, and Eli had moved away from the toxic metal as I raised it.

He gave me a strange look when I didn't send a pulse of

magic to find the again-walker I sought, but my magic had been like a malformed pipe these days. Sometimes, I tried for a trickle and ended up with a flood. Sometimes, I tried for a stream and received a few droplets. Better to use my regular sight.

I could hear the bells that were tied to the *draugr*, but I wasn't keen on standing still and waiting. I motioned to Eli, who followed with the sort of stealth that made me think of tigers or panthers.

We rounded a corner, and there, between a grave topped with a lamb and one with a weeping angel of death, was a *draugr*. The late Mr. Chaddock looked like his photograph, seventies and well-dressed, but he was still coated in soil and concrete dust from the vault he had shattered to escape. Logic wasn't present yet, and the newly perverted were hungry for any life they could drink. In time, he'd be genuinely sentient. Right now, he was a newborn who knew only hunger.

He lunged, moving with the serpentine flow that typically only came with age and experience. He was one place and then the next, faster than a newly arisen *draugr* had ever been. Something was wrong here. He was too fast for the newly risen.

I tugged on the magic inside my bones, as if it was a tangible thing that nestled in my marrow when unused.

To bind.

To hold.

Barely visible tendrils twisted around Chaddock's feet, holding him to the soil even as he tugged to tear free.

I whispered a prayer as I lifted my sword, and then added, "I am sorry for your loss."

Perhaps my prayers and words eased no one's pain but my own, but I still needed to offer them.

My first swing missed because somehow Chaddock was able to break free and *flow*. He should not be able to do that. He ought to be lumbering.

I heard Eli's muttered curse, as he shoved me out of Chaddock's suddenly-too-close reach.

Fear for Eli and for myself made me foolish. I *flowed*, too, and my magic flared into tendrils that would make Jack's fabled beanstalk look puny.

Then, I swung my sword again. My blade glanced off Chaddock's upper arm. I let more magic fill me, calm me, strengthen me. I hadn't ever needed it for the recently dead before now. I should not have needed it with Alvin Chaddock, but I did.

Inhale. Anticipate. Swing.

Finally, my blade slid through flesh.

"Dust to dust," I whispered in relief as I severed the head of the late businessman from his torso.

The head landed with a meaty sound, and the late Alvin Chaddock stared at my boot through once-more lifeless eyes.

Chaddock was mushier than most first-waking *draugr*, but he didn't drift into nothings like the older ones did. Eli and I now had a rapidly decomposing corpse, and we needed to redeposit him in his grave before it got too much messier.

Eli took a quick photograph for the client, and then he scooped the majority of the corpse into his arms, leaving the head for me.

"Should be about six rows back. Grave already disturbed. They said the stone was an angel," I said as I lifted the head by the short grey hair and followed. I was grateful not to need to take pictures. I understood the request for proof, but it seemed ghoulish to me.

Once we found the grave, I handed Eli the head. Then I unzipped a pocket and pulled out a few handfuls of salt. The salt could keep the dead out . . . or in. Here, I was hoping it would help tether Chaddock to the earth. At home, I lined every wall, window, and ledge with industrial quantities of salt.

"Hurry," I urged and ran toward the office.

This was always the hardest part of jobs like this: the newly dead were dispatched easily enough if you had the strength to avoid their ravenous bites. Most people didn't. For me, it was easier than falling into a refreshing lake. The danger for me was getting out before I woke the properly dead. They always felt my presence if I stood on grave dirt.

Tonight, that danger was worse. I'd actually used my magic in a field of dead. I could feel eyes opened in the soil. Ears listening for my call. They were aware of me. They were waking.

"Rest," I whispered to them.

Eli would be digging enough of a hole to put the corpse in the ground by now.

I broke the doorknob and let myself into the office where the security cameras were. This cemetery's security was handled by Abraxxas Monitoring. I exhaled in relief. They stored footage on site, not at a main hub, so I could access and delete the footage here.

I grabbed the talisman that hung around my neck and hoped I wasn't going to fuck this up. More magic near graves. It wasn't ideal when the dead were already waking. And for reasons I couldn't understand, my magic had been increasingly off the past few weeks. Simple spells resulted in extreme energy bursts. A minor summoning last month had woken an entire potter's field. As soon as I was able, I was going to have to see if my mother had any insights.

But it was either magic to erase the footage or stab the machine. One of those would result in fines for destruction of property if I got caught—and since I was *hired* to be here, someone knew I was on site.

Magic it was. I sent an electrical pulse into the machines and overloaded the circuits. I knew from experience that the most recent footage would be recorded over. I needed there to be no video of Mr. Chaddock's decapitation. Simple. Easy. Magic I could do before I was old enough to get a period.

Tonight, however, my magic was not listening to my will.

Again. The simple electrical surge flashed into a purple flare that radiated outward. I felt the knot holding my hair in place vanish. Tendrils lifted, as if the magic made the air around me lighter. I knew without a mirror that my eyes had changed, too. They were my father's reptilian eyes. The only thing he'd ever done for me was accidentally augment the magic I inherited from my witchy mother. My vision shifted as I saw trails of energy, the whispers of deaths, and—if I looked—I'd see the auras of anything living.

I felt bodies in the soil stirring, shifting, rising.

I'd used far, far more magic than I'd intended to summon.

"Shit. Double shit. Shit balls!" I was out the door and running as the shifting forms under the soil grew increasingly restless.

"Eli!" I called, despite the need for stealth. If anyone else heard me, there were plenty of excuses I could give if we were all still intact. And I couldn't guarantee we would be if this energy kept growing.

I could feel hundreds of corpses listening for me and reaching out their hands.

Sleep! I urged them.

Their voices slipped through soil and stone, rising up on wind that should not be.

"Madre."

"Mere."

"Mathair."

"Mother."

Rest! I ordered.

"We come." Their voices tangled together into a symphony of affectionate whispers. "We *come* to you, mother."

"Eli!" I called again. I could see him patting down the dirt over Mr. Chaddock's grave. He glanced up.

"Now. Go now," I managed to say. "Dead. Waking."

His expression was one I rarely saw: shock. He was strong, but the dead were resistant to everything but time and magic. He could sever their limbs, and the arms would roll toward me and feet would hop.

"Go!" I repeated.

The dead heard my order, too. I felt them growing increasingly *together.* Flesh and muscles knitted together atop bones as my extra surge of magic gave them temporary life.

I heard them, creatures I had called to life again, calling to me.

"Mati."

"Moeder."

"*Rest,*" I said, spoke, thought, urged.

"We go. Go with you," they insisted.

Eli was up and moving, but so was the soil. Ripples moved as the earth looked suddenly liquid. Fingers, arms, and legs were poking through the roiling ground as plentiful as spring flowers. A roll of moving earth followed us as we ran to the fence.

"Don't stop." Eli cupped his hands for my foot. "Over."

I didn't argue. The best I could do was try not to let my sword hilt touch him. No steel should be on the pretty faery. He could handle it because he wasn't full fae, but it hurt him.

"Plug the energy, Geneviève," Eli urged. "Release it. Do *something.*"

I put my foot in his hands, knee against his chest, and hand on his shoulder. My breasts were at his face, and I looked down at him. Eli glowed like a small star had been sewn inside the shape of a man. With my magic, I could see that he was brighter than anything in the city.

"You're beautiful," I said, all but sighing the words.

"Now is *not* the time." Eli lifted me then, half-shoving me over the fence. "Go on, Geneviève. Over. The dead will come as long as you are in reach."

I couldn't speak around the voices that crowded my mind, but even in that blur, I knew I trusted Eli. I grabbed the fence and hauled myself the rest of the way over, despite the voices begging me to stay with them. The truly dead called to me in a way that was as close to maternal as I would ever be. I wanted to heal them, save them, swear to them that they would be okay.

I landed in a crouch outside the fence and waited. I wanted to run, but I couldn't leave Eli to be torn apart by creatures I'd summoned. I straightened and looked at Eli as he shook free of a hand that had grabbed his boots.

"*He is mine*," I thought at them, words surging on my magic. *You do not touch what is mine.*

The hand retracted.

"Yours."

"Be yours."

"Mother."

"Sleep, children. Sleep." My words were edging into desperation.

If the dead returned to their bodies at my whispers, they were souls caught in some midway point where they were neither alive nor in an afterlife. They had something to share, some task to finish, and I wasn't sure if that task was making amends to someone else who was dead or avenging their own murder. I could spend an eternity trying to shepherd the souls that lingered —or I could chain them to my will. I opted to do neither.

I had nowhere to house a home full of walking dead. I hadn't quite mastered taking care of my cat reliably, and somehow, I was fairly sure that taking care of the dead wasn't going to be as easy as installing a cat door.

I could see hands and heads pushing through the soil nearest the fence as Eli scaled the fence. My magic animated them, and if they stayed near me, their hearts would beat again, their lungs would draw air, and they'd follow my orders and--if possible-- they'd settle their own unfinished business.

But if I left, they'd drop back to their graves, as if the soil was reclaiming them. I just needed to get out of range.

Once he was beside me, I took Eli's gloved hand in mine and

began to run. The further we went, the more the voices lowered to whispers.

We stopped two blocks away.

"What just happened?" Eli asked quietly.

"He was stronger than he should have been," I pointed out. "I needed excess grave magic."

"And it slipped?"

I nodded. Talking about my inability to harness my own energy wasn't going to lead to a calmer me. I needed to relax.

"Any *draugr* nearby?" Eli asked after a longer than normal pause.

I sighed and listened. Of course there were: The sun had set, and the reawakened were always around in New Orleans. I just didn't know how many yet, so I sent out a gentle "hello, dead things" message with a surge of my excess magic, directing some of the energy I had summoned into a wave I scattered for an eight-block radius.

"Three? Four?" I waved my hand in the general direction of the corpses. "Two are together. The others are solo."

"I can take you to safety," Eli offered.

"Lead the way." I drew my sword. Walking after dark in New Orleans was always risky. Doing it with my particular allure for the dead was often an adventure. Tonight, though, with grave energy radiating from me, it was dangerous.

"As you command, truffle."

I rolled my eyes, but followed my sometimes-partner as he led us to whatever safehouse he'd undoubtedly located.

Chapter Six

I WATCHED FOR THE DEAD AS WE WALKED. I FELT THEM LESS
and less as I locked my magic in tightly. Corpses ambling after me
wasn't on my to-do list, and as much as I was okay killing more
draugr, I was exhausted already, and everything felt like too much.
My magic being off meant that scents were growing harder to
ignore. I'd always brewed a few concoctions to keep them muted,
but lately, it wasn't enough. Cigars, pot, or woodsmoke couldn't
be muted. I guess it was a generic fire awareness—which, considering how often witches were put to the flame in history, might
not be a bad thing.

Tonight, the scent of smoke from recent cigars mixed with
the vaguely wet smell of city streets. No earthy scents of recent
dead. Nothing alarming. I exhaled loudly in relief.

On the street, the dead could be recently gnawing, growling
shamblers or they could be powerful, elegant, and centuries old.
The older they were, the faster and more articulate they were.
And while Eli was stronger than humans, and I was capable of
feats I'd rather not broadcast, it was still risky to walk around

with my impossible-to-silence magic sending out a come-hither-dead-things beacon.

My body ached like my skin was too thin to contain me. That only happened when my magic was out of control—which was far too often lately. I needed to hold everything in check while watching for the dead. That meant that I didn't want to speak.

We walked about a mile before Eli stopped at a building in the Garden District that looked like it could have been one of the first in the city. A fence, stone not iron, surrounded a house that had the shimmer of old magic to it, as if the city was built around it, drawn to the echoes of power that the stones whispered. The house itself had no balcony or gallery, no porch or Ionic columns. It was almost so plain as to be unnoticed—which required magic in this area.

I glanced at him. "May I?"

He nodded, and I stepped closer.

I knew the moment I touched the exterior that it had fae protections woven into the foundation so securely that living in it was beyond my paygrade *and* whatever my future highest paygrade would be, too.

"What is this?"

"Be welcome in my home, Genèvieve Crowe." Eli bowed his head. "I offer you my hearth."

I paused. "Your *home*? I thought we were going to a safehouse."

"There is nowhere safer in New Orleans," Eli said. "The bones once belonged to my great-gran."

I reached out and touched the building again, placing both hands on the stone. As I did, I let another small pulse of magic slide from my skin into the wall. I really didn't need to have Eli's dead grandmother step out of the walls. I felt for bones, hoping they were restful and ancient, wanting them to be deep asleep.

Nothing answered my pulse.

I had no idea how old Eli was, so his great-grandmother's

death could have been centuries ago. Or perhaps she was full fae and wouldn't hear my call. I'd never woken the dead fae.

I pushed a little more forcefully, sending the grave magic out in waves that rippled and returned to me.

"No bones," I said lightly, still not entering the building. "Are they ground? Treated? Dust?"

"Bones of the blackhouse where she lived, cupcake," he said with a laugh threaded into the words. "Not *her* bones. What kind of monster do you take me for?"

The grave was still too close to my surface, or maybe the thought of being in Eli's house clouded my judgment. Either way, I asked, "Do the fae leave actual bones that can wake?"

"Gran was human." He opened the door and gestured for me to enter in front of him.

Peace beckoned as I stood in the foyer. The floor was marble so polished it could be glass. I couldn't feel its origin, but the wood under the bannister reached back to me as I slid my hand over it. I felt new shoots start to press outward, buds curling at the tips of branches as if they were feeling spring rains.

My eyes fell shut at the energy that still rolled through my blood. Pausing here was like finding a forest in the middle of the city. In nature, I could let go, send my magic into the earth. The natural elements here tempted me to do the same. Cautiously, I relaxed more—until I felt my magic brush against Eli.

That glancing touch was enough to make my body flush. He was the very opposite of the grave. I wanted to roll around in that. I let my energy move toward him, feeling my entire being burn at the nature that was contained in Eli.

"Geneviève," Eli said.

I opened my eyes to find him a moment from touching me. Up close, his eyes looked like tiny lights danced in them. I should have retreated, but I needed to know more. I inhaled, pulling the essence that was Eli into my body.

Hunger. Longing. Power.

"What do you long for?" I whispered, my hands on his chest, my body leaning into his, as if closeness would answer. Humans were easier to read. *Draugr* were probably easier. With Eli, I could feel magic pressing on walls that seemed impenetrable.

But I glimpsed *Elphame*. Elf Home. His world. It was vibrant and inviting, and I felt his longing. *Home.*

"Why not go home?" I stared at him.

After a longer than normal pause, Eli said, "Someday, I will tell you, but I would rather you know my secrets from my lips than stolen from my flesh."

I swallowed and stared at his lips. Unconsciously, I licked my lips.

A wave of desire rose up and crashed over us both. The longing was not just for home. He wanted *me* in a way that was equal to his desire to go home. "Me? Why?"

"Geneviève . . . you aren't ready to hear these answers."

I stepped back, jerked my hands away, and summoned my self-control. Maybe he was right. I didn't particularly like being told what I was ready for or felt or needed. I didn't like it as a child when my mother did it, and I sure as fuck didn't like it as a grown woman.

"Shall I tell you what I long for? What I *need?*" Eli asked in a voice that was thick with the same desire I'd glimpsed.

I took another step backward. At the thought of what he undoubtedly would offer if I said the word, energy surged out of me in a wave that rattled the ground under us.

"Or shall we drop this line of conversation?" he asked lightly.

"I can't. We . . . we cannot," I said, although I wasn't sure which of us I was trying to convince.

I wanted him. I doubt that anyone could be on the receiving end of Eli's charm and not consider it. Maybe if he spoke to me like he did to the women he took to the back room at the bar, or even if he offered the excuse that it would mean nothing, I could give in. He never gave me that, though. No fae-lies. No excuses.

He didn't move away like he usually did. "Many believe the fae are gifted in touch. Some even say that there is no magic to being faery-struck, simply the fact that no lover is as thorough as a faery."

Despite myself, I said, "Being faery-struck is a scientifically proven phenomena. Some mortals are simply overwhelmed and cannot return to *human* lovers."

He laughed and motioned for me to ascend the stairs.

"Are you admitting to being more fae than you claim, Eli?" I glanced back at him.

His laughter vanished, and he stared at me intently. "Would that change anything? My heritage? Or my secrets? Or perhaps my full disclosure? Is that your price?"

"Eli . . ." I swallowed and whispered, "You want something I can never give you."

"Do you truly want to debate this, Geneviève?"

I refused to answer, choosing instead to look away and continue up the stairs to the second floor of the building. This was a bad line of conversation.

"I can't do this," I admitted. "I can't lose you."

"And yet, I am *here*." He kissed the air near my face, close enough that I shivered. It wasn't just sexual. It was so very much more. And I knew then that he meant more than in my life. He was in my life, my world, my city. He was at my side.

Then he motioned me forward. That mask, the vaguely amused beautiful face, was back in place, but I saw the things behind it—and I was terrified. To be fae was to want a family. I would never have children. I knew what I was, and I could not pass that on. Not with Eli. Not with anyone.

Most of the time, that decision didn't hurt. With Eli, it did. Maybe it was his feelings that were making me feel this way. The image of being with Eli wasn't something I could allow myself. Not even for a moment.

Eli and I were connected as surely as I was to my two closest female friends and my oldest, dearest friend, Jesse. If I were an animal, I'd consider them my pack. If I were a regular human, I would think of them as my team, my squad, my family. All I knew was that they had my sword as long as I lived—or beyond if I stayed animate after death. They were *mine*.

Eli was mine, in the way Jesse and Sera and Christy were. He could not be more than that. I wasn't able to give that to anyone. I wasn't sure what I truly was, so attempting a relationship was out of the question—especially with someone I cared about too much to hurt by leading him on.

Best not to ever risk developing feelings at all.

Chapter Seven

I STOPPED AT THE SECOND-FLOOR LANDING OF ELI'S HOME. IN front of me was an ornate door, wood inlaid with silver and brass. To enter Eli's home required entry into the building—and I *had* noticed the formal words to lower whatever barrier the door held beyond physical—and now another door. Two doors and acceptance verbally. He had three points of opening simply to enter his home.

"Look back," Eli said lightly.

Behind us, his polished stair-railing was covered in buds and blossoms. It was chaotic and beautiful, but it interrupted the polished look of his foyer. I wasn't sure if I ought to apologize or expect gratitude. Either way, I felt awkward.

"It was an accident."

Eli gave another of his shrugs. "The magic must go somewhere. Best to fight or fuck it out, if not for its intended purpose." He paused until I met his eyes. "And you are unwilling to invite me to do either, correct?"

"Eli . . ." I had done well resisting him so far. Most of the time, we were better at being just friends, but just now, I had to lie, avoid, or run.

"You *can* leave, Geneviève. I will not stop you," he reassured me, speaking in that tone that said he knew and accepted my flight urges. "If you want to go, you are free to. There is no trap. I give you my word of honor."

Eli was strong enough to give me a better fight than anything other than older *draugr*. Most people had no idea just how physically strong the fae were. Even I hadn't realized it, and the excess power in Eli's wiry body made me question how well I'd hold up against a full-blood fae if Eli was no more than half.

"Don't do this tonight, Eli. Don't be so . . . *you* when I'm already energized."

He nodded, somber as he rarely was. "I shall not imply so overtly that I desire you."

"That's a very fae way to say that."

"If you want to speak without restraint, we will speak of everything. I will answer any question—or demonstrate. Say yes, Geneviève, and I will do anything you ask of me."

"No." I swallowed my fears for a moment, and before I could second-guess myself too much, I admitted, "I just . . . I can't. If you meant nothing to me, I'd already have taped your smart mouth shut and fucked you until we couldn't move. You know that, don't you?"

He stepped closer to me before the words were fully said, reaching around me to unlock his door. "You won't want my mouth taped when we are finally together."

I could have moved aside. I *should* have moved. I needed Eli's friendship. I needed the ease of someone who saw what I could truly do and still thought I was safe and good. I hid parts of myself from Jesse, from Christy and Sera, but with Eli I was more wholly myself than with anyone else I'd met in my life. I couldn't give that up, not even for what would undoubtedly be fabulous sex.

"If," I managed to say. "*If* we are."

"And if you were insignificant to me," he said hoarsely. "I'd have seduced you by now. I adhere to your rules, Geneviève, because you are important to me. But *when* we are, you'll wish you hadn't delayed."

We stood that way, me in the open embrace of his arms and him close enough that my magic wanted to surge into him, follow the air he'd exhaled into my hair back into his lungs, to know him inside.

"Don't." His words were barely a flutter against my neck. "If I must keep my words and mouth away from you, you cannot touch me with magic again. You've asked me to play nice. You must do the same, Geneviève."

His reaction to my magic exploring him seemed oddly dangerous. With most people, I did so as reflexively as asking their names. A quick scan told me what I needed to know.

Maybe it was different with Eli because of what he was or what we were.

I stepped forward, into his home, and said in the lightest tone I could muster, "Drink?"

Being in his home was new, but he made me relax and I treasured that. My magic felt erratic, and there was literally no one else in New Orleans who knew what could happen if I wasn't fast enough to contain my calls to the dead. Eli steadied me. He was strong enough to defend himself against many threats, and he had a knack for getting me to listen to reason.

"Vodka? Gin? Tequila?" He nodded to an inset to our left when we went further inside his home. Gleaming bottles, some so rare I wanted to stay right there and examine all of them, beckoned me forward.

"Damn."

Eli smiled proudly. "Perhaps a single malt? Wine?"

"All of it?" I looked at the options. There were bars that weren't as well stocked as his liquor cabinet.

I pulled my gaze away from the liquor and took in the larger room. Stone and earth. Light-blocking drapes—currently opened to the light of streets and stars. I felt the age in the building materials of the building. This was a structure with minimal steel, the sort of place even a full fae could visit comfortably.

"Your home is incredible."

"I've worked to create a haven," Eli said. "I am . . . happy to be in New Orleans, but I do like my creature comforts. I miss nature more than I expected. The courtyard here helps. Some of my interior architecture does, too."

"Could you go—"

"Home?" He gave me a wry smile. "To *Elphame?*"

I nodded, not sure if I had already crossed a line and afraid that the wrong move or word would shatter the moment. I felt like my entire body was in stasis, not breathing, no heart beating.

"There are obligations I would need to address," he said. "My uncle and I have an accord. I agreed to begin the process of fulfilling my duty on our next meeting. He does not ever leave *Elphame*. As long as I do not visit, the clock does not begin to tick."

"You're in exile." I stared at him. "I had no idea. I'm so—"

"Self-imposed. I have not been cast out." Eli gave me a fierce look. "I choose not to see my brethren. That is the choice I have accepted."

I couldn't say I completely understood. I could, technically, go to my childhood home. I could visit my mother, although I had to keep my visits short for her safety. And I had Jesse—who was like a brother—here with me in New Orleans, too. Like Eli, I had limited choices. I thought about home more and more these days. I couldn't live there, or even visit there long.

"I miss fields," I admitted. "I grew up in a space where the soil was clean. There were no surprise dead under the ground there."

He nodded. "But there are no places in the fields to hide your beacon from the unclean ones."

I accepted the ornate textured glass he offered, enjoying the weight of the heavy glass, and stepped back to the liquor choices. "The barriers my mother erected with her magic stopped working when I was eight. I woke most days to *draugr* and shambling, dead animals surrounding the house. My nature carried from root to stem, dew drop to stream."

"And they came." He poured himself a single malt. I knew what it was by the scent, although the name on the bottle was unfamiliar to me.

"We are both exiled in our way," Eli said.

I grabbed a bottle of tequila. "And not truly by choice."

"Let us drink then." He lifted his glass. "To exile."

We drank and stood in silence, both lost in our own thoughts. I considered asking for a bit of juice so I could actually feel intoxicated. Straight liquor was like water for me, nourishing and refreshing; the taste was simply a pleasure. No liquor I'd found would leave me drunk. Wine could offer a light buzz, but that required a full bottle. I didn't publicize that fact. I'd rather look like a bad-ass with a hollow leg than admit that booze wasn't limiting to me—but that *fruit* was.

"As my dear dead gran isn't in the walls to summon," Eli announced suddenly, "perhaps we could relax here until you are ready to visit the family. I have two showers and a pair of tubs. I will need one of the showers after carrying the deceased. What would you prefer?"

The appeal of sinking into a tub must have been obvious on my face. Eli led me to a room that seemed impossible, but so utterly *him*. Plants bloomed, and moonlight filtered in through skylights. The ground appeared to be grass. I bent to pet it.

"I'd ask that you wear no clothes or shoes past this foyer," he said. "Some of the plants are sensitive, and we were in the dirt and blood."

He motioned to a wooden cabinet. "There are clean clothes here. Identical to items you wear often."

"In my size? Or . . ."

"Yes." He said no more, but I opened it and glanced in. It wasn't as if he had many clothes, of many sizes or styles. Just mine.

"Eli—"

"I lack shoes for you, but . . ." He shrugged. "I was not expecting to need those."

"My boots are fine." I bent and removed them.

"Shower to rinse first if you want." He gestured to a marble rainfall shower behind plants. "However, the tub filters the water at all times. The controls are on the wall near it, but it is already at a temperature comfortable for you."

In the far end of the room was the largest tub I'd ever seen. It was cut of stone, and a small waterfall poured down the wall as if nature had been captured inside. It seemed more like an indoor pond. At least four grown adults could fit inside it.

I glanced at Eli, thinking about him joining me. "Where will you be?"

"Another room." He didn't respond to my look: no flirtation, no offers. He took a drink of his whisky and walked away.

When the door closed, I stripped and walked closer to the tub. At the bottom were massive smooth rocks. I sank into the already warm water and tried not to think about my magic's irregularities or the way I wanted to lean into my body's response to Eli.

I was going to drink and wash the gross away instead. I appreciated the way Eli looked and acted, and he appreciated something about me he was kind enough not to say. Ours was still a simple, clear relationship—which was how I liked everything in my life. Clear. Well-defined boundaries.

I just needed to figure out how to keep it that way.

Chapter Eight

WHEN I RETURNED FROM BATHING, DRESSED IN A NICER
version of my standard jeans and shirt, Eli was settled in at a
plush chair by the window, reading a tattered book of what
appeared to be Gaelic poetry. His hair was damp, and his clothes
were clean. I resisted the urge to remark on his reasons for having
clothes here for me, or even the fact that my magic was calmer
after having a few moments to find my own ways to take the edge
off the sexual tension I couldn't release with him.

"Better?" he asked. The question felt loaded, and I wondered
how much his fae senses told him—or if he just knew me.

I nodded. I was a witch, tied to nature, life, and death. There
weren't many of us in the world. The only one I knew well was my
mother. I'd met two or three others in my childhood. None of
them were particularly reserved women. Life and nature and
death were all raw, messy, and dealing with that didn't leave a lot
of room for being a prude.

My mother's version of the "birds and bees" was along the
lines of "witches who refuse their primal energy can't work magic

well." Nudity was natural. In this, Eli and I were pleasantly at ease. The fae weren't any more prudish than witches.

"I am calmer as well," he said with a rough voice and wicked smile that made me quite certain that he had taken the edge off his tension much as I had done.

And just like that, my needs were back. I walked over to the bar, grabbed another drink, and tried not to think about naked Eli.

I glanced at Eli, who had placed my weapons on a cloth on the floor beside the window.

"Do you have oil I could use? An old rag?"

"An *old rag*? For your sword?" Eli looked scandalized when he lifted his gaze from his book and motioned to the bottom shelf of a massive case. "There is a box in the bottom shelf for you. It is labeled."

"A box . . . for me?"

This time Eli didn't look at me. His eyes were fixed on the page as he said, "Weapon care supplies. Bone setting implements. Sooner or later, I knew you would be here."

He had left an opening to talk about so many things, and again, I was not going to take it. Silently, I walked over to the bookcase in question, and there was a wooden crate with a hinge. On the outside, in ornate script letters, were the words "Decadent Golden Cream Delight. Unwrap carefully."

I looked over at him, and he offered the sort of smile that said he was aware of my response even as I said nothing at all. I wished fervently just then that I disliked him. Hate fucks or casual fucks with him sounded better by the month. Sadly, he wasn't offering me those. Everything I would enjoy in a man was composed before me, but I had a lifelong "no relationships" policy. Casual sex was lovely. I had only two rules: no dead things and no serious relationships.

Cleaning my sword would take far less time than I'd like, especially since Eli had a well-stocked kit. All I truly needed was to wipe it down, and re-sharpen it. The box on Eli's shelf held oil, cleaning rags, cotton swabs for the grooves of the inlay, as well as a new whetstone. No unnecessary liquids or fluff that was sold to the unknowing fool. Aside from a spell sachet, the kit he'd prepared was exactly what I would have assembled.

Eli was damn good at the details.

Blood, especially *draugr* blood and flesh, would corrode the blade. Liquids weren't great for steel either, though. Even with effort and care, my sword would only last a year or so before replacement. Less if not for magic. So, I went through quite a few swords before I started infusing them with various magic.

I considered my weapons as I removed a bit of rotted flesh that had started to dry. I liked to use a two-hander, a single-hander, and revolver as my default weapons. If folks wouldn't look at me like I was vaguely terrifying and cross the street to avoid me, I might carry a halberd or even a battle axe, too. It might seem like overkill, but I liked to keep a good distance from *draugr* teeth—and venom.

The venom was what worried me.

Not every bite was one with venom; some were even "dry" bites—no venom injected and no blood taken. There was no way to predict that, however, and I had no idea what venom would do to me. In the living, it could kill. It could also reanimate. Enough bites with venom would turn a person. It was incentive for a lot of people to live behind fences, and it reduced the number of people willing to fight *draugr*.

It simply made me extra thorough. I could handle what many could not. I'd never come close to being bitten. If I did, though, I wasn't sure of the consequences.

Humanity had spent billions on injections, surgeries, pills, and every manner of way to deceive the eye and appear younger. Who knew that an old Icelandic magic was the answer so many people had sought? I didn't think a decade of ravenous mindlessness was worth extra years in the world, but *draugr* forgot much of their first decade or two. That was common knowledge. They were stumbling, mindless eating machines.

By forty years post-death, they were fully articulate. They were monstrosities, and I wanted no part of building a rapport with them, as some politicians and religions suggested.

If anything, they seemed more like reptiles. Cold. Borrowed heat from outside themselves. Hunted well in the dark. The only difference was that reptiles served a purpose in the ecosystem. *Draugr* were a blight.

Forty years into the reveal of the *draugr*, the laws were still struggling to make sense of what it meant. After a few years, they were sentient, but what was to be done between death and sentient minds? Do we let them rise? Do we have social services for the care of the ravenous? If not, were we saying eternity was only for the wealthy? The Re-Animation Advocates had already managed to ban cremation unless pre-planned, notarized in the year prior to death. This modification was valid for the next century "while the legality of life in the post-living is assessed." The objective, in theory, was to prohibit family members from undoing choices made by the decedent before passing.

The rest of the laws were in flux. What happened to inheritances when the dead were re-animated? Were prenups violated? Could a *draugr* own property? What about taxes? Do they owe more because they were still sentient? Or less because they weren't using the universal healthcare?

I would never find out firsthand. I glanced at Eli, only to find that he was watching me. He was the one I'd ask to kill me if I was envenomated. He could do it. He was strong enough to end my existence if I woke up shambling and trying to bite my friends. I just wasn't sure when—or how—to ask him to kill me if the time came.

Hey, Eli, could you kill me if I wake a draugr? I have money to pay you.

And now, I had a lot more than I used to with all of my recent clients. This month alone I'd had three wealthy businessmen. I finished cleaning my blade and was pondering the uptick in work when I felt Eli's gaze on me like a physical thing. He still held his book, but he was obviously not reading.

"Stop staring at me."

"After a job, you are different. It is an honor to see you so." He lowered his book, surrendering his pretense of reading. "I find myself wanting to procure antique weapons for your hands."

"I thought you weren't going to flirt."

He stilled. "I am *not* flirting, Geneviève. I am remarking that you are a warrior in ways that should be honored."

My hand curled around my hilt as if expecting the appearance of an enemy I could slay. Fighting made sense. Kill. Protect. It felt natural. I could summon an *army* of walking corpses. Violence was in my nature. That was part of why we could never be together.

I slid to the floor and boxed my cleaning supplies, my *new* ones that Eli had collected. Whatever he was offering, flattery of my work and useful supplies did more than all of his pastry-based nicknames.

I did not look away from the box's contents as I said, "I don't know the rules that will make our friendship work."

"I would ask that you tell me when you are panicking next time rather than refuse my aid." His voice took on a raw edge as he added, "I would be . . . not be well if you were injured, especially if it were because you are afraid that I cannot observe your rules. I will not force you to accept my affection. I will not plan to seduce you. You can rely on me."

I nodded once because I couldn't trust my voice just then. I glanced at him. Elegant. Handsome. No longer hiding his dark hair under a cap or under the magic he used to dull it in public.

I needed to focus on my immediate task: collecting for the

Chaddock job. Sometimes collecting was tedious. Retainers were easy. Fear of the dead motivates a lot of people. Afterwards? There were often excuses. People were, by their very natures, deceitful. They doubted my word. *Unlike the fae,* a traitorous part of my brain whispered. Fae things didn't lie outright.

"Would you accompany me to meet the client, Eli?" I asked as I returned the box to the shelf. He'd never accompanied me to meet clients before this, but it seemed foolish to exclude him. I had enough areas of my life that were off-limits to him. This one did not have to be.

He rose to his feet with a grace he never showed in public. "I would be honored by such trust."

"I do trust you." I cleared my suddenly-dry throat. "But. . ."

"You find me attractive."

I met his gaze. "Of course, I do. Are there straight women who don't?"

"I had wondered, since you have selected not to pursue the immense potential we have."

"Would it mean something to you? Personally? Culturally? If we—"

"Yes."

"Then, yes, I am ignoring the potential," I said carefully. "Be my friend. My right hand with my work."

"I will accept your terms for a fee."

"A fee?" I echoed.

"One kiss."

I shook my head. "Eli—"

"You know I am not human, Geneviève," he said bluntly. He had dropped whatever glamour he still had in that moment. His skin glimmered as much as his hair, as if he was cut from the rarest of opals. "You have offered a bargain to one whose *heritage* requires an exchange. Do not offer a bargain to a faery without expecting a term in exchange. I require a kiss freely given at the time of my choosing."

In some ways, his lowering of defenses and disguises with me was still more alluring than his words—and those were increasingly hard to ignore.

"Where?" I asked suspiciously.

He laughed. "Have you been researching bargains, bonbon?"

I felt the heat rise in my cheeks. "Which part of my body do you intend to kiss?"

"My fee is one, unfettered kiss here." His fingertip lightly brushed my lips. "You can release your magic if you choose, and whatever decisions you make at that point, I shall accept. Even if it is to use me thoroughly and then discard me."

"Eli . . ."

"You could satisfy your curiosity, and I would forgive you. I will still be here. I will never eject you from my life, Geneviève. It's an advantageous bargain," he tempted.

I licked my lips, tasting the honeysuckle sweetness that his skin seemed to exude. "Why?"

"Because I believe it will answer your questions," he said lightly. "And I believe that there is a not insignificant chance that I will gain at least one night exactly where we both want me to be."

I gasped involuntarily at the thought. "I accept."

We stood there close enough that I could feel the heat of his skin, and if he couldn't hear my heartbeat, I'd be stunned. I waited. After several years, were we finally going to kiss?

"Your deal is accepted," he said, and turned away without kissing me.

Disappointment crashed through me. "Clearly, I didn't do enough research," I muttered.

He chuckled. "At the time of *my* choosing," he reminded me.

I'd wanted that kiss, wanted to know if it would melt my mind as I expected it to. I'd also hoped—perhaps irrationally—that it would fizzle and the tension between us would disappear. One kiss and I could, maybe, move on. I was braced, ready—and, yes, damn it, I was excited.

Now he had the right to kiss me, and I had to either think about it constantly to brace for it or be caught unawares. Either way, I was fucked. I'd done as every human in history had when they made a bargain with a fae: believed I was clever enough to come out the winner.

But, in reality, I'd just handed him all the power.

Chapter Nine

We left Eli's place in a strange silence, and I was fascinated with how peaceful he seemed. Something I wasn't yet understanding had transpired. I wanted to know why the bargain calmed him—or maybe it was the promise of a kiss. Whatever it was, Eli was relaxed now, and I wasn't going to disrupt our peace by asking questions.

That silence continued as we took Eli's modified-for-fae car to Esplanade Ridge. The gearshift was like a barrier between us, and there was no backseat, but Eli's car was exceedingly comfortable with its leather seats and wood inlay. Somehow, he'd turned a machine into just enough nature to seem fitting for him and topped it with a powerful engine. I didn't know much about cars, but I knew there was a metric shit ton of magic woven into this one. Eli had explained in passing once--before I'd asked for help on the first job together--that there were ways to make steel tolerable—but that the cost was prohibitive. He'd paid for it at the bar and in his sleek blue car.

And it had done nothing to hamper the obscene speed he could get out of the machine as he darted around the taxis and car service vehicles that made up almost all of the traffic in the city. At this hour, they were scarce, though. His little blue convertible moved with a near-silent engine, unless Eli was in the mood to make it growl. The one time I'd driven it, I had such a fit of sportscar lust that I think I drooled. I'd never thought I was a car person, but I may confess to dating a man or three just to drive their cars after that day.

It didn't hurt that the car, much like Eli did, blended in with the sort of people who lived in the neighborhood we were visiting. I was relieved that he was at my side for this, as I felt out of place when meeting most of my clients. I hadn't grown up destitute, but I'd been raised with simplicity and nature. In New Orleans, most money meant layers of demonstration of their deep pockets. Houses. Cars. Clothes. Those who hired me typically were the sort of people I'd never otherwise encounter.

This row of houses was nothing but old estates, stately homes, or squatting palatial mansions that looked foreboding. It felt stifling. And I felt tense just being there.

"What do you need of me?" Eli prompted.

"Be charming," I said as we approached the gate to be buzzed into the Chaddock Estate. "The widow is young . . . with crocodile tears on command. She hired me because her *stepson* contested the will and filed a case of decedent rights where he would control the estate until his father could fully return to the company."

"So, the Chaddock son knew his father would rise." Eli's tone held all the same questions I'd had when I realized that detail. The dead could be safely housed, warehoused with medical personnel and feeding tubes. It was an expensive stay, but if money isn't an object, some families were all in. Accidents still happened, though, and people still died.

"The court filing was a prelim motion, an 'in-case-of-rising.' She was not to know it was filed, but . . ."

Eli shook his head. "So, the widow had her husband killed a

second time to keep from spending it on Transitional Care Homes."

"*Draugr* are not alive, so I didn't actually kill him." I shot Eli an angrier than usual look.

We didn't agree on this. Not truly. Newly infected *draugr* were dangerous enough that I questioned if these well-to-do medical facilities had any chance of success. They had been founded to drain the accounts of the foolish, and they employed the desperate. The pay at the T-Cell Houses was exceptional, but so was the risk of death.

"Maybe she had him returned to his grave, but that's not *murder*."

"I know your views, divinity."

"Divinity? How is that a baked—"

"It's a candy-fudge confection. Sweet and dizzyingly heady." Eli depressed the buzzer before I could reply and announced, "Ms. Crowe and her associate to see Ms. Chaddock."

The gate unlocked with a loud clank as I whispered, "I need professionalism toward me and charm toward her, as if you could see her as a paramour, but without being sleazy."

"Of course, Ms. Crowe." Then he added, "Later, I'll bake some desserts for you. That one is rich enough to make your neighbor's teeth ache."

I should be irritated with him after our bargaining, but I found myself smiling as we walked up a cobblestone driveway to the house. Gun on one hip. Short blade on my other. I looked like the wrong sort of woman to approach such a house, but at least I had charm personified walking with me. There was definite appeal in having a fae-blood with a devastating smile that I could use against my current employer.

A young woman with an impeccable uniform opened the door before we could reach out to knock.

"Ms. Crowe to see Ms. Chaddock," Eli said, as if announcing royalty.

The woman led us to a parlor that was ostentatious in the way that screamed old money and gestured at masculine posturing all at once. The heads of dead animals stared out through glassy eyes from wall mounts, and several smaller mammals were intact and caged under glass. The furniture—white, of course, and immaculate—was stiff and unwelcoming. One particularly atrocious ottoman appeared to be made of an elephant's foot. It was topped with thick gold tassels and a thin cushion. Everything in the room spoke of death and money.

"She paid the retainer, but she owes me the balance," I said, forcing my gaze away from the dead things on display.

Eli nodded once. "Yes, Ms. Crowe."

He met my gaze and then glanced to the mantle where I caught the flicker of light in the eye of a bear.

We were being recorded.

I noticed the moment Eli decided to make use of the camera.

"Ms. Crowe," Eli said for the camera, "I know you would dislike doing such a thing, but if the client does not settle her account, your particular magic would enable the deceased to rise."

I frowned.

With his back to the camera, Eli mouthed, "Agree."

"It seems wrong."

Eli smiled. The camera wouldn't know that I was referring to *lying* being wrong. He did, though.

Momentarily, the door flung open to reveal the grieving widow. Mrs. Chaddock was, at most, thirty. Her late husband was in his seventies. Such matches resulting from love were not impossible, but I had a suspicion that Mrs. Chaddock might have had other more motivating interests.

"Geneviève, dear, was it . . . did he, you *know*, crawl out of his vault?" The widow reached out for my hands and asked breathily, "Was it horrible? Did he smell?"

I'd met more disagreeable women, but it had been a while. Her shoes, jeans, and blouse were all high-end designers. I might not know the brands, but I did notice material and cut. The gems on her ears, wrists, and throat would pay for several *draugr* containments. The ring alone would pay for at least a year's worth of my work.

"It was painless," I said politely.

"So, my sweetness didn't suffer?"

Eli clearly had no patience for the show that the widow seemed determined to put on. He bluntly said, "Mrs. Chaddock, the deceased was *already* dead. Ms. Crowe simply guaranteed that he would stay that way rather than gnaw on your throat."

I shot him a scowl and mouthed "charm!" at him.

Eli forced a smile, and then he added, "And Ms. Crowe underestimates the difficulty of her work, due to her mastery of weapons and unique magic. I can assure you that she was in peril. I can further attest to the truth that had any other person been dispatched there, your late husband would have killed them. He was uncommonly agile for a newly turned *draugr*."

I couldn't decide if I was more flattered or irritated. I didn't like my oddity being noticed. On the other hand, I liked the way I looked in his eyes. Not a killer. Not a monster. A woman who was a warrior. It made me feel all mushy in my heart space.

But then the widow gave him an appraisingly look. "Is *that* what she told you?"

"It is what I saw," Eli corrected. "I was there to assist. Your husband was uncommonly violent. The newly risen are usually less aggressive, but he moved with speed and hostility."

"Truly?" the widow prompted.

"He was more agile than normal," I allowed. I tried again to muzzle my irritation, and I reminded myself that *I* didn't want to wake as a *draugr*. But the fact was that the widow was only fake mourning. It made me dislike her.

"I see. Violent. Fast. And we are all saved by the incredible Miss Crowe." The widow Chaddock was far from appreciative in her tone.

"You weren't in peril," I reminded her. "You were here in your gated secure home."

"And it's *Ms.* Crowe," Eli corrected with a smile. "Now . . . I believe you owe my employer compensation for her services. Do you have a check drafted to Crowe Enterprises? For the agreed amount?"

Mrs. Chaddock made a disgruntled noise, but she withdrew a check from her pocket and extended it to me. I hated this part. I didn't necessarily *love* the violence inherent in the service I offered, but it *was* a service. I did what I did because I was uniquely qualified to do so.

Eli stepped in and plucked it from her hand. "Let me handle this, ma'am."

He immediately pulled out a phone and pen, electronically deposited the funds into to my account. I'd agreed to the process because I hated accounting. Letting Eli sort payments out was far more efficient than my magnets-on-the-fridge system until I got around to visiting a bank machine.

"All done," Eli said, pocketing the already-deposited check.

"I had no idea you had a . . . what are you?" She stared at Eli, as if he was an insect that had crept into her mansion.

"I'm her associate." Eli smiled as warmly as he could. "I assist her in handling the parts that I am able to."

The widow sat. "But what *are* you?"

"Excuse me?"

"Look at him!" Mrs. Chaddock gestured at Eli. "He's gorgeous, but he's barely noticed me. He *must* be something inhuman."

Eli stepped closer to me.

"Eli is my associate," I said. "Why would his . . . ancestry *matter*?"

The widow sighed. "Alvin and I met at the Society Against Fae and Reanimated Individuals." She crossed her ankles primly.

"There was no way my Alvin would have allowed himself to be poisoned with *venom*. He was a lifetime SAFARI member."

"The Society . . ." I shook my head. "Are you seriously lumping the *fae* in with walking fucking corpses?"

"They are not human."

"But witches are fine?"

"I wouldn't have relations with one," the widow said.

My temper was frayed after the last week. My hand went to the hilt of the short sword at my hip .

"Cream puff," Eli murmured quietly, turning to face me and putting his back to the widow as his worry overrode professionalism.

"What?"

"No." He put his hand over mine on the sword hilt. "She has paid you. Our business here is done."

"Fine." I took my hand off the sword hilt, trying not to be grateful for the gloves he wore. Then I looked at Mrs. Chaddock and said, "He's a better person than you. Or me."

Eli smothered his smile and turned to face the widow. "Thank you for selecting Crowe Enterprises. We'll see ourselves out."

I attempted to motion Eli forward so he was in front of me, away from the widow.

"Hush, cupcake. I am not unused to fear." Eli's hand hovered close to my low back, not touching, but there should he need to stop me from turning back. "You will not get referrals from your clients if—"

"Fuck referrals." I met his gaze. Then I glanced at the widow. "I ought to summon your husband back from the grave and bring him to your door."

She blanched. "Can you do that?"

I pointed at myself. "Witch." Then I pointed at her. "Bitch."

Eli chuckled.

I wouldn't do it. The dead didn't deserve that kind of abuse. The widow Chaddock didn't know that, though.

We all have our fears—I was afraid of myself, and of dead things hurting my loved ones, but the fae were sequestered in their homeland. They didn't snack on humans, enslave, or otherwise injure people. They bought art, and they returned back to their own world where they were at peace.

Unlike humans who regularly hurt other humans, and *draugr* who ate them.

Chapter Ten

"Miss Crowe?" A man who looked at most a few years older than the widow stepped in front of me in the foyer. "Might I have a word with you?"

Eli glanced at his watch and muttered, "Does anyone in this city ever sleep?"

I grinned. It was coming up on 5am. Eli's bedtime. The joy of my genetics was that I knew what his watch said without asking. Just call me a sword-swinging sundial.

I released a pulse of energy. If the new man noticed me reading him, I wasn't concerned. He was a Chaddock or employee of them. So far, the two Chaddocks I'd met were a *draugr* and a bigot. I wanted to know what this man was.

The glimmer of my energy pulse was a bit more obvious than I meant for it to be, but I'd had a rough night. It made me sloppy. The young Chaddock would have a touch of a migraine soon. He paused and smiled tightly as my energy slid into his skin.

Human.

No magic. A touch of death that made me pause, but mostly,

he was simply an average thirty-something man in an expensive suit.

Even so, his family seemed rife with hatred. I met the man's gaze and asked, "Are you a member of SAFARI? Because if you are, I have nothing to say to you."

"No. That was my father's particular brand of hatred in his later years." The younger Mr. Chaddock extended a hand to Eli. "I do apologize for . . . Alice."

"Alice?" I echoed.

Eli shook young Mr. Chaddock's hand in silence.

"My father's most recent bride." He inclined his chin toward the doorway where the widow stood watching us. "We went to the same school, so calling her 'stepmother' would be awkward."

"Tres." Mrs. Chaddock's demeanor shifted noticeably. She sounded positively kind as she said, "I wasn't aware that you were here."

"It is my house, Alice."

"Of course. And it's my *home*," she added.

"According to the will," Tres said mildly, "it will only remain so as long as you are not a burden on his children. Do you suppose the court would consider murdering my father a burden on us?"

"He would not want to be a monster." The widow's pretty face darkened. "Someone injected him with that poison and—"

"I didn't do it, Alice. None of us did. We've gone over this. I want to know who did it, too, but you had him murdered—"

I raised my hands. "Whoa. Halt. *Injected?* Murdered?"

The man, Tres, rubbed his face as if he could wipe away his frustration. It was obvious that he was short on sleep.

"There was an injection site. The mortician who prepared the, err, body asked about it. I intended to hire a physician's team, as I wanted my father to be able to become sentient enough to tell us if he was freely dosed or if his death was a result of poison." Tres glanced at the widow. "And if he knew who did it."

"Don't you look at me that way!" The widow's anger revealed a thick rural accent. "I took good care of my husband. Day and night. *Every* need. And I would've kept doing so until his natural death."

Tres spoke over her, saying, "Dad was generous to a fault with every single one of his six wives. Housing, jewelry, money." Tres shook his head, and then he looked at me. "My father was a good man, Ms. Crowe and . . . what was your name?"

"Eli."

"Right. Eli." Tres smiled at him. "My father was a true romantic. He wanted to believe in love, and he married a lot of women over the years in search of what he had with my mother."

"Who hasn't made foolish choices for love?" Eli glanced at me, even though I made a point not to notice it.

Tres continued, "The widow—whichever one was the current one—was well provided for in the event of my father's death. Far more so than during the terms of the prenup."

The current widow turned on her kitten-heeled foot and walked away like a petulant child. "I did not kill him."

"Which time?" Tres asked. "With the injection or"— he gestured at me—"by hiring a killer?"

I wilted a little. Technically, I *was* a killer. It was, quite literally, how I paid my bills. That didn't mean I liked the implications of the word in this case.

No one spoke for a moment. The widow didn't defend herself, and neither did I. There was little I could say, and it was obvious that they had very different opinions on how to deal with the *draugr* issue.

Finally, Tres asked, "Would you join me in my office, Miss Crowe? Eli?"

After exchanging a look, Eli and I walked into the small, elegant room. Hard wood floors. A heavy wooden desk. A surprisingly comfortable brocade settee. Eli gestured to it, and I sat on the edge. He stood at my side like a guard.

The widow Chaddock attempted to follow us into the room,

but Tres stopped her at the door. "I'm sure you understand that this is a private meeting, Allie. After all, you've met with Miss Crowe without me. It's only fair."

He shut and locked the door, leaving an angry Alice Chaddock hammering on the door for several moments. Once she stopped, Tres sighed and looked at the door. "We each take shifts with the wives. We have since my mother passed on unexpectedly."

"How many—"

"Wives?" Tres grinned in the way of those who can either see the humor or develop bitterness. "My father *really* liked romance. Five wives after mom. Each one younger and bustier than the last. They were women in need of a dashing knight, and my father . . ." Tres shook his head. "He wanted to be young and in love."

All I wanted was to leave. Guilt was rising up. If the late Mr. Chaddock was murdered, there was little he could tell us now. Death was traumatic, especially if it was murder. Not that I thought waiting ten to fifteen years for answers would make it better, but I had ended the possibility of answers for the Chaddocks.

"I'm sorry," I offered. "For your loss. And your current situation."

Eli looked between me and Tres. His expression was not damning, but I knew him as well as he knew me. He heard my guilt—and possibly the fact that I felt slightly kinder because of it.

"We should depart, Geneviève." He motioned toward the door.

"Miss Crowe?" Tres stepped closer. "Could I call upon you? My father didn't decide to be a mindless corpse. He loved his wife, and he was a good businessman. Smart. Ruthless. There was no way he was going to give up either hobby."

Eli's tone of disapproval was abundantly clear even though all he said was "Geneviève . . ."

I held up my hand. If Tres was right, I shouldn't have been hired to behead Alvin Chaddock. Although they would have needed to warehouse Chaddock senior for at least a decade, they could have had their answers.

"It was a standard contract," I explained gently. "The 'make sure my loved one doesn't eat me or someone else' deal. Usually, the family hires me, tells me where the deceased is interred, death date, and I verify that they *are* family. You couldn't hire me to behead anyone other than a relative. She's his *widow*. I just did the job."

Tres sighed. "I don't blame *you*, Miss Crowe, and I actually understand why Alice hired you. I am well aware that my father would have been opposed to being resurrected, but . . . he wasn't ill. He should be alive still. Properly alive."

"I'm sorry for your loss," I said, meaning it. "I'm not sure I can help, though. I'm a hired gun, not a detective."

"If you come across another corpse that seems unlikely to have requested envenomation, will you let me know? I need to know who murdered my father."

I nodded at him. I didn't ask what he intended to do. Maybe he was law abiding. Maybe he wasn't. It wasn't my business.

After a tense moment, Eli spoke. "There will be a retainer fee, of course, if you want Ms. Crowe to seek intelligence of use to you."

I shot a look at him.

Eli continued, "And we will require a list of the members of your father's club. I can set up alerts on the obits for them."

"Sure. Wait right here." Tres stood and left us there alone.

"A retainer?" I glared at Eli. "Since when do I get a retainer for sending a text or whatever?"

"Since you're making decisions out of guilt." Eli grabbed my hand in his gloved one and squeezed.

I felt deflated. My anger washed away, and I closed my eyes.

Eli and I waited in silence for another few moments.

Tres returned with a sheaf of pages. There were far more members of the hate-group than I'd have expected. Hundreds of people had joined together not only to share hate but to act on it. That might not be what they told themselves they were doing, but once you put your money and time into a group to talk about hate, eventually actions would follow. The worst part was that perfectly "nice" people were capable of irrational hate that destroyed others' lives or careers.

While I glanced at the sheaf of names in horror, Eli simply took the pages and gave Tres a business card. "Please, let us know if you—or your associates—will need to contact Crowe Services. I can send you a bill for the retainer in this case."

"Thank you, Eli." Tres handed Eli his card as well.

I stood.

Tres looked at me and held out another card. Eli reached over and plucked it from Tres' hand. Apparently, he wasn't allowing me the courtesy of a number to contact Tres. Obviously, I wasn't going to be a bitch in front of a client, but I glanced at Eli with anger in my eyes.

Tres added, "It was a pleasure, Geneviève, despite the circum-stances."

"Sure." I felt like a dunce the moment I said it. *Sure?* Super professional.

"Perhaps we could meet for lunch to discuss matters?"

"Perhaps," I agreed.

"Geneviève," Eli said coldly.

I gave Tres an apologetic smile and followed Eli out of the office. There was not much else to say in front of him.

In a matter of moments, Eli and I were outside, and he was opening the passenger door for me. As ever, Eli was a gentleman, even with a killer as his passenger. I gave him a chilly smile.

I could feel dawn start to come creeping toward us. Within the hour, it would be here. "Give me the card."

"I shall investigate any leads on the injections," Eli said.

"Fine." I paused and held out my hand. "Card."

Eli handed it to me, and I shoved the card in my pocket.

When we reached my building, I looked at Eli before he could turn off the engine and said, "I'm not a tool to cover up murder."

His lips pressed together, as if there were words he was refusing to say.

"You were hired. You did a job." He opened his door and got out to open mine.

I tried to open mine and get out, but he'd locked it. When he opened it, he offered me his glove-covered hand as if nothing was amiss.

I tensed. "I'm frustrated. I can't just . . . what if the widow killed him?"

"Are you an officer of the law?"

"No."

"Did you cover up a crime?"

"No, but—"

"You take the world on your shoulders." He hugged me. "You cannot feel responsible for other people's misdeeds."

I knew he was right, but I still felt like I had to help Tres. I didn't *know* him, but I wanted to set things right—even though I couldn't truly do so. Maybe it was the touch of death on Tres that beckoned. Maybe it was worry that I was an unwitting participant in something heinous. Either way, I felt like a mother bear with no target to maul.

Eli motioned toward my building. "Ask me into your home. Let me take care of you."

"No." I folded my arms. "I'm fine. I just . . ."

"Feel like you must save people?"

"Yes."

"You don't," he said. "Let me deal with Chaddock."

"Fine." I nodded, and then walked to my building door.

I waved over my shoulder because I knew that behind me, Eli was watching. He always waited until I was inside. I didn't need to look to verify it, but I still did once I opened the door. And he smiled at me.

And despite the way he understood me, I was definitely not sleeping with Eli. Breaking both of our hearts seemed like a terrible idea.

Chapter Eleven

After the Chaddock job, life resumed something closer to the calm I often preferred. I went looking for Marie Chevalier, watching the usual news sources—which these days included various social media accounts and hashtags. No *draugr* sightings or suspicious kills came across my news. I didn't find anything when I went out seeking trouble either. In truth, the newly-corrupted *draugr* weren't exactly daily events, but there ought to be something. Someone. Instead, everything was silent.

I was in my apartment, pausing between work-outs and toying with Tres' card. I could call him, if not for the fact that I'd left my phone in Eli's car. I'd need to borrow a phone or go to a public phone.

For the moment, I would let Eli deal with Tres. That meant I waited to hear about new *draugr*, and I waited for some sort of information on the injection thing. Unless I got a call on a job or one of my paid-informants who passed on leads said something, I was at a loss. I didn't get any new job offers. I rested and didn't leave my home much, not that staying in was a hardship.

My apartment was a full floor of the building, but that's

because no one else wants to live on a ground floor unit. There were plenty of other people who lived in the building, just not low enough for the dead to look in the windows easily. Me? I liked the closer distance to the soil, and there wasn't any chance that anyone could be buried in the foundation of the building when I lived down there. Yes, that really was something I worried about. Walking dead inside the building could be awkward, at the least.

So, I bought the units next to mine when they came open. Eventually, I owned the whole floor and was little-by-little undertaking a reconstruction that meshed them all. For now, some of the floor was living space, some was work-out space, and one far end unit was basically an intact apartment. I half-planned for my mother moving in there some day. Sooner or later, even the indominable Mama Lauren would grow too old to live on her own in the Outs. Probably.

I was back to attacking my poor practice dummies when Christy stopped by my place midday on the third day. I only knew Christy was there because I saw her on the monitors. My music was loud enough to wake the neighbors a block over if not for my extra insulation and sound-proofing.

Christy Zehr was smarter than ninety-eight percent of the people you'll meet in life, and pretty as the fairy tale princess you wanted to hate but couldn't because she'd just given you a dusty page with the antidote to a witch's spell. She was a towering Black woman who researched freelance and hustled pool, and if I needed to have an alibi, she'd already have called me up and offered it before I'd realized I needed it. Like Jesse and Sera, she was someone I trusted wholly. Unlike Jesse and Sera, she wasn't a meddler. Jesse was subtle at it, but he was always attuned to me. Sera wasn't subtle. Christy was somewhere between them, but until I asked a question, she wasn't usually intrusive.

Christy looked me up and down when I opened the thick

door that separated my living space from the stairwell. "What's wrong?"

We went inside, and I flicked the row of locks on the door. "With me?"

She looked around. My gym was filled with weapons and training dummies. I'd been whaling on the dummies the last couple of days every time I thought about the "Eli situation"— which meant I'd worked out a lot. I was sweaty and gross and no closer to clarity than when I'd started thinking about Eli's claims that I was being unfair to him.

"You seem off." Christy followed me into the gym portion of my home.

"Everything okay?"

"Maybe?" I was dripping in sweat, magic zinging around my work-out space like hopped up fireflies. These two units had been stripped to the concrete. I'd covered part of it with wood, but I'd left some of it at crude concrete. Carpet was shit for workouts, and the smell of sweat collected in the fiber.

She looked at me, the magic strobe show, and shook her head. "I'll listen."

"Am I wrong—?"

"Often," she interjected as she plopped down on the floor, toed off her shoes, and made a "continue" gesture.

"About dead things. Am I wrong about doubting that dead things ought to be out and about like they're you or me?" I grabbed my water-bottle, which was filled with diluted vodka to hydrate my body and organs. I needed both in excess lately.

Christy looked up at me and said, "I like tigers. Beautiful but deadly things."

"Very different. Corpses aren't pretty, Chris."

She waved my objection away. "Work with me."

I nodded.

"I *like* tigers," she stressed. "If I could, I'd have a predator as my pet. Let it eat my enemies. Probably get a dumb-assed collar and nice cage for it. Buy it good steak."

"Okay."

"But if the cage door opens and it eats me, people wouldn't be shocked. Damn stupid if I forgot what it was."

"Still with you," I said.

"T-Cell Houses are cages." Christy rolled her shoulders. "We call them hospitals, but they are prisons for *draugr*."

I frowned and punched one of the dummies that was suspended from my ceiling like a fluffy windchime.

"You don't go into the cages and kill," she said.

She made sense, but it wasn't the same. Not really. "I wouldn't kill a tiger, though. And they don't *talk*."

"What if a tiger gets a taste for human instead of filet?" she asked. "Prowling New Orleans . . ."

"Fair."

"If tigers had been trying to eat you your whole life, you'd want to kill them even in cages, but you don't kill *every draugr*. You think of yourself as a killer, but you only kill the *draugr* that attack." Christy shrugged. "That reminds me: Jesse said he needed to talk to you about a blood bag hanging around at the shop."

And that was the thing that the people in their posh houses didn't get; when you live outside the fences and answer your own door or even just have a job without a secretary, the dead can reach you. *If* they stayed in their little T-Cell cages and *if* they agreed to a bagged lunch diet forever, maybe they'd be sort of okay, but Christy had a good point. If the tiger got out of the zoo, it would eat you and your kid because even fresh filets weren't enough. Tigers hunt, and we're all just filet with feet.

Christy hopped to her feet after a minute. "Want to go to the bar? Or you staying in to brood?"

"I need to check on Jesse," I said, but then it occurred to me again that Eli had my phone.

I'd left it in his car, and he hadn't dropped it off. I could've gone to his house to get it except that meant seeing Eli, and I wasn't ready for that. I could've gone to the bar. I didn't. I needed a break from him, too, and if an urgent job came up, I knew he'd tell me. No one called my phone other than someone offering work, Christy, Sera, or Jesse. They all either had my address or Eli would answer and tell them I left it behind. It was far from the first time I'd left the damn thing behind.

I wasn't about to tell Christy where my phone was, so I held out my hand.

"Can I text Jesse? I left my phone somewhere again." I gestured around the apartment, as if it was there. "Battery dead or ringer off."

Christy rolled her eyes but handed her phone to me.

"You okay?" I texted.

"Fanger. Bit customer," Jesse replied.

"Inbound. B.D." I handed the phone back before Jesse could piss me off reminding me that "before dusk" wasn't the same as arriving *at* dusk. His bookshop was in Gentilly, a good five miles away.

Then without thinking much on it, I texted Tres. "Geneviève here. Friend's phone. Lunch Saturday?"

He needed my help, and I was failing at the urge to resist finding a way to help him. It wasn't like me to be like this, but it wasn't an urge that was passing.

I grabbed a quick shower and walked out with Christy, who drove me partway.

"Tomorrow?" she asked when she dropped me off.

"Day after that. I promise." I paused and added, "I texted Tres on your phone. If he replies to it, will you let him know I'm available Saturday?"

"Tres?"

"He's a client."

Christy shrugged. "Friday night?"

"I'll meet you at the bar," I swore.

It was late enough that I wanted to be sure she had time to get home safely, and I felt better with a couple miles of walking.

I headed out to look after Jesse, my mood lighter from a few minutes chatting with a friend. When I arrived at the bookshop, Jesse filled me in. A *draugr*, at least ten to twelve years risen, was coming into the shop every night. It had bitten a customer, who had to be hospitalized for blood loss.

"That must be killing business," I joked.

"Seriously, Gen?" Jesse scowled at my attempt at levity. "You might not be here behind the counter or tracking inventory, but it's your shop, too."

"On paper," I reminded him, for what must have been the hundred and twenty-seventh time. I fronted the start-up costs the first year, and since then, Jesse had paid me enough to more than cover it. As far as I was concerned, we were square.

These days, Jesse was refusing to remove my name, and I was refusing to cash his checks. Eventually, checks expire, so in the end, the money stayed in his account. "I shredded the last check."

"Just fix this," he muttered when I stood grinning at him.

"Upstairs." I pulled my sword out and dropped it on the wooden counter.

Then I shooed him away.

Jesse was the sort of man who looked like he wasn't afraid of much. Muscles. Deep eyes. Dark skin. Gorgeous. Fortunately, Jesse was also secure enough in his manhood that he didn't object to me being the one with the gun and the sword. He was my brother in heart, and my oldest, dearest friend if we needed to get technical.

He was also completely human, and if there was one person I'd slaughter the world to protect, it was him. We were friends in childhood. Friends as teens. Aside from one very awkward attempt at kissing, we had a long history of being the kind of friends that seem like cousins. And since my mother was an only child and my bio-father was dead, twice dead now, I didn't have any relatives I knew of. Jesse was the only person, other than my mother, who had been in my life for most of my earliest memories.

Jesse was as protective of me as I was of him, but in vaguely overbearing-big-brothering ways—which was why I still hadn't told him or Christy *or* Sera that Eli had been with me at the cemetery. They liked that I had back-up, but they'd seen the way time with Eli got me twisted up. I wanted him. I cared about him. And that made life complicated.

I never told my friends what I was, but they knew where I stood on relationships—and children. And anyone with eyes could tell that Eli was fae enough to need to father a kid or two. The one man I wouldn't mind keeping around for a while was *also* the one man I shouldn't want. It made me surly—and then Eli and I argued. Rinse. Repeat. I knew better.

I also knew that Eli was the only person who could have my back in a fight, and with my magic being unpredictable, I needed the help. It was a case of the proverbial fucked every direction dilemma I seemed to excel at finding.

So, I wasn't going to tell my friends that Eli had helped me with the Chaddock case. Avoid. Ignore. It was one of my favorite solutions when bash-and-behead wasn't an option.

I was at the counter at Tomes and Tea, and Jesse was tucked away upstairs watching me on his security cameras. Sometimes I thought Jesse would love to have had magic or something just to be able to keep me safer, but I was grateful that he was wholly human.

I glanced up at the camera and smiled in what I hoped was a reassuring way when the *draugr* strolled in.

The ones old enough to be semi-sentient evoked the kind of aversion I usually reserved for weddings and lectures. Tall, dark, and dead came through the door of the bookstore like he thought he was alive. I was expecting him, of course, but no amount of expectation quelled my disgust when the infected ones approached me.

"This store is off-limits to *draugr* under the age of twenty," I said. "You fed on a customer."

"Hello," he said.

"I will not allow you to eat people," I stressed.

Somehow the big-assed sword on the counter wasn't a clue. I mean, no one really thinks of me and says "oh, she's *subtle*." At least after tonight I could claim that someone—or something— thought I was understated because my combo of sword and "off-limits" still earned me a friendly look.

He smiled in what I guessed he thought was an alluring manner. He had all his teeth plus the two shiny extra teeth that dead things grew, and if you could overlook the icy skin and vague scent of death, maybe a *draugr* could be attractive.

Somewhere in his malfunctioning mind, *he* thought he was sexy.

I mean, okay, more than a few living humans seemed to enjoy banging the dead. I just couldn't grasp it. Maybe if my heart wasn't thumping in irritation and agitation, I would be the sort of woman who thought blood-breath was an aphrodisiac. My mother certainly had.

Sadly, for him, I hadn't inherited her perverse streak—just her temper.

"You are not welcome here," I added in a louder voice.

He nodded and then took another step. This one had to be trying to live off a blood-bank diet. No one much discussed it, but dead blood diets seemed to make *draugr* little better than Hollywood zombies. Faster, of course, than the shambling zombies on screen, but not much for thinking.

"This store doesn't serve the recently dead," I explained calmly.

He nodded again, as if he understood, but he wasn't retreating.

"You know there are laws, right? And you *bit* a customer." I reached under the counter, hand searching for the button that would summon the police. Protocol. Every public encounter with an aggressive *draugr* outside a registered graveyard or cemetery had to be reported. Stores and streetlamps had alarms mounted in reach. All a human had to do was press an alarm so the police could be aware of attacks, potential attacks, and self-defense events. It was all recorded, charted, mapped.

Most of the time, pushing that button was the last act of a person's life. Me? I might have the record for successful post-button life.

Button depressed, I said, "The online stores will ship to—"

"You aren't like them."

I reassessed its age to closer to fifteen. It spoke clearly, but with obvious effort. Someone had been babysitting this one for it to live this long.

"You smell," it said as it sniffed so hard it looked like a feral pig. No tusks, mind you, but definite pig snout face.

I grabbed the gun under the counter. I preferred the up-close reliability of steel, but some nights I was impatient. Pointing out that I seemed not-quite-human brought my foul streak out faster than anything other than blind-dates.

"I would like you to leave and not return." I pulled a little grave dust magic to my surface and into my skin. It was like cocking a gun—primed but not yet engaged. I just wanted to be ready if it was old enough to be faster than my aim. Freshly awakened ones were predictable. I knew how old they were. On the street or in a store, it was a guessing game. It felt closer to fifteen, but I couldn't be certain.

It lunged at me, grabbing for my arm and stretching over the counter.

I lifted the gun and squeezed the trigger, aiming to the left of where it stood and hoping I guessed correctly. Just in case, I fired a second shot to the right as quickly as I could. More and more I felt which way they were about to flow before they did. Those were the good nights.

This was a good night.

The round I'd fired on the left hit the thing. The stench of old death was instantaneous. Congealed blood started to ooze from the hole that was trying and failing to seal. Heart shot. Now that the thing wasn't able to flow into the speed that it relied on to escape, I emptied three more rounds into it. Eye. Eye. Throat. Four hits, one loss, and one spare in the chamber in case it had a friend.

I shifted the gun into my left hand and grabbed my sword with my right. I leaned down and beheaded it before it could repair itself enough to rise. Once it was well and truly dead, I watched the door. I always worried that they had friends. Contrary to what we used to whisper in the dark about the creatures that lived on blood, they weren't pack beings. No nests or families. They were typically loners.

But even loners got urges for the occasional friend or fuck.

I stared at the door as I called out, "Roll doors."

The clattering of the metal shutters dropping over the windows and doors was loud, but comforting in the way of steel at the end of the day. I watched the creature, making sure that it couldn't flow, as I listened to the solid thunk of the doors slotting into the anchors.

The latches all clacked, sealing us in.

The store phone line lit up.

"Tomes and Tea. How can I help you?" I said cheerily as if there was any chance it wasn't the police.

"We had an alarm from your store—"

"It's dead. The *draugr*, not me, I mean."

"How many other fatalities?"

"None."

The bullets weren't ejected from the body on the floor, so the thing was, in fact, dead. I watched the decaying process, as if time sped. The bodies not only stopped moving, biting, screwing, and whatever else they did. They also raced through the years between their first death and this permanent one. The oldest of their kind faded to ashy powder rather than stopping at bone.

"Geneviève?" the officer on the line asked after a pause. "Is this Miss Crowe?"

"Yes," I said softly.

"You know witches aren't immune to their venom," the officer on the line said. "This is the fifth *draugr* you killed in the last two months."

Ninth, I silently corrected. Some were jobs. Some were awkward side effects of the job. Either way, there were nine dead-again bodies in the last eight weeks. It was a wonder I wasn't *more* exhausted.

I closed my eyes and suggested, "I guess I keep ending up at the wrong place."

The officer snorted. Murdering the dead wasn't illegal. *Hiring* people to do it or being hired was. Those who pulled it off were usually lucky or had encountered an exhausted one—or one still asleep.

I only killed to keep people safe. What I never said aloud, though, was that I *liked* it. I worried that it made me too much like them. There was a satisfaction I found when I killed that I couldn't explain. It didn't feed me, but it sometimes took the edge off my temper.

And *that* frightened me.

I wasn't a sociopath. I just enjoyed protecting my city, and there was sometimes a satisfying jolt inside my body when I fought and didn't die.

"Miss Crowe," the officer said. "Seems like a lot of body retrievals around the places you go."

"Are you suggesting I shouldn't call them in?" I asked lightly.

"No." The officer on the line sighed. "I'm suggesting that you stop seeking them out. You're as able to die as the rest of us."

"Uh-huh." I hoped he was right, but I had good reason to doubt it. I really tried not to lie outright unless I had to do so. Too much time around Eli? Too much time studying ethics? I wasn't sure, and I had no desire to ponder it.

Life was easier unexamined.

"We'll send the Con Crew at dawn," the officer said. "You'll need to make a statement this time."

I smothered a sigh. "Dead guy tried to grab me. I shot him. There! Statement made."

"Tell that to the retrieval officer at dawn."

We disconnected, and I glared at the corpse. I hated being trapped, but since I apparently had to be the one to talk to the Con Crew, I was stuck at the shop. I think it was their way of keeping me off the streets.

That meant being around Jesse and not slipping and saying anything about Eli—or how much work I'd had lately.

Chapter Twelve

RIGHT NOW, THE CORPSE WAS DECAYED TO NOTHING BUT BONES and some sinew. It, at least, was dead. Finally. I never understood whatever venom or genetic wrongness caused them to walk after death, but I'd learned how to tell when their spark left.

It was dead.

I was trapped.

One of those was better than the other.

But the Contamination Crew collected at dawn. They weren't going to drive around at night scooping up supposedly dead *draugr*. There wasn't always a good way to check if they were dead. Even animated, they had no pulse. No one wanted to bend down—throat in their line of sight and scent—and lift them. In the early days, more than one of the Con Crews had died that way.

Protocol mattered, especially in New Orleans.

And my offer to go behead the dead for them went over poorly. I seemed too gleeful or some shit. Or maybe the liability insurance was too much. Either way, they did it their way. I did it mine.

My city wasn't a place where nights were safe for most people. Some parts of the country were supposedly safe, or so the news stations all swore. To get into those gated areas required being born there *or* a blood test, seven generations of verifiable lineage, exceptional traits, and a donation that had more zeros in it than I could see clear to hand over even if I had the rest.

And I didn't have the rest. My blood test would create an international panic. I would spend my life in a facility with a lot of security to keep me inside—or they'd simply kill me on the spot. So, I stayed in New Orleans. Honestly, I wasn't sure I could leave anyhow. It was an incredible city with music, booze, and a river.

I glanced over my shoulder as the steel door behind me unlocked and opened.

"You're sure?" Jesse asked as he came up behind me.

"I'm sure." I pointed at the decaying corpse on the plastic tarps that Jesse had put down before I arrived. Blood and quickly contracting flesh puddled there. "It smells like wet ass."

Jesse laughed and handed me a plastic baggie with a menthol-soaked cloth. I covered my mouth and nose.

"I don't know how you stand it."

"It barely smells, Gen," he said quietly.

"Uh huh." I tied the rag over my face. "I'll hang out here for the night if that's okay. Con Crew insists."

He gave me a sympathetic look and motioned to the store. "Load a bag. It's not much but you won't take your cut of sales *and* you did this—"

"Handling it took five minutes." I shrugged.

I was several steps away when he said, "You know I'll accept you no matter what, right?"

"Sure." I stared at the thing on the floor. I wasn't much different. Living and dead all at once. I was technically alive, but no one knew what happened to the child of a *draugr*. The women who got pregnant to them typically aborted or miscarried.

Draugr, obviously, could impregnate women. I existed, so it was an irrefutable fact. I just hadn't ever heard of any of their offspring living to adulthood. Lucky me.

"My mother was a witch," I argued, as if that was a valid explanation. "I'm quick. Good at defense. I'm not sure what there is to accept. Lot of witches out there, Jess."

Jesse said nothing at first, but after a moment, he added, "Witches don't *flow*."

I glanced back "I didn't—"

"The first time I saw you do it was when I was falling out of that tree. We were . . . what? Ten maybe?" He shook his head. "I should have cracked my head, but suddenly there was a damn sofa cushion. Right there under me. A cushion from my living room in the middle of the backyard. You know there was no other way to explain it."

"We brought it out earlier. You just forg—"

"No. I didn't forget." Jesse looked at me intently. "That wasn't the only time either. I wasn't sure until I saw one of them the first time. Those *draugr* that showed up at the river. Do you remember? I suspected you were different, but I wasn't sure. That night, I knew. You *flow*, Gen."

I stared at him. For most of my twenty-nine and change years, Jesse was my constant. My rock. My shelter. My best friend.

"We were eighteen when I figured it out for sure," he said mildly as he wrapped the corpse up in the tarp and duct taped it shut like it was some strange gift. He stood up. "Been a minute since I knew. If it was going to change something with us, it would've happened years ago. You're still my family."

And I stood there watching him, trying to figure out how this conversation had happened after all this time.

"Gen?"

I met his gaze.

"Do you want to admit that Eli is hunting with you again while we're clearing the air?"

I shook my head. "I was going to tell you."

"I know. He told me accidentally, though." Jesse stared like he was trying to will understanding directly into my mind. We both knew Eli did exactly nothing by accident.

"How?"

"I met Christy last night and—"

"Oh?" I'd been trying to set them up for a year.

"Yep." Jesse said, popping the 'p,' but he didn't spill any details. Instead, he said, "Eli asked about you. He gets a tone when he's irritated with you."

"So, you knew he saw me because he sounded irritated?" I glared at Jesse.

"When you two are around each other, he's irritable, and you are happier." Jesse grinned. "If I liked him more, I'd feel bad for him."

"He's likeable," I muttered.

"You're my only family, Gen. I'm honor-bound to dislike any man who looks at you like he does. And he looks. He wants to screw my *sister*, so I must hate him. It's like a law or something."

I sighed. I loved him in a way I doubted I could love another human, but sometimes I understood why siblings fought. He watched me as if I needed to defend myself or Eli. I wasn't doing either.

After a tense moment, I pointed at the remains. "It's dead, but I'd still feel better if you slept upstairs. I can stay down here to be sure—"

"No." Jesse rolled his eyes. "It's been reduced to *bones* now. Find some books. There's a fifteenth century *Book of Relics* that I stowed in a hex box for you, but grab whatever else catches your eye."

Despite the rest, my attention perked up. I had an excellent collection of esoteric magic and mysticism books thanks to Jesse. Some months, I was sure my book buys were what kept the shop afloat. The sensitive books were on display in enhanced glass boxes that were soldered to silver and steel pedestals. They couldn't be removed without the keys that were woven into his skin and mine, so to buy any of those, either the buyer had to be an already approved customer or I had to vet them.

"And an illuminated cook book," Jesse added.

"What year?"

My best friend laughed at my undisguised hope. "Not that one, I'm afraid. Still looking for it."

I'd been searching for a seventh-century potion that I thought might yield a few new defenses. At least, I thought it was seventh-century. Record keeping was questionable with magic workers, and rumors were intentionally created. Still, all reliable data I'd found said that the seventh-century book was the real deal. I just needed to find the damn thing.

"Grab your new books." Jesse pointed. "We'll go up and get some rest. I already changed the linens in your room."

"Not my room," I muttered.

"The 'guest'"—he made air quotes— "room that no one else ever uses because you keep clothes and swords and weird smelling tea bags in it."

"Tea bags?" I laughed. "I'd like to see someone drink tea out of a spell bag. Wake up with a fucking bunny tail or who the hell knows!"

"Books, Gen." Jesse waved me forward.

And then he stood there waiting until I'd retrieved my payment and accompanied him up to the apartment that was my second home.

I was hoping that we weren't going to have a heart-to-heart about the fact that I would likely live on in some way after my heart stopped beating. Because the sheer truth was that my second life would only last as long as it took to starve. I wasn't eating people. My earth-magic mother raised me as a g'damn vegetarian. If I couldn't eat the flesh of a cow, how was I to eat people? No. Hard fucking no.

Sooner or later, I needed a plan for what I'd do after I died. Short of buying the working guillotine I'd found on an auction site, I couldn't handle it myself. And somehow, I felt like replacing my sofa with a guillotine would send an alarming message to my friends. That meant I needed a friend or friends who could behead me when the time came—or find a guillotine that was accessible to the public.

Chapter Thirteen

I TYPICALLY NEEDED ABOUT AS MUCH SLEEP AS A JUNKIE ON A good long bender. It wasn't that I never grew tired, but I had the peculiar metabolism that meant that I could do a low-grade activity while my body recharged. Watch a show? Take a bath? It was as if by powering down my brain, I was somehow recharging muscle and organs. It made me particularly efficient, but it was sometimes lonely.

But for actively sleeping, eyes closed and body reclined, I only needed maybe four hours a day unless I was injured. So, the guest room—which Jesse called my room—had a stack of books that were designed to numb me to sleep, as well as a bizarre assortment of chamomile teas and lavender bath bombs. He had long allowed me to claim that I had insomnia. What else was I to call it? "Lack of metabolic need to sleep" sounded less than human. "Fucked up" sounded negative. So, we called it "insomnia" and treated it with relaxation tricks.

When we lived in Algiers Point, roommates for real then, I roamed at night. There was something joyous in that, creeping through yards and sliding into tree tops and onto roofs. I felt magical, and I saw a part of the world that I missed now that we were on the other side of the river.

As a kid in the Outs, in what was once a town called Slidell, I didn't know that the things that made me that way were monstrous. As a twenty-year-old, I was in denial. I told myself it was how witches were. When I was twenty-four, I found out about the necrophilia that resulted in my mother's pregnancy. I was disgusted—not with my mother for screwing a dead guy, but with myself for being the child of a dead guy.

My mother's ability to rationalize anything meant she thought she wasn't lying all those times when she said my father was dead. I could see her argument to a point, but I guess I wanted to think he'd been alive when I was conceived. I had no words for my shock. Sure, there were people who slept with *draugr*. I'd thought they were the ones who looked macabre or something. My mom was the sweetest, liveliest person I'd met. She grew herbs and tended flowers. I mean, if there was ever a human stand-in for a cartoon princess with birds and mice at her side, that was my mother.

I would never understand how she decided to sleep with a corpse.

They were a "fling." It was "just a thing that happened." They "would've had a chance," but he "refused to adopt a vegetarian lifestyle." That one I couldn't even process. *Draugr* required blood. When I asked if she meant eating actual *vegetables* or eating *vegetable eaters* instead of people, she was mad enough that she didn't speak to me for a month.

Mom had her version of answers; I had anger. Either way, she forbade me from seeing him—and him from seeing me.

But he came to see me when I turned twenty-five, and I killed him.

Mom and I have still not recovered from that, but the last

thing I wanted was a dead—as well as deadbeat—dad. Maybe he wasn't always a monster. Mom argued that he was a good-hearted man once. Maybe there was a time and place where he was different. All I knew was that his plans for me were the sort of thing that would get any man or monster shot.

I shoved that line of thought away and stared at the ceiling, letting my brain slide into that space that was my version of sleeping. It was a lot easier during the day when the light was so bright that I wanted to close my eyes anyhow. Nights were hard. My body wanted to roam. My mind was active.

But at some point, I must have actually drifted into sleep because I felt the sunrise at the same time as my door opened.

"Dawn. Get up." Jesse stood there pelting me with grapes. There was a reason for that. After I'd gone from sound asleep to crouched over him with a knife at his neck when we were twenty and roommates, he'd taken to throwing things like grapes, candy or, my least favorite pick to date, canned vegetables. Who liked to have slippery, slimy, wax beans tossed in their face?

"You're lucky I don't wake *you* this way," I muttered, eyes still closed.

Jesse laughed. "Feeding me grapes for breakfast? Oh, the horror! Your threats are so scary, Gen. I quake in . . ."

I was up, plucking a fruity projectile out of the air and shoving a grape in his mouth at a speed I wouldn't have willingly shared yesterday unless it was to protect him.

". . . fear," he finished around the grape in his mouth. Then he grinned, popped a grape into my mouth and added, "Con Crew should be here in about five minutes."

I spat out the grape. "Five. . .? What the fuck, Jesse! You couldn't wake me?"

"You aren't usually asleep at night, so how would I know you slept?" He turned and walked away. "Do you want water or vodka for breakfast?"

"So, we're just going to put it all on the table? You need to show me how much you figured out?"

"Best. Friend." He called back at me. "Very fucking patient best friend, I might add."

I followed him.

"I waited. I waited some more. I hinted. You pretended. So"—he tossed another grape at me with no warning—"yeah."

I dodged, and the grape landed with a *plink* on the wooden floor of the room. I scooped it up and teased, "I might have liked you more when I thought you were stupid."

Jesse gave me an incredulous look. "My apartment is filled with plants and hardwood floors on every room. Do you honestly think I *accidentally* created a nest for you? Magic core elements in every room. Nature-filled. Salt-lined windows. And your mattress is filled with sacred earth and lavender."

My mouth dropped open.

"You rest well in *your room* because I figured out what Mama Lauren used in your mattress at home," Jesse explained as if I was the one who was utterly sans clues. He wasn't magic, but he'd trailed behind my mother at my side often enough that I wasn't able to be shocked that he'd figured out what she'd stuffed in my mattress.

I gaped at him, though. "How did you get the soil?"

"It's harder to get that much stealthily these days, so I was bringing it back a satchel at time, but...I know a guy. He brought a pickup bed full, and I carried it upstairs." He held out a glass of straight vodka. "And little by little I add it to your mattress at your apartment, too."

The buzzer downstairs saved me from needing to reply. A quick look at the street cam revealed the local Con Crew standing at the rolldown. Jesse pushed a few buttons on his remote. It had codes for every door, window, rolldown, as well as for the security boxes for books in the shop.

I snagged the bottle of vodka from Jesse's kitchen counter

and one of my holsters. Then we went down to welcome them into the store.

Unlike the night before, I hung back from the front of the shop. The first few hours of daylight had started to make me queasy over the last year or so. It wasn't impossible to handle, but I saw no need to get too close to the door and that disgusting brightness.

I slid my sunglasses on and leaned into the doorway.

"Hang-over again, Gen?" one of the guys teased.

I lifted the bottle of vodka. "Still drinking."

If I wanted to *actually* get a buzz, I'd drink one of those fruity drinks with a slice or two of citrus or cherries in it. Or eat the grapes Jesse was noshing on like they were a breakfast food.

"Don't see any point in being sober when the dead guy is properly dead," I added. "He can't hurt me now. So, *l'chaim!*"

"Is that a spell?"

"No, man. It's Hebrew," the second member of the Con Crew, Gary, said lightly. "Gen's a Jewish witch."

"A . . . *what?*"

"My Jewish mother found Pan or Gaia or something, so she raised me both. It makes for complicated holidays," I said cheerily. "Also, *L'chaim* means 'to life.'"

"To life, kid." Gary echoed. Then he shook his head and looked at the blue-tarped body with its duct tape seal. "That our corpse?"

I nodded.

"If you keep putting tarps down *before* you kill them, Gen, they look premeditated." Gary said.

"Jesse was about to dust the fans." I pointed up at the gently spinning, dust-free fans. "Don't want to get dirt on the books, do we?"

Gary and the other guy whose name I hadn't learned yet both looked at me and sighed. Then Gary asked, "You think you have your magicked-up bullets and that's enough?"

"Nah, I think I'm a witch with a few sharp swords," I said. "No law against killing *draugr*."

"That all you kill?"

I shrugged. "If I find something or someone trying to hurt innocents while I'm strolling home from the bar, I'm going to do my civic duty."

Gary looked at Jesse, who was staying silent.

At that, Gary shook his head. "Not your responsibility to save the city, Gen."

I shrugged. I kind of felt like it *was*. I had gifts. If I didn't find some way to use them, wasn't I as bad as a monster? I slid one of my swords out. "Steel and silver." I tilted it so the shop lights bounced off it. "With spells embedded in the silver. And you know what my rounds do to a *draugr*."

Gary sighed again. "Try not to die, kid, okay? I know you've been lucky, but you aren't always going to be fast enough."

I nodded because I did try not to lie more than necessary. Omitting details was a lot easier than outright lying. I mean, I *could* lie. I just felt guilt when I did it, so I tried to keep my lies to a minimum. Killing, on the other hand, didn't bother me at all.

I didn't know what that meant about me. I thought about it a lot, and I guess I was coping by living a blend of my mother's faith and my own Jewish leanings. In both cases, there was an idea that we were here to make the world a better place. Nothing wrong with other faiths, but those that focused on a hell or heaven as a motivator weren't a good match for me. I wasn't likely to ever be able to knock on any extra-worldly doors, and even if I could, I didn't really dig the notion that my choices ought to be guided by carrots or sticks.

I might not know why an abomination like me existed, but I figured there was a Plan. I just needed to try to make the best of it. Be a force of good in the world. Silly, maybe, but that was my goal.

Not like I was so arrogant to think I was a soldier for some higher being, no great mission or role for me. But I was here, and I had skills, so I used them. The way I used them was often brutal, like Torah and Christian Old Testament brutal, but to suggest only forgiveness in the face of hate or murderous intent was a stance that was not for me. I preferred an old-fashioned sword to the throat or heart most days. When that wasn't viable, I went for my modified rounds and a reliable pistol.

I killed more monsters with bloody, cold violence than magic —although I let the New Orleans Police Department think otherwise.

My magic was earth-based. My rounds worked because they healed, and the life of it was incompatible with *draugr*. It was also why the dead woke after my magic flashed out. It was why they regrew their flesh and followed me like puppies needing a home. Somehow, I was born of magic and death, but my magic was life giving.

No one asked a lot of questions, though, so I kept that tidbit to myself. I was what I was, and I trusted that I was working to make the world a better place. It let me sleep well most nights.

Today, Jesse stayed at my side as we watched them tote the tarp-wrapped *draugr* into their wagon. There was one other there, but it was rare to see more than a couple of them sent off to the incinerator. Once they were bagged, tagged, and delivered, the Con Crew would toss them in the re-purposed cremation facility, and then once a day, all the ashes would be mixed with sacred soil and scattered in a field designated for that purpose.

The paranoia about the regenerative skills of their sort led to a lot of safeguards.

And I understood it. The wrong sort of bullets did little damage, but figuring out the right way to injure them required a captive *draugr* —or someone foolish enough to test new rounds on the street.

"Gary," I called out, carefully avoiding going too far into the sunlight. It didn't injure me. I just disliked the headaches that it left behind. I beckoned him over.

Then, stealthily, I held out a few of my newest high caliber rounds. "Just keep these in your back-up gun in case one of them isn't all the way dead."

Gary looked at me, scowled. "My paycheck doesn't come close to covering those."

"Then it's your gift for not asking a lot of questions," I said casually. After so many pick-ups lately, I'd seen Gary more than most of my friends that month. "And . . . if there are any rogue *draugr* that you hear about, I'd like a call."

He looked at me in what I supposed was meant to be a fatherly way. I hadn't had that experience from my actual father, who was more interested in discussing my abnormalities and breeding me with a few of his kind to see what we could "add" to my theoretical offspring.

"Try to stay alive," Gary murmured, but he took the proffered rounds in his hand.

It was as close to agreeing to my terms as I could hope. "You, too," I said. "I wouldn't like it if you died."

The police in New Orleans were peculiar. It took a special sort of person to want to work here. We had a higher population of dead things than anywhere else in the nation. I couldn't fathom what drove most men and women to come here seeking work. I was here because there were no other options, but many of the police officers chose it. They got signing bonuses, and the pay was incredible, but it was a gamble. The mortality rate was high. Every time I saw them, it was always a chance it would be the last time.

Gary and his newest partner left, and I hoped they'd still be living next time I called for a pick-up. They might not consider my job the same as theirs if they knew about it, but I felt like we were connected.

Jesse closed the door and locked it. The store wouldn't open for another hour or so. Most everyone in the city started their work day not long after the sunrise. Come dusk, the sidewalk might as well be rolled up and tucked away.

"I'm going to grab a mop, and—"

"I'm out." I flashed him a grin and kissed his cheek. Then I went upstairs to grab one of my books, my bag, and a pair of the special-order dark glasses I had stashed here. Getting home before I had to face the midday sun would decrease my odds of another migraine. It was go now or stay until afternoon.

When I came downstairs, Jesse had a mop and bucket in hand. There was no ooze from the death. His floor was fine, but I understood the impulse. Cleaning up after a murder seemed reasonable.

"You could stay and watch me clean," Jesse said in that light voice he adopted more and more with me. It made me feel like I suspected a feral cat would, intrigued but not exactly eager to chance it.

"Nope. I'm going over a few job things. The last dead guy was injected. His son thinks it was what killed him."

Jesse stuffed the mop into the bucket and watched me. "I don't like how Eli looks at you, but if something's weird out there . . . well, weirder than normal, I'm glad you're taking him with you."

"Eli's not bad," I pointed out.

"He wants to get my little sister naked. It's my sibling right to want to punch him." Jesse grinned.

"Little sister?"

"Two months, Gen. My birthday is a full two months before yours. It counts."

"Whatever." I grabbed the vodka and took another drink. "Thanks for breakfast, Jesse."

Then I slipped my glasses on and headed out the door. Tomorrow, I would get back my phone and start to see what I had to do and where I was going next.

Today, though, I was going to visit my mother. I wasn't going to tell Jesse in case he decided to tag along, but I needed maternal insight on what was wrong with my magic. If anyone in the world had theories about my fucked-up biology, it would be Mama Lauren.

Chapter Fourteen

I WALKED TO THE BUS DEPOT AND BOARDED ONE OF THE THREE buses headed across Lake Pontchartrain over to what we now called the "Outs." The driver, a man with plenty of tattoos and a few wrinkles, had a shotgun jutting out the left window. It was mounted in what appeared to be a homemade rig that would give steadiness and wide range to shoot anything on the left of the bus. Soldered to the driver's chair on the right was a holster. Stepping onto the bus meant the pistol was eye-level to each passenger. The driver's hand rested on the butt of the gun. If anything unwelcome entered the bus door, he could stop it—or at least stall it. I suppose it depended on what was loaded in the chambers of the revolver.

Most busses weren't driven by folks who were so public with their weapons. I paused and gestured at the guns. "Expecting problems?"

"Not lately, but I do like to take precautions." He motioned to my weapons belt. A short sword and gun hung on either side of my hips. He asked, "You? Running from or toward trouble?"

"Neither. Just prepared if trouble crosses my path."

We exchanged nods, and I walked to the back of the bus, glad I was early enough to avoid walking through a crowded bus with weapons visible. Sometimes people got nervous at the sight of me. I blamed it on my weapons, but Jesse argued that I simply don't smile enough.

Several busses crossed the ghost zone on day trips to the outskirts every morning around dawn. They started bringing people back mid-afternoon. Despite the inherent appeal of nature, no one stayed out of New Orleans after dusk. There was no sheriff, no police, and the few souls who lived in the Outs were mostly unpredictable.

Jesse and I grew up in the Outs, so I was at ease there— despite the "Wild West" attitude that prevailed in the Outs. It was home, and weird as fuck or boring as watching paint dry, home was always special in some way. I grinned at the thought of being barefoot in a field in a few short hours.

The bus crossed through the city walls into the ghost zone. It was the first casualty of the *draugr* reveal. A few people dismembered at a park-and-ride lot made international news. *Draugr* had existed for centuries, but for reasons no one knew, one random Thursday a bunch of violent newly-infected dead folks started attacking across the country. People moved in mass exodus to cities, and a lot of cities had found ways to be completely *draugr* free.

Blood tests. Wealth. And a shit ton of laws. Those cities weren't for me—and to be completely honest, even if my blood was pure, I wouldn't trade my weapons for such an existence. Walls were made to go over or under, and the idea of total trust in any faceless governing body made me cringe.

Others had vacated entire towns. Either way, the suburbs were completely emptied in mere weeks. Too widespread to wall and too filled with anxiety to stay. Every city had a ghost zone now— and *draugr* claimed whichever vacant houses they wanted.

People watched out closed windows anxiously. A few *draugr*

watched the bus from the shaded porches of stolen houses. And I tried not to shudder at the feeling of so very many dead things gathered near.

The more miles between New Orleans and the lake, the more open it was. Windows opened, and the unmistakable scents of nature filled the bus. Trees, soil, and flowers. It was a kind of dizzying perfume that cities couldn't offer. Beyond the ghost zone was the Outs—where I had been born and raised.

The few people who lived here now held as much land as they wanted, but it wasn't part of a town or city. No utility services. No sheriff. No law. To live in the Outs meant you handled your own law. If not for my allure to the dead, I'd prefer being outside society. Solar or wind power, well water, your own self-defense. In this, I was my mother's daughter. I saw the appeal in that sort of life.

Mama Lauren was handy with a gun, and now she had roll-downs for every window, door, chicken coop, and greenhouse on her farm. Some of those were added after she had me. The first time she found a cluster of *draugr* napping in the barn and one under her chicken coop, she added more roll-downs.

The roads became dirt and gravel about ten miles outside New Orleans, and the street lights were replaced by trees. Now that we'd passed the ghost zone, nature was all there was. The murmurs of the others on the bus grew louder. Families brought their children out here, and seniors went to sit on benches at the lake or walk along the short trails there. During the day, it was perfect. *Draugr* weren't all trapped by sunlight, but the newly-infected ravenous ones were.

The bus pulled in with a rattle and *whoosh*.

The driver repeated the same announcement that all the bus drivers made each day: "First bus back will be here at 4PM. Last bus thirty minutes before dusk."

The busses were consistent in their schedule. They made sure to count each passenger to be sure no one was left behind in the dark. For the most part, that was for the best. I waited until everyone else was gone before I stood and walked to the front of the bus.

"I won't be on any of the return busses tonight."

"Miss, you can't stay out here. I see you're armed but—" He stared at me in the way of those who think they're dealing with the very stupid or very depressed. He wasn't sure which. "There are things out there."

"*Draugr.* I know, but—"

"Let me take you back. It's suicide to go out there in the dark."

"I know what I'm doing," I explained.

And he very obviously took my words wrong. His face slid toward a kindness that made me hope he was quick enough to keep himself safe. Good people made me hope that for them.

"There are other choices," he said as he reached out a wrinkled hand. "Whatever happened. Whatever brought you to this. Remember: Bleak days pass."

I had a momentary urge to hug him, but instead I accepted his outstretched hand. "I'm not suicidal. I'm a witch, and my mother lives out there. I'll be back tomorrow. Tonight, I'll be tucked in with gross tea and steel roll-downs."

When I lifted my chin in the direction of home, the man stared at me with a new understanding. "You're Lauren's baby girl?"

I nodded.

He laughed. "That explains everything. That woman's as stubborn as a herd of mules."

"And I am my mother's daughter," I said lightly.

"Get there before dusk at least." He waited until I nodded again and then sighed in a way that said that he had met my mother more than once. "Tell her Bud sends regards."

Then he waved me off.

I couldn't *flow* with Bud watching me, so I walked at a brisk pace until I was hidden by the copse of trees that grew thick and strong without humans interfering. People enjoyed short trips to nature, but by and large, they weren't comfortable too long outside the walls of cities. Nature was rebounding without the litter and greed of humanity. If I slowed, I knew there were wolves, foxes, birds, and any number of prey animals in the thick undergrowth of the forest. As a child, I'd taken glee in playing near them, comforted by the knowledge that my speed and magic would prevent the larger ones from eating me.

It was not nature that scared me. The unnatural *draugr* and the fearful man, those frightened me. Nature made sense.

As I started to *flow* toward my mother's house, I knew that her magic was why I felt such trust in nature. She'd given me a gift, a regard for life and all the slithering, crawling, running, flying, or swimming things in it.

I recognized that gift, but my relationship with my mother was still strained. Not on *her* side, mind you. My mother, bless her sweet heart, was fairly sure I was goddess-sent or G-d-sent, depending on which faith she was leaning into that week. Mama Lauren was raised Jewish, discovered paganism, and honestly, argued convincingly that the two faiths worked remarkably well together on a lot of practical matters. Vegan witch wasn't much different than kosher Jew. Some of the ethos fused well, too: make the world a better place and "harm none." In some ways, it made for an idyllic childhood.

My mother stood in a garden in front of the tidy little A-frame house where I grew up. When I came home, I could forget that I'd ever left. Home was a constant, my mother surrounded by plants or herbs or brewing something while she danced through the house. As usual her hair, barely gray still, was tied up in the sort of untidy knot that looked somehow elegant. I could've been any age from two until now, and my mother still wore the same basic thing: tall boots, dress, and a pair of pistols holstered at her hips. She was all about life and love, but she was aware of the world, too. Her hand went to the butt of one of those guns at the same time as she lifted her head. If I was a human meaning her harm, I'd be dead before I reached her.

When she saw it was me, her hand dropped away from her gun. "Genny! What a lovely surprise!"

It wasn't just her voice that filled with joy. My mother lit up at the sight of me, arms open for an embrace, and I couldn't refuse. Honestly, I don't go broadcasting it because I fear someone using her to hurt me, but I always felt like pleasing my mother was my life's mission. Sometimes, I thought that was part of the strain between us: Mama Lauren never quite saw me as I *was*.

To her, I was a miracle, a gift, a mission, and I just wanted to be a girl.

"The cards said you'd visit, but I wasn't expecting you so soon," Mama Lauren said in a tone that felt like reproach. "You could have let me know."

I stepped away, but let her take my hand in hers. "You don't have a phone. How was I to let you know?"

My mother let out a pulse of magic that I felt like a sizzle on my skin. She said nothing, though. She'd answered my question. I could have sent a message. We were both witches.

"I don't exactly like broadcasting where I am or where *you* are."

She gave me a look that used to send me cringing in fear.

"Fine. I suppose I could've sent a message when I was on the bus," I murmured.

She made a *hmm* noise and smiled. It wasn't simply that she used her non-answers like weapons. My mother was an artist at emoting. She embraced a school of thought that basically said that illness comes from repressed emotion. And yes, it was just about as anxiety-inducing in childhood as it sounded. Every feeling, every possible emotion, was to be shared.

"I worry," she said, as if that was news.

"I know." I let her tug me to her patio where there was a table with a pot of tea, a bottle of homemade moonshine, and two sturdy teacups.

She released my hand and looked me over, cataloguing things I didn't need to know. I squirmed as she brushed my hair back and stared at my face. I stayed still, though, when she put her fingers under my eyes and tugged so she could examine my eyes more closely.

When she smoothed her hands over my temples and jaw, I asked, "Any wrinkles yet?"

She frowned and swatted my arm. "Don't be cheeky. Your iron is low."

I winced. My mother had any number of herbal drinks that she'd concocted over the years to try to offset my peculiar diet. Sometimes I'd rather be low on multiple things than be forced to drink a cup of whatever gritty sludge fixed my daily deficiencies.

"I'll eat later, and grab a few vitamins, too."

She made the same *hmm* noise and gestured for me to sit. Dutifully, I did, and my mother went over to a raised garden bed and pulled out a tuber that looked like the beet's uglier cousin. A sharp knife from her pocket, and she sliced the root into slivers that she dropped into a tea cup.

Then she topped it off with a spoonful of what looked like sugar and a splash of moonshine. "Drink."

I sighed and accepted the cup of dirty root and homemade booze. There was no sense arguing with her. I could be a hundred, and she'd still be mixing up things that most mothers wouldn't give a child *but* know damn well that it was precisely what my weird body required. She could read me with the same ease she had with the soil in her various gardens. Sometimes, I suspect the truth was that she parented the plants or maybe gardened me. To her, it was one and the same. Who's to say she was wrong?

It was salt, not sugar, in my cup. Salt, dirt, root, and booze. It was weird, but her concoctions always were. The damned gritty root cocktail was making me feel better already. I lifted the cup and said, "It's helping."

"Well, of course it is." She patted my arm. "Don't forget salt, child. You're low."

We sat and enjoyed the afternoon sun, chatting and drinking moonshine, and I felt a lot of my stress slip away. There was a lot of my life I questioned, but no matter what went wrong or right or somewhere in between, I always knew I was loved and accepted unconditionally. Some days, that was everything.

Other days, it was a pressure, a weight I didn't want. I had fear that my very soul was tied to her, and if I were injured it would break her—but we had agreed not to discuss that. She'd made sacrifices to have me, and I couldn't get an answer as to how deep the costs were.

"Jesse okay?" she asked after we'd relaxed long enough for her patience to wear thin.

"He is."

"The girls?"

"Good, too."

"Work?" Her tone was identical to the first questions, but I saw her hands tighten around her cup.

"It's good, Mama." I reached out and took her hand. "I'm safe. Careful. I have Eli helping, too."

I didn't feel compelled to mention that I'd rejected Eli's help for months, or that it was just recently that I gave in. There were things best not said, and any version of what she'd hear as "I've been being reckless" was always on that list. In this, Sera and my mother saw eye-to-eye.

"Eli? The bartender?"

"Bar owner," I corrected. "He's strong."

My mother nodded, and I would typically leave it at that, but I couldn't ask more if I didn't come clean. She was the only person other than Eli who knew of otherworldly things. Witches weren't exactly common, and everyone said that the true fae were all tucked away in Elphame.

"He's half-fae," I whispered.

Mama Lauren made that humming noise in her throat. "He is?"

I nodded. "I've needed him to help because . . . my magic is off."

My mother leaned back in her seat and smiled at me with the same look that she gave her prize vegetable or moonshine. "Well, then. It's about time! *Eli* explains why your magic is off, doesn't it?"

"Eli's ancestry?"

"No, dear. The feelings you have for him." She walked over to a short citrus tree, plucked a hybrid fruit of some sort. She stood staring at the fields and holding this bright pink thing that was lime-sized. Her back was to me, and I felt that she'd just used some sort of magic.

"Mama?"

She tossed the remains of her tea into the garden and refilled both of our glasses with moonshine. She looked at me. "I'm guessing you're feeling erratic? Magic surges? Waking up corpses by accident?"

"Yes."

"Mmm." Mama Lauren tore the rind off the fruit and squeezed the pulp into my glass of liquor. "This calls for being a little tipsy." Then she lifted hers and said, "To secrets unveiled. Goddess have mercy."

I drained my glass, and she did the same.

"Baby girl, you're going to be upset with me, but" —she looked away for a moment, cleared her throat, and met my gaze again as she announced—"hear me out. I made a bargain. It was the only way to keep you safe when you were younger."

I refilled my glass and dropped the rest of the weird pink fruit into it. "What sort of bargain?"

"I tamped your magic down until you found a real partner," she said shakily, not looking at me as she spoke. "I meant to tell you, and eventually, I would have. You know that . . . but you said you weren't dating. I ask Jesse's parents every time I see them. I used to think it would be him, you know? Close as you two were? I was afraid I'd done all that only to have you find your intended as a teenager. Most people never find their perfect mate, Gen."

"My perfect . . . *Eli?*" I was careful as I explained, "We're friends."

She smiled.

And I laughed. Despite the sheer exhaustion of my mother's overprotectiveness, I could still laugh at the idea of Eli and I as perfect mates. We were something, but perfect? I could never give him what he'd need. I wasn't that person. I never would be.

The thought, though, of having Eli in a permanent way did weird things to my heart.

I looked at my mother and explained, "We might be compatible in bed—although I don't know because I haven't gone there —but he's half-*fae*, Mama. He'll want children. He *has* to have at least one child of his blood."

"You might be able—"

"Not happening," I said coldly. "Whatever perversion of nature I am, I'm not passing it on to a baby, and he isn't going to violate his people's law for me. That's not fair."

"Geneviève!" My mother had tears in her eyes now.

But I was not going to console her. Not now. I stood and stepped away to prevent myself from hugging her. "What were the *exact* terms of the bargain, Mama?"

"'Your beacon to the grave would be tamped down. Your *draugr* traits tamped down. Until you met a true partner, loyal and able to stand at your side. So mote it be.'" She spoke the words like a recitation.

"That's not romantic in wording!" I turned and hugged her. "Eli is my business *partner*. Your wording left room for interpretation. He's safe."

"Geneviève . . ."

"This is fine." I kissed her head. "So, it's just a learning curve, right? Like puberty." I thought about all the corpses I summoned my first few periods and winced. "Hopefully, not *quite* like that! But I get more juice since I have a business partner."

Now that I knew the words she'd used, I felt relieved. I wasn't sure I wanted to tell Eli, but I suppose I probably needed to. He was the one who'd had to deal with my come-here-dead-things pulse the other night—and my temper being touchier. He deserved to know about this. Well, parts of it. He didn't need to know that for just a moment the thought that the decision was out of my hands made me practically quake with a twisted mess of fear and desire and hope. If we were bound, I'd have to face whatever this was. We weren't, though. *Partners.*

"Geneviève, honey." Mama Lauren pulled me close and put her hands on my face. "That bargain was intended to be about being loved, about you not being alone once I die. I asked for your *bashert*, your soulmate."

"Those weren't the exact words of the bargain, though, and faery bargains are notoriously unreliable. You were had. You might have been seeking my destiny, but Eli is my business partner. I used that word, and this is the result," I insisted, shoving the thought of being loved by Eli far away. I gave Mama Lauren a tight smile and said, "I'm going to enjoy the farm before sunset."

"Geneviève?"

I paused and looked at her, half-daring her to argue, but she just sighed and said, "I'll freshen your room. Stay away from the bayou."

And I went to ramble the fields where I'd grown up. I could roam, and with my speed, I'd be at the water. Sometimes, when I was a little girl, my mother allowed it. It made her nervous, despite my best intentions. If I would *flow*, she couldn't keep up.

It hit me that this was what I was with bindings. I wasn't

going to think about what it would mean to be unbound. I wasn't going to think about bad faery bargains. I'd called Eli my partner more than once. The bargain was worded as "partner," and that was that.

The alternative, the thought that she could trap him with her bargain and I could cost him his heritage, filled me with sorrow. And in my deepest of hearts, I could admit that there was a fear that if I had the chance to be fully loved by Eli I'd be destroyed by losing it—and I would have to lose it. People near me were at risk. Even my friends were kept at a distance. What if I lost control? What if my ancestry changed me little-by-little? What if I couldn't stop from summoning the dead? I was too dangerous to love, and caring about Eli—which I could admit to—meant making sure he didn't get too close to me. My mother had the right of it living alone. I followed her example these days. No roommates. No permanent relationships. Limit time with loved ones, including my own mother. There was no way to know what I would evolve into, but I had a pretty good idea that it wasn't going to be cute and cuddly.

I kicked off my shoes and stepped into the grassy soil that nourished me. Coming home wasn't easy, but it had perks. Rich soil and open space, fresh moonshine and Mama Lauren, I wished briefly that I could stay. I supposed it was hiding, but I preferred to think of it as a retreat. Strategic withdrawal. Returning home.

I was stronger, and maybe there was a way to stay here now.

Tonight, I was going to enjoy a little country peace. If I was wrong about the bargain, I'd burn that bridge when I got there. And if all else failed, I knew a faery. Maybe I could make a new bargain to bind my cursed traits.

Chapter Fifteen

THE NEXT MORNING, I FELT REFRESHED AND OPTIMISTIC. MY mother's tinctures and teas—and the secret she spilled—made me feel better than I had in months. My magic being erratic was temporary. Hell, maybe once the dust settled, I'd be stronger and surer.

By early afternoon, I felt positively energized.

"You understand why I did it, then?" Mama Lauren asked again. "You were just so young, and I was hiding you. They started showing up when you weren't even teething yet, and I was a single mother and . . . scared."

There was no way this conversation was going to good places. She was a single mother to an aberration by her own choice. She took fertility teas for months and actively tried to conceive me with a *draugr.* I wasn't a miracle baby, an oops, or even a birth control failure. She chose me.

"I don't blame you for binding me," I said. I kept the list of things I did blame her for to myself. We both knew it was there just under the surface.

"No child has been as wanted as you were, Geneviève." My

mother stared at me, and there was no way to deny the sheer love in her expression. She had wanted me enough to break the laws of nature. There was power in her that few people realized. She had done the impossible.

I knew, though. She was a terrifying woman, a powerful witch, and a devoted mother. I would rather face a field of angry corpses than my mother when she was angry. I still asked the detail she'd pointedly ignored addressing: "What did you give in exchange?"

"It doesn't matter, Geneviève." She waved her hand as if she could physically ward off my words. She could, but to get her anger to the point of silencing my voice was a thing I hadn't managed since killing the corpse that fathered me—and intended to use me like breeding stock whether I agreed to it or not.

I shoved that thought back into the recesses of my mind to address more pressing issues. "So . . . the fee was huge then?"

"Geneviève!" Mama Lauren looked at me and sighed. "It's a favor for a faery called Doran. That's all."

"To do what?"

"Whatever is asked of me," she said quietly. "No restrictions."

I took several deep breaths. Then I repeated the process. I folded my arms over my chest. And in the calmest voice I could summon, which admittedly was like angry *bean sidhe* on a bender, I asked, "To clarify, you gave an open-ended vow for an unspecified favor to a faery?"

"Yes." My mother tilted her chin up and stared at me. "You are my baby, Geneviève. I would carve out my heart for you if that was what it took to protect you. Those corpses and the *draugr,* they were everywhere. Like maggots on rot. And they weren't like your father. They were terrifying."

I closed my eyes. "We will not discuss him. You agreed."

"Fine!" Mama Lauren touched my face. "You are my world though, Geneviève. Surely you understand. When you're a mother, you'll—"

"Please. Don't." My voice cracked. "If you are contacted, you tell them to find me. Whatever faery it is, I need to be present. I want you to be safe. Agree to that, and . . . and I'll *forgive* you."

"You have my word," my mother said softly.

I nodded. Her madness over motherhood wasn't a thing I understood. Maybe it was a Jewish thing, or a pagan one. Both faiths uphold maternity as nearly holy. Maybe it was just her. Some women felt the call to mother as if it was their divine function. Whatever it was, the one and only thing she ever wanted out of this lifetime was to be a mom. She insisted everyone call her Mama Lauren. Not just me. It was her identity.

And me? I never wanted children. All I could think of was passing my own wrongness on. And I suppose it didn't help that the dead man who helped her in her quest for motherhood wanted to use me as an incubator for *draugr* reproduction. To me, motherhood was a trap, and to her it was a gift. We would not agree on this.

"I'm heading out." I pretended not to see the heartbreak on her face, but I still hugged her tighter than any human could do and reminded her, "No mother has been as loving as mine, and I am the luckiest child to have you as a mom. I know that."

She sniffled. "I love you."

"I know." I kissed her on both cheeks and her nose. "I love you, too. If you hear anything, let me know? Something is wrong with the rise in new *draugr*."

Mama Lauren nodded. She might not always make sense to me, but when it came to lending a hand—or a spell—I could count on her. No human could gather information from the otherworldly quite like a witch. A *draugr* was previously-human. A faery only looked human. Witches were *both* human and other-worldly.

And then I let myself *flow* back to the park to catch the first bus back to New Orleans. I felt better physically, and I had a few answers, but I had new questions, too.

Tonight, I'd see my friends. Tomorrow, I'd meet Tres. And in the middle, I'd pretend not to know secrets I ought to share with Eli.

———

UNTIL RECENTLY, FINDING STEADY WORK HAD BEEN HARDER than I'd like. Then, in the last two months, I had more removal jobs than time to do them. Part of me wondered why. *Draugr* weren't keen on creating an excess of mouths to feed on the population. They'd kept themselves a secret for centuries, so they were well-aware of how many of their kind they could feed and hide.

So why was there a bump in newly-infected *draugr*? Had one of them freed Marie Chevalier? And who injected Chaddock? Was the woman with the syringe there because of Marie? Had *Marie* been injected, too? Why?

The injections mentioned by Tres certainly set off alarms, but he was one man with one theory. Alvin Chaddock could have been getting injections for pain medicine or vitamins. I had no reason to believe that there was a conspiracy or that the injection was tied to his death or the increase in beheadings I had to do. And sure, Chaddock was weirdly alert, and he'd seemed strong— but I was tired and my magic was wonky. Three days of rest and one night in the relaxing bed at Jesse's flat had calmed my worries. The visit to the Outs had me feeling like I was invincible.

The need to help Tres pressed at the back of my mind, and I decided to reach out to the police. Subtly. The fucking lectures Gary had already given me were my ceiling for well-intentioned worry. And I wasn't about to hang out an old-school detective shingle. I was making a few calls. Asking Mama Lauren. Monitoring obits. But I was still me—just a woman with weapons and the skill to use them.

Tonight, though, I was ready to relax with my friends—and get my phone back from Eli. Maybe I'd call Tres to follow up and see if he'd learned anything. There was no reason to wait until lunch tomorrow. We could meet later tonight. I could see what he'd learned and—

I paused. My desire to help Tres felt like more than guilt. I wasn't sure *why*, but the list of things that made no sense was growing too long.

"Fucksicles."

Having my magic untethered was making me off kilter in way too many ways. I needed stability, and that meant seeing my friends. I could sort out the rest later.First, I'd drink and see friends at Eli's bar. I needed friendship and liquor, and I thought they needed to see me, too. Both Christy and Sera were worrying in their own ways, and I felt guilty for not talking to them about my magic being weird—and about my feelings for Eli. I just tried to limit what I told them about my job. No sense making their stress levels higher.

I'd delayed later than I should've, stayed inside out of the glaring sun, and now I was scurrying through the streets at a pace just shy of flowing. Sometimes, I would call myself careful. Tonight wasn't such a time. I could feel tendrils of energy, a sort of low hum that told me *draugr* were near. The warehouse district was two blocks away, and somewhere there was a group of dead things. They felt like gaps in the world, pockets of vacancy. I couldn't feel just one with pinpoint accuracy, but if several were together, I sensed it much as hearing sirens or smelling cigars.

The sirens lifted and fell like a strange song. Voices rose in anger, in greetings, in excitement. And things that skittered on paws and claws ran nearby. My mind sorted through the sounds faster than I registered most of them.

And with my internal sundial, I realized how close to careless I was tonight. Put me in a windowless room, and I'd still know. Sunset was in three minutes.

Three g'damn minutes.

I slammed open the doors to Bill's like I was running from a pride of hungry lions.

"Slow down," Eli grumbled as his hand stopped one of the doors from contact with his face.

"Life's short," I said drolly.

"We're all going to die, cupcake," he said. "I'd rather not die because you kill me with my own door."

I grinned. "No murder, bonbon. Just trying to make your perfect face match your flawed personality."

He made a noise that wasn't quite a laugh. Honestly, we both knew I wouldn't want to kill him, most days. Maybe I liked Eli *because* he wasn't going to die of natural causes. Fae creatures lived longer than most *draugr*. I wasn't sure if *I* was going to live longer than a human, but if I did, it would be nice to have a few familiar faces.

Perfect partner, a little voice whispered. It sounded like Mama Lauren, but it was my own neurosis, not her magic. I needed to tell him—maybe ask about Doran, too.

I wasn't about to discuss it here, though. Tonight, I wanted to pretend I was plain old run of the mill human. Witches were human, and humans died. I'd be gone long before a faery.

"Afraid of the dark?" Eli asked as he looked into the dusk behind me before pushing the door shut, as if it would trap the bad things outside. "Or something in it tonight?"

"Sometimes. Or maybe how much I enjoy what I do in it."

"Your job doesn't define you, Geneviève," Eli said quietly. "You hunt in the dark, but *you* are not dark."

I laughed in a combination of relief and amusement. I loved that Eli called what I did "hunting." I leaned in and said, "I *kill* in the dark. It's very different than mere hunting."

"And you are radiant as you do so," he said, unperturbed by my words.

"I am *not*."

He pressed his lips together as if trapping words from

escaping again. He did that more and more. Silently, he opened a box on the table and handed me my phone.

I looked at it. Four messages from Tres.

Eli's disapproval was beyond obvious. "His messaging feels more obsessive than normal."

"He's grieving. People do that differently."

"Send me a bottle?" I asked in a flirtier tone than I should have, pointedly shoving the phone in my back pocket. Eli had read the texts, and that meant I didn't need to read them just now. Tonight was a night out with friends—and maybe a little careful flirting with Eli.

I cleared my throat. "Join us for a drink later?"

"Of course, my dear meringue."

"Good." I paused before adding, "I like being around you."

"I know." He gave me a wicked smile. Then he passed by me closer than comfortable and whispered, "Sunglasses."

I pulled my shades off, and winced at the loss of detail that followed. But as I left him there, I was smiling. I liked us this way. Easy. Light. We simply weren't suited for long conversations right now. Perhaps we never would be.

Perfect partner, my ass. We'd be a disaster.

Eli motioned to the bartender as I scanned the room, looking for my two closest female friends. Honestly, I was suspicious of the sort of women who lacked good female friends. Mine were people I'd easily kill for or die to protect. Hell, I'd even sit through pedicures for them, and that was a lot less fun to me than killing.

The bar was dim in the way of my preferred bars. I saw better in the dark, and if I had my way, the only kind of place I'd be in would be dark rooms, darker rooms, and carefully chosen areas on nights with a New Moon. Those were a sort of perfection that I wished I could enjoy without being aware of what else was in the dark with me. The world took on a kind of clarity that only happened when the sky was perfectly dark.

In the darkest corner of the bar, I saw Christy and Sera beside a pool table. Several old men watched them. I wasn't sure if it was because Christy was running the table or because she was bent low and wearing a shirt with a lot of cleavage. She had several degrees in esoteric shit, but research didn't pay the way her pool hustling could.

Consciously slowing myself, I slid between tables and wait-resses, bodies and beers. Sera sighed in relief at the sight of me.

"Thought you weren't going to make it," she said as she stood and hugged me.

Christy's gaze lifted from the table, assessed me, and that was that. We didn't talk when she was earning the rent, and goddess love 'em, tourist after tourist bought her sweet and fumbling act most nights. She was adept at a lot of things, but an affinity for physics meant that she steered pool balls like she had a magic wand instead of a pool cue.

I settled in at a table to watch.

"Dinner." Sera slid a glass of whisky, neat, toward me. Not a dram. Not some terrible "water added" nonsense. A generous tumbler of booze.

I put my hand on my heart and said, "I love you best in the whole world."

"As you should." Sera slid a plate of greasy, onion-and-bacon-coated fries toward me.

I did eat. Solid food, too, just like a regular person. Okay, *mostly* like a regular person.

"Bless you," I said.

Sera and I watched Christy fleece the fool who agreed to play against her. The old men in the corner chortled and high-fived her. I swear I hadn't figured out yet if they were more entertained by watching her because she was such a curvy girl or because they were in on the secret. Either way, she paused to talk to them as she folded her cash and tucked it into her cleavage.

"Where were you the last two nights?" Sera asked.

I shrugged. "Work?"

"I heard from a friend at the station," she pronounced, as if she'd caught me in a lie. "Jesse's place?"

"Still work."

"Both nights?"

"Outs last night," I whispered. "Needed to see Mama Lauren."

Sera looked ready to say something more, but Eli paused at our table with a bottle just then. I knew not to remark on the fact that he delivered it himself. Everything with the damn fae had meanings, ritual in old ways that I was still trying to learn.

"Well, aren't you sweet?" Sera murmured. "Or are you just sweet on Gen?"

Eli's mouth curved into a smile, transforming his face in a way that screamed "not human." It wasn't exactly a secret, but in that moment, it was glaringly obvious.

"I don't believe one could be 'sweet' on a creature such as Geneviève." Eli opened the bottle, cracking the seal in front of me. "In awe? Frightened? Fascinated? I dare say that no other creature in all of New Orleans is quite so rich in contradictions as she is."

Christy came over mid-proclamation.

"House cut," she said, withdrawing a folded bill from her cleavage. "Left them drinking cash this time too."

"Be still my winged heart," Eli murmured.

The doors opened without a sound, but I didn't need sound to tell me what had walked into the building. I felt their tug on my skin, tightening muscles as my body wanted to *flow*. Like called to like.

Tonight, though, they were trying to read me. Tendrils of grave magic pounded against my mental shields. I was on my feet without knowing how or when I moved.

Eli stayed at my side. "Sugar frost, I believe you have a small duty before relaxing. May I assist?"

Short sword already in hand, I glanced at my friends. "Guard them."

"As you wish," he murmured. *Draugr* were pleasantly frightened of fae blood until they reached around a century old. By then, they could control themselves. Fae blood looked a lot like liquid silver, and in any dose but a quick sip, it acted like silver, too, leaving the *draugr* sickened and ravenous all at once. Eli had an innate safety with most of these, but not this one. *She* was old, and that meant Eli was in need of protection, too.

And without thinking about the consequences, I let myself *flow*. In the flicker of a moment, I was at the front of the bar, sword in one hand and gun in the other.

Chapter Sixteen

"YOU NEED TO COME WITH US," THE FRONT *DRAUGR* SAID. HE had the perpetually elongated teeth of an again-walker in his second-decade. It made him harder to understand, but at least he was more articulate than grunts.

Behind him were three more walking corpses and one who stood drooling around the gag in her mouth. One of the *draugr* held onto the prisoner, who appeared to be a nice grandmother with a growling and hissing problem.

The two *draugr* not guarding a prisoner stood on either side of a woman who was dressed like she'd watched *Interview with a Vampire* far too often. Added to that was make-up that looked like she was prepping for her own funeral. She was old, though; the sort of old that told me I wasn't fast enough to shoot her. My bones tingled at the chill she radiated. When she died, there would be no need for a Con Crew pick-up. Dust and air would be all that remained of her.

And I wasn't sure I could kill her even if I was prepared, even if I was facing *just* her.

My hand was wrapped around the hilt of my single-handed

sword, and the blade was resting on my left shoulder. Only the forward edge and a few inches at the curved tip were sharp, so it was more comfortable to rest the blunt edge on my shoulder than hold it aloft. A standard weight sword was only two pounds. Still, I felt better with it in a waiting position—and less silly than standing poised to attack.

"I've been over this with almost a dozen of you." I sighed and met several dead-eyed stares. "You all need a social media site or newsletter. This is *my* bar, and anything other than a human has to have *my* permission to be here."

I ignored the technicality that it was Eli's bar. It was mine only in the sense that I was happy here.

"We need to talk to you, Geneviève," the older woman in the center of their clutch said. She was the most articulate monster I'd met, more so than most humans. It still didn't mean I wanted to chat.

"I have nothing to say," I told her.

"Darius," the one in front said.

Maybe because it was my so-called father's name, or maybe it was because the dead guy reached out. Either way, I brought my sword down reflexively. His hand flopped to the ground, a rotting putrid lump. It looked like week-old meat.

"Newly infected, aren't you?" I muttered.

"Reborn," the woman said. "He was reborn during your lifetime."

"Potato, pa-tah-to." I didn't lift my sword or my gun.

Her gaze was still fixed on me, and I realized that her fangs were retracted. There was nothing but control in her form and face. Her voice was steady, and she gazed upon me with the surety that she had no reason to fear. I'd never met a *draugr* as old as her. If she wanted to kill everyone in the bar, we would die.

I still said, "Exit now, or we'll need to call the body bus."

The woman pressed her lips together. She looked around, and

I resisted the amateurish impulse to see where her gaze fell. *Watch the scary lady*. Eli could tell me later what she'd been studying.

When her attention re-settled on me, she said, "I knew your father, Geneviève."

"Cool. That makes one of us." I pasted a smile on my face.

Two of the *draugr* laughed. Lucky me. I was amusing to corpses. It wasn't exactly a life goal, but to be honest, I wasn't sure what my goals were. Don't die? Don't wake up a walking corpse? It was more of an *un*-list than a to-do list. I really ought to have a bucket list that contained things other than "don't kick the bucket."

"You're special, Geneviève," the dead woman said. "A hy--"

"No." My sword raising ended her words. "I am a witch, one who very much dislikes dead things."

"We can speak about your heritage here, or we can sit down like civilized women and address it later. We *will* address it," the woman said in a tone very much like an order.

I really disliked orders.

"Not here. Not now." I didn't add "not later" aloud although I had exactly zero interest in talking to her later either. I had a lousy temper, and chatting with something old enough to kill me with her elegant pinky finger wasn't a great plan.

"We shall plan a luncheon," the dead lady said. "I will answer your questions, and you will not attack me."

One of her corpse guards moved forward, and I was left in the unenviable position of deciding how much I wanted to expose myself and how much I wanted to avoid being touched. Most of the people in the bar weren't looking at me. Fear blurred recall anyhow, so I could explain away my speed.

I opted for expediency, and raised my gun.

"We did not inject those people, Geneviève," she said. "I wanted to tell you myself, so you would understand the serious-ness of it. I've watched you and respected your work from afar, but I require your aid directly."

"*What?*"

"I am hiring you. Several of my subjects were kidnapped. Milked like serpents." The *draugr* woman sounded increasingly agitated. "And left to starve to death. Do you have any idea what they must have suffered?"

I swallowed. It sounded awful. I could admit that. Mildly, I said, "My kills are always clean."

She nodded. "Yes. I do find your work for us helpful, Geneviève. I would gladly compensate you for it, but I was worried that you'd be affronted."

I faltered at that. "What?"

"Pay? Donate?" The *draugr* woman frowned. "Be your patron? What is the word?"

"For . . ."

"Cleaning up the troublesome ones." She smiled, showing blood-stained teeth. "You are a most effective *bougie*-man." She paused, frowned again at the shortened version of bourgeois. "Not bougie. Booger-man? You are a good threat."

I gaped at her, truly at a loss in that moment. Bougie? Booger? I was neither bourgeois or snot. I shouldn't be amused by a corpse attempting slang either. I killed her kind, had lopped off a *draugr's* hand a few moments ago. Now she was offering to pay me.

"I am called Beatrice," she pronounced. "When you have knowledge of this problem, speak my name, and they shall find me. You may not consider yourself my subject, but you are of me and I am your ally in this. I've brought you a gift as a token of my regard."

"Subject?" I echoed. "Gift?"

I was fairly sure I didn't want to ask the question at the tip of my tongue. Still, I needed confirmation. "What are you? Who?"

"Don't be daft, Geneviève. For now, however, you may simply consider me your patron." She looked at me with a vaguely amused look and withdrew an envelope which she tossed to me.

I let it fall to the floor. My hands were occupied with weapons. "My . . . patron."

Then the woman, Beatrice, ripped the head off the woman, the *draugr* prisoner. "Marie Chevalier. She was let loose after an unwilling transformation. Injected."

Beatrice dropped the head next to the corpse's body and said to the remaining draugr, "Guard my exit. Do not injure her even if she strikes you."

I felt more than saw Beatrice *flow*. She was there, and then gone. The ease of her exit was like a gentle ocean current, and with it, I felt an underlying certainty that she could shift that gentle ripple into the edge of a storm. I'd once thought that the corpse that impregnated my mother was old. He was an infant next to Beatrice.

The young corpses stayed for a moment, and then turned to walk away once she was a few blocks away. I felt her pause and send a pulse of energy toward me, an energy I'd thought of as solely my maternal heritage.

And then I was standing alone in the doorway with a sword in my hand and a lot of questions in my mind.

I called dispatch. "No human injuries." I paused. "Marie Chevalier. Recent walker. Killed a security guard at Cypress Grove a couple nights ago. I didn't kill her."

I disconnected. Honestly, I wasn't sure what to say. Dead lady brought me a gift? My surprise patron saint beheaded another *draugr* for me? I grabbed the envelope Beatrice had tossed to me, and then I stood clutching my phone.

When my phone buzzed, I stared at it and then at Eli. It rang. Buzzed again. Patrons in the bar were freaking out in general, and I heard Eli's staff going around verifying that no pictures had been taken. Honestly, I couldn't process the events of the last few moments.

I walked toward my friends.

"Cupcake?" Eli prompted.

A message from Tres appeared. *Associate dead. At morgue in 15 min. Injection. Come?*

"Geneviève?"

I held up a hand to Eli. I needed to process the mystery of Beatrice, but right now, I'd have to hold off on that.

In his recent message, Tres was all business, but I scrolled to see the other texts he'd sent. One per day. Friendly, slightly flirty, and then simply, "Grab a drink?"

I lifted my gaze to Eli. I hated to admit it, but Tres' reaction to me was a bit beyond weird. I had no information for him. I didn't *know* him.

"Tres texted. Again."

"Twice in one day?" Eli said. "Do you not find it . . . strange?"

"Who's Tres?" Sera asked.

"Son of a dead man," Eli said.

"Client." I stared at Eli and added, "I'm meeting him tomorrow."

"Geneviève," Eli started.

And part of me thought I was making a mistake. There was something off. "Donkey balls."

Sera met my gaze. "Eli worrying for a reason?"

"I don't know. I just . . . wanted to help him, but . . ."

"He's fixating on Geneviève," Eli said.

"Shit crackers." I sighed and nodded. "First situation first. . . The dead chick back there says their kind aren't injecting anyone. She paid me." I motioned to the money I'd dropped on the table. I wasn't going to leave a thick bundle of cash on the floor either.

Eli pocketed it. "I will handle this."

"Police will come by for . . ." I gestured at the body.

Eli nodded.

I glanced over as one of the bartenders spread a sheet over the remains.

Honestly, I should've done that, but I wasn't sure what to do. Being hired by the same kind of thing I killed was weird as fuck.

How was Mrs. Chevalier connected? To Chaddock? Why inject people with venom? I glanced back toward the door. One weird thing at a time, or maybe the same weird thing. Either way, I needed to deal with the next dilemma on the list.

"Tres texted about another body with an injection site," I said.

Eli glanced at Christy. He withdrew the same folded stack of cash that she had handed him from pool hustling before the *draugr* arrived. He extended it to her. "Mind the bar?"

She nodded and took the cash.

Even though I knew better, I started, "I could handle it—"

"Do. Not." Eli snapped. "You know something is peculiar here, and I accompany you for work."

I hesitated. Texted Jesse: "Job thing came up. S and C at bar. Come to them?" I paused, sighed, and added, "Eli with me."

"Be right there," Jesse texted back.

I held my gun out to Sera, butt first, and said, "It's loaded with my special bullets."

Both of them opened bags and pulled out their own guns. Christy said, "We're good. Keep your gun."

————

I WASN'T QUITE READY TO CONFRONT MY FEELINGS ABOUT MY *draugr* encounter. I was equally unable to address my feelings about Eli. And I hated to admit that Tres wasn't the only one acting strangely. I had a nagging urge to help him, see him, rescue him. It made no sense. Why was everything so complicated? I walked to the passenger door of Eli's car. He was there, opening it, treating me the way he always did.

When he got in, I said, "You confuse me."

"You infuriate me," he replied in the same tone.

I sighed as he steered us into traffic. New Orleans, like anywhere at night, had traffic that was wretched at the best of times. Almost no one walked in the dark.

"What?" I asked.

"Your guilt is unnatural."

I stared out the window. "I know."

"I want to help, but you push me away."

"I cannot—"

"*Will* not," he interjected. "You *will* not let me in. Nothing and no one is stopping you. You, Geneviève, are making this choice *for me*. You decided I couldn't handle it. My opinion doesn't factor into the decision. Only yours."

"So, I should do what? Risk our friendship? Use you until there are too many feelings? Should I be with you knowing it will hurt you eventually?"

Eli glanced at me. "Yes."

I wanted to hit him. I knew better. Punching someone because they pissed you off was shitty. Doing it while he was driving was even stupider.

"Go enjoy your boy toys, and in the end, you'll see that I could have been here all along. The fae are not so . . . *narrow*. I do not begrudge you the flings you need to find peace."

"Liar."

He drove in silence for several minutes. "I do not lie to you."

My anger bubbled inside me. I knew the fae didn't lie.

So, when he pulled into the morgue parking lot and put on his gloves, I decided to test my theories. He opened my door. I stepped out, but instead of taking his steadying hand, I wrapped my arms around him. He didn't resist as I turned him so my back was to the half-lit lot.

I shoved him a bit forcefully into the side of his car and took a wrist in each hand, squeezed them, and held him in place. Electric surges, magic that grew between us like sparks before an inferno, threatened to overwhelm me. I didn't retreat.

When Eli opened his mouth to speak, I kissed him.

And he didn't refuse me. He parted his lips and let me have control. I gave him none of the affection he deserved. No kindness. No soft touches. No words of regard. I told myself he was no different than a stranger in a bar.

But he tasted like honeysuckle wine, and I wanted more. It wasn't Eli who couldn't handle what we could be. It was *me*. I wanted Eli. Even in the moment, I couldn't tell myself he was anyone else. I wanted him. No one else.

My body pressed into him, toe to hip. We were sealed tightly together. I felt his muscles hard against me, and the realization that he might be able to overpower me made me moan a little. So few people could overcome me physically with my fucked-up ancestry. Eli could. If he knew I wanted that, he would.

And he wouldn't judge me for it.

My hand slid into his silken hair, clutching to be sure he wouldn't escape.

No mercy.

My magic was the only thing I kept in check.

I felt his body respond, so I hitched my leg up, pressing closer to his obvious arousal. He made a noise that eroded a little more of my self-control. I tried to pretend he was not Eli. I tried to pretend we didn't fit. I was simply proving a point. I was using him. He was just a body, replaceable, meaningless. I wasn't emotional.

Eli might not lie, but in this, I was. Eli *mattered* to me. I knew that, and now that we were hip-to-hip and mouth-to-mouth, I also knew that the chemistry we had was extreme.

I was . . . so very fucked.

Nothing had felt as natural as kissing Eli. I kept my eyes closed, but I could smell the unique scent of Eli, taste him, and my body was awash in need that was more than simply sexual. It made me pause.

As soon as I felt his arms lift, his hands grip my hips to hold me to him, I tried to step away. I managed to pull back enough to stare at him. He looked as shaken as I felt.

"Still right here, peach," he said lightly. His grip tightened, and he bit my throat gently, kissed my neck, and whispered into my ear, "I'm still here. Trust me. Trust *this*."

Casually, or at least as casual as I could be, I said, "If I can't use my magic, and you can't leave your hands where I put them, it wouldn't work, so stop pretending it could."

I stepped away, and he let go. I wanted to prove that he couldn't accept being used, that he'd demand more, that he wouldn't give me that kind of control. So, I turned and walked away from the pretty little blue sports car and the gorgeous man leaning against it.

Honestly, I needed distance or I wouldn't stop touching him —and he needed *not* to know that. My attempt to prove that he wouldn't settle as he claimed he would was far from well-advised. If I hadn't retreated, I'd have shoved him onto the hood of the car and made a spectacular and very public mistake.

That was the secret I'd kept from him—and myself. I might not do relationships or feelings, but I was already there. If I went any closer, I'd break at least one of our hearts. I'd spent so long claiming I was protecting him, but the reality was that letting Eli into my heart or my bed would destroy me in the end.

I was three steps away when he answered, "If you don't trust my control, I suppose you'll need to use handcuffs then."

Chapter Seventeen

✦❦✦

My pace quickened as I walked across the dark and light patches of the parking lot without replying to Eli. I was not running. Clearly. I was simply walking quickly. And what was there to say to *that*? The image of Eli handcuffed to my bed was enough to short-circuit my already lust-soaked brain. Eli wasn't the one to finally kiss me, despite the fact that I'd granted him a kiss in a bargain. He'd kept his word. He didn't cross the lines I'd drawn. That was all on me.

And now my lips tasted of honeysuckle wine. His kiss was on my lips like a lingering drink of liquor. I licked my lips, trying to drink the last drops of his kiss.

A moment later, Eli was at my back as I walked. He hummed to himself, as if we were out for a walk at the park instead of going to see a corpse. A guilty whisper in my mind reminded me that I ought to have a little more respect for the dead. This wasn't a date. Nice girls don't go to the morgue on their dates.

Or practically dry hump their friends in parking lots.

Of course, if I was a nice girl, a lot of things in my life would be different. I was who I was, and for the most part, I was fine with it. No walk of shame here. Not now, not ever. I straightened my shoulders and strolled across the badly rippled and cracked asphalt. I kept my lazy saunter up until I was at the side entrance to the morgue.

Three men in suits waited at the door like rumpled male Fates who weren't sure which of them had the scissors. Two of the three looked confused and wary as I approached. The third, Tres, looked at me in hope.

"Miss Crowe," he said warmly. "I was starting to think you hadn't received my messages."

I nodded and cleared my throat. "I had work to handle."

"Are we still meeting tomorrow?" Tres asked as his gaze raked over me.

I squirmed, wondering what exactly the three men had seen. I wasn't embarrassed, but it was a bit unprofessional to stop and maul my associate as I had. Perhaps, though, it was no worse than planning to meet my client for reasons that had nothing to do with the case.

"Shall we continue?" Eli said from behind me.

My body heard that question differently than the people with us, and I repressed a shiver of need.

"Lead the way, Mr. Chaddock," I said as I motioned to the building. The door itself was atypical for the city—it appeared to be a basement floor entry. The illusion was a result of the way the asphalt was built up in the front of the building. There were no deep basements in a city prone to floods, but the morgue was in a new building with architectural oddities, so the men had descended several steps. In the mini stairwell, they were tucked in where they were reasonably secure, illuminated by the greenish light over the thick steel door. It was foolish to be outside in the dark.

"Why aren't you inside?" I asked.

Tres smiled, and it looked a little creeptastic. Then he sobered and said, "I just arrived, and when I saw the car, I waited for you. That is quite a memorable vehicle."

"Mr. Chaddock." Eli stepped forward, ignoring the flattering remark on his car. "Thank you for letting us know about the latest development."

His professional-sounding voice reminded me that this was a work call. My body might feel half-high on the honeysuckle kiss I just had, but . . . I paused, glanced at Eli, and realized that I *did* feel off. This wasn't the place to address it, but I would need to address it later. A warm glow had eased over the edges of my usual attitude. I felt calmer, languid, as if I'd been soaked in hot honey until every muscle was loose.

"Can we go inside?" I said bluntly, trying to at least sound like myself despite the mellow feeling which was most likely a side-effect of kissing Eli.

"Of course," Tres said.

One of the suits opened the door he'd been propping open with his foot. Obviously, at least one of them had been inside. Both men entered in front of Tres, either to lead him or guard him. It wasn't clear.

I followed behind Tres, and Eli was behind me. The hallway had the sterile look of cheap government buildings. Walls of mint green were illuminated by the harsh lights that buzzed faintly.

"It locks automatically," Suit One said.

I made a point of pushing the door, so Eli didn't need to touch it. He had gloves on, knowing where we were headed, but even with gloves, steel was unpleasant for him.

"Geneviève," Eli said softly.

I slowed so Eli could walk at my side.

"Are you . . . well?"

I nodded once, but I mouthed, "Very calm." Then I leaned in close enough that my lips were almost touching his ear and whispered, "You taste like honeysuckle wine."

Despite common sense, I flicked his ear with my tongue while I was there, and for a blink of a moment, I wondered if we could get this done and go somewhere else. Naked Eli. I had a strong suspicion that Naked Eli would be one of my favorite kinds of Eli. Logic tried to shove traitorous thoughts away, but I was standing still, staring at Eli.

"Is everything in order, Miss Crowe?" Tres asked.

"We were at a bar when you contacted us," Eli said, nudging me to continue walking. "Relaxing with friends."

"I'm a little tipsy," I said in a softer than normal voice, an almost girlish sound that really ought to belong to someone else.

"Tipsy?" Tres echoed.

I took a few seconds to focus myself, correct my voice and posture, and added, "Tipsy, not *drunk*. I'm relaxed but more than sober enough to work, Tres." I met his gaze unflinchingly. "I am fine. The job will be fine. Even if I were drunk—and I am not— Eli is completely sober, and he is more than adept at gathering the information you have."

I gave Eli the sort of smile that probably made it seem like we were lovers, but fuck it, I was being honest. He was capable. Maybe I needed to bottle whatever wine Eli had been drinking. I felt lighter, giddier, happier than I'd ever felt before. Sex was a great mood leveler for me. Witch, right? But this was different. A kiss shouldn't relax me this much.

"I'm the slash and kill part of this team," I added cheerily. I mean, technically, I was *all* of the team until recently. For years, it was just me. Eli was a very recent addition, but it sounded better this way, and my drunk brain wanted to sound professional.

"I see," Tres said. "Well, perhaps then, *Eli* can notice the evidence that you will need to know when you are ready to work."

"What do you mean by—"

"Do not question her ability, Chaddock." Eli stepped forward as if I needed shielding. "Even slightly inebriated, Geneviève is more adept at understanding death than the rest of us combined. She's easing your worries, but a few sips of something intoxicating will not decrease anything other than her manners."

"You say the sweetest things," I murmured. "Do you remember when I came to the bar with a broken ulna jutting out of my thigh?"

"Do you mean a femur?" one of the suits asked.

I laughed because, really, a femur? A bone that big would've severed an artery if I got stabbed with it.

"No. Ulna." I pointed to my forearm. "Arm bone."

"It was not Ms. Crowe's bone," Eli said, clarifying what I thought was obvious already.

Why would my *own* ulna be jabbed in my leg?

"One of the *draugr* used it to stab me after his friend went all goop and bone. That one hurt," I explained. "I lost so much blood I was like a stumbling drunk. I think I actually crawled into the bar that night after I finished the job."

Eli glanced at me. "It was more of a roll than a crawl."

I looked at Tres and his lackies and smiled. "Anyhow, a little blood loss or booze doesn't really stop me from getting the job done. I still got it done that night. I was just a little rough the next few days. So, no worries."

I met their gazes, offering reassuring smiles at each man. Weirdly, they didn't look comforted. I was going to offer more examples, but Eli said, "Let us see their evidence and get you home."

The three men continued on to a closed door. I didn't need to hear their explanations to know there were multiple corpses in the room.

I felt the answers before they opened the door. One of the corpses was likely to wake, to be an again-walker. Like the light in the hall, there was a soft hum of energy around it, as if the spark wasn't there completely.

I wanted to sit and watch, a wake for the not-properly-dead. I wondered if someone would sit shiva for me one day. *Eli.* I'd need to ask it of him, not to mourn but to protect my mother and friends if I woke. I really ought to have done it before now. I looked at him and asked, "If I die, stay with my body for mourning. Not at a morgue."

"Are you in peril here?" Eli stepped close. "Geneviève?"

"Not really. Maybe?" I shot him a look and a smile. "Aren't we always?"

He nodded. "I will attend your wake if you exit the world of the living."

It was enough for now. He wasn't asking questions I'd rather avoid. Maybe doing the hard conversations during disasters was the trick. And I was starting to think this was going to be a disaster.

I stepped into the room. The dead man before me hummed, and I felt like a moth trying to ignore a bright light. My magic wanted to explore. It was a rare thing to be so near to a *draugr* before it stood. I could feel it, a sort of low noise of awareness that buzzed over the skin of the corpse. There was a spark of energy hovering in wait, and I wanted to catch it. I felt like I was Dr. Frankenstein about to catch lightning.

My magic could do that with corpses, call them back to our world. They weren't alive, though. They were animated dead, and the moment they were too far from me, they crumbled as they were when they were raised. They weren't *alive* when I brought them back to our world. They weren't tethered. No food. No drink.

On the other hand, they were a lot more sentient than the average *draugr*.

The *draugr* before me would wake with or without me. It would walk, eat, destroy, and eventually, it would gain sentience.

With the truly dead, the only spark was me. When I called flesh and sinew to knit over bones, I felt a warmth in my belly like I'd just had a long drink of hot cider. I felt as if I had a hearth for them to gather near. I *was* the hearth. This was different. The closest comparison I could draw was a rattlesnake, coiled, poised, vibrating so fast that the possibility of motion felt tangible. I wanted to understand, but I didn't want to be on the receiving end of fangs.

I drew my sword.

"Geneviève?" Eli asked.

"Alert," I explained. "It's alert now."

"Do not behead it," he reminded me.

"It shouldn't want to wake yet, but I *feel* it. It wants to come talk to me." I felt my eyes trying to shift, to slid into those slits that would bring me the vision of the grave. "Mind the humans, please."

Eli nodded. "Gentlemen, Ms. Crowe needs a little bit of space to assess the deceased."

I glanced at the pair of men with Tres. They were average, middling men who wore the sort of suits that were clearly off the rack—the cheap rack, to be specific. Most of my clothes were thrift, so I wasn't judging. I was merely trying to get a sense of who they were. The one on the left, Suit Two, had a weak valve in his heart.

"See a heart doctor soon," I told him.

Suit Two frowned, gaze unhealthier than I realized until now.

"You're dying." I pressed my magic along his heart, sliding it like a fingertip over the wet warm thing that pumped his blood. It stuttered. I wanted to pet it into health, but I wasn't a physician. Experimenting with my unexpected surge in abilities seemed like a wretched idea. Was this part of the break of binding my mother had created?

I could tell the suit, though, that his heart wasn't strong. "Three years, tops."

"Miss Crowe," Tres said. He didn't move away as I approached. It wasn't the sound of a stranger greeting me. His voice was deep and friendly, and I knew that he was responding to the pulse of magic that was slowly drifting toward the covered bodies on the tables.

I let my magic slide over him, feeling the shape of him. His heart was strong. Muscles taut. I blinked at the longing radiating from him, and then I felt his body respond to my magic.

"Miss Crowe?" Tres's voice held awe, not just interest, but something closer to devotion.

"Geneviève," I offered, almost against my will. Perhaps it was the proximity to the corpse, but he was eliciting the same protective urge that the dead did.

Tres smiled, and then he looked guiltily at the suits and the covered corpses. The suits were already looking at me with the same fondness I suspect they'd show maggots. I wasn't surprised. My eyes were reptilian, not human, and my knowledge wasn't the sort I ought to have. More than a few people hated witches, and goodness knows, a barbeque or two had been suggested to me over the years.

"The dead don't mind," I assured Tres, who was looking appalled when he realized he was nearly flirting over a corpse.

Either way, Tres wouldn't be smiling in a moment. Most men only found me attractive or interesting when they hadn't seen my affinity with death. The new abilities were interesting, but they didn't undo what I was.

I stepped closer to the corpse I was there to see. "Uncover him."

One of them asked, "How did you know which—"

"I can feel his infection." I watched as he peeled the sheet back. My grave vision is uncommonly useful with the recently infected. I could see the venom under his skin, like green light. "Between the toes, right? That's where the injection is. Tell me about him."

"Mr. Odem was an associate of my father's," Tres began, sounding serious and businesslike now. "His widow, three daughters, and seven grandchildren are in mourning. There was no reason to expect him to be...changed." He paused, awkwardly, as if guilty, and then he said, "I've made considerable donations. Legal, of course, but I asked to be notified of any injection sites on recent deceased."

"No judgment." I glanced at Tres. "It's your money now."

Tres said nothing further, so I let myself draw on even more of my grave magic, letting it drift over the corpse. I found no other traces. Most *draugr* had a limited capacity for venom. To fully infect the living took several envenomations. They had a limited food supply, so evolutionarily speaking, they were remarkable. There were a lot of fail-safes to prevent overpopulation. *Draugr* were the apex predator, and much like a shark on a reef, they needed to have enough food to support them. If every bite was contagious, that would quickly complicate the balance of food to predator. Venom could kill, or weaken, but transformation required a choice.

Aside from the obvious, *draugr* sure as fuck couldn't bite someone between the toes.

One of the suits spread the toes of the deceased to look for a mark. "She's right."

With my grave vision, I could see the vibrant green of venom. Without my vision, I suspect it looked almost unnoticeable, a minute blemish between the toes. For an older man with a cardiac history, a post mortem exam was probably not as thorough as in the case of a suspicious death. Money changed hands to get this exam and to get me into the morgue.

Eli leaned in, took a picture of the injection, and stepped back. "No diabetes? Social drug use? Vitamin shots even?"

He knew the answer, but it was form to ask.

"Jimmy Odem was a respectable man," Suit One said.

"And a member of SAFARI?" Eli asked. I knew by the tone of his voice that he recalled the man's name from the list.

"He was," Tres confirmed.

I still had my sword at ready, but I was curious. I let magic fill me until I felt like my skin was going to split and spill the energy onto the world. When I could stand no more, I released it in the direction of the late Mr. Odem. I was the conduit from the grave to the living, or in some cases, a conduit from the far side of the grave to our side. Either way, undead magic filled me to the point that my vision slid into that place where the world looked like a dream, hazy and ethereal, as if I'd become a ghost for a moment —not that ghosts were real, mind you. They were just like shapeshifters and cyborgs and tentacled aliens: merely the stuff of fiction. I enjoyed reading of them, but not of witches or *draugr*. I had the ability to see the world with such an eerie vision that any horror director would be jealous.

With that grave vision, I saw that Tres burned with a light, but his glow was a flicker next to the shining glow that made Eli look like he'd swallowed a city-sized menorah on the night of the last candle.

"They're dead," I said, gesturing at the other corpses in the room. "Truly gone, but I could summon—"

"No. They are unrelated," Eli said. "They have nothing to tell us."

He was right, and until recently, the resting dead could not be summoned. I felt enough power flowing into my skin tonight that I wanted to try. Eli's voice stopped me, though. I trusted him, and experimenting as I'd been doing was dangerous.

I tapped my sword tip on the sheet covering the late Mr. Odem. "He knows things."

I pressed grave magic into him, filling him from the soles of his feet to the crinkles on his balding head. I'd never tried to speak to the dead who were at a crossroad like this. Not full dead like the corpses I drew together. Not awake yet as a regular *draugr* would be a few days after death.

"Geneviève?" Eli asked. "What are you doing?"

I was about to tell him that I had it under control, but the dead man sat up. He slid to the edge of the table and stood with a sudden lurch. He leaned against the edge of it, but he had pushed to his feet and opened his eyes.

"Talk to me," I ordered. "Tell me what I seek."

I let my magic carry questions: the visual of the injection, the dead Chaddock, the conversation snippet of Tres telling me someone had murdered his father.

When the corpse of Odem tried to speak, he noticed that his lips were sewn shut—as all corpses' were. He frowned, looked around, and then the naked dead man walked over to a counter, grabbed a scalpel and sliced the threads sealing his mouth.

"What is the meaning of this?" The re-animated Mr. Odem gestured at all of us with the scalpel.

One of the suits fainted.

I held my sword at ready.

What had I done? The dead man ought to be a muttering, hungry corpse, no more sentient than any other newborn. This was unexpected. I tried to keep myself positioned, so I was between the dead and the living. Eli, Tres, and the suits ought to leave so I could . . . what was I to do? Odem seemed coherent.

"Mr. Odem?" Tres asked. "James?"

"Chaddock." The late Mr. Odem stepped forward. "What are you doing here? I was sorry to hear about Alvin, but . . ." He paused, glanced down, and frowned. "Why am I standing here starkers?"

"Geneviève?" Eli walked up to my side. "What just happened?"

James Odem was alert, dead, and sounded very much like he'd skipped the entire decade-plus of drooling, starving nonsense that *draugr* all had.

I cleared my throat and admitted, "I think I, umm, accidentally fixed a *draugr*."

Chapter Eighteen

TRES LOOKED AT ME AND THEN THE DEAD MAN WHO WAS wrapping a morgue sheet around himself like a cheap toga. The suits, who were both upright now, gaped at me. Their expressions were horror-filled. Tres, however, had a look of awe on his face that frightened me more than I could explain.

"You did that." Tres gazed at me, all semblance of calm businessman long gone. He watched me in the way of zealots—and not the predictable pitchforks-and-torches sort. This was worse. He looked more like he might build me a temple than a pyre.

"You, boy." Mr. Odem gestured at one of the suits, who were both watching him warily. Neither man moved, but they both looked at Odem. The old man held out a very steady hand and ordered, "Jacket."

"I need to get out of here," I whispered to Eli. Tres' reaction had been odd before, but this?

"Could you bring my father back?" Tres reached for my arm.

"I cut his *head* off."

"Could a plastic surgeon or"—he gestured to the morgue —"pick a new body. Something younger."

"The fuck . . .? They're not *cars*, Tres." I backed away from him. "Eli?"

"Chaddock, step out into the hall with us."

When Tres joined us in the hall, he was no longer looking at me in any way remotely resembling normal. He looked at me the way folks looked on prophets or false messiahs.

"Do you want to deal with Odem or should I behead him . . .?" I asked Tres.

Tres laughed. "You restored *him*. The possibilities, Geneviève! Can you—"

"So, you'll stay here and deal with the police and whatnot?" I glanced into the room where Odem was holding court. One disaster of shit-storm potential at a time. Odem was first. He might be alert now, but I had my concerns about what this all meant. Would he stay alert? Could he be trusted to go home? Would the police find a house full of mutilated corpses if he did?

"You could save so many people." Tres tried to take my hand, but I jerked away. He dropped to his knees and stared up at me. "You created life, Geneviève."

Eli shook his head.

"Does that mean you will protect my secret?" I tried to sound holy, but I felt like I mostly sounded constipated. "No one can know, Tres."

"Why wouldn't you want people to know?" He stared at me in confusion.

"We could kill you," Eli said mildly. "Them, too. All that happened here was that the old man must have had some experimental drug before dying. *That's* what happened."

"No." Tres glared at him. "St. Geneviève—"

"Oh, hell no." I stepped back. "Your vow, Tres. Swear you won't tell anyone what you think happened."

"My kind take vows seriously, Chaddock. You do not want to face the consequences of breaking a vow." Eli tugged off his glove and flicked the steel sword in my hand. The sizzle of his flesh made my stomach turn, but Eli was lowering his own defenses to the fae-deadly metal to make a point about what he was.

I kept my worry to myself. I wouldn't undo his point.

"There are consequences," Eli said. "And I have vows of my own." He stepped forward, so he was between me and the still-kneeling Tres. "I would slaughter the whole city to protect Geneviève."

I was startled at that revelation, but Eli wasn't done.

"Swear that you protect her secret unless you would prefer the grave," Eli demanded.

Tres stared at me as he swore, "I will never betray Geneviève." He stood finally and glanced into the room. "Neither will they. I'll see to it."

"Good. Your vow is accepted in exchange for your life. Should you break this trust, I will kill you slowly."

"Understood," Tres said. He sounded a bit frightened, but then he met my gaze briefly. His voice softened as he said, "I hope to see you tomorrow, Geneviève. I've cleared my entire weekend in hopes . . ." Tres bowed his head to me and returned to the room.

I stared at Eli for several moments. "What the fuck was *that?*"

Eli shrugged. "We are in accord that this new skill is one that ought to be held in secret. The young Mr. Chaddock was given incentive to protect your secret."

"But . . . he's . . . what's going on with him?" I glanced back. "That was fucking drunk monkeyballs levels of weird, right?"

"It was." Eli held my gaze. "If he becomes a threat . . . I do not enjoy killing, Geneviève, but I will do so to protect you."

I nodded and then let out a deep sigh. "Putting a pin in the zealot businessman. I need to figure out what the fuck I just did with Odem."

"Healed him, I think," Eli said. "Are there solutions other than eliminating the dead or binding them to you?"

I looked away. Short of killing them, there truly was no other solution with a *draugr*.

"What if it's temporary, though?" I asked. "What if he just . . . goes back to a normal *draugr*? Like the dead do when I'm out of range?"

"Then I will not need to kill the young Mr. Chaddock to keep his silence." Eli shrugged.

I knew he was not a heartless person, but he was fae. Perhaps telling me so bluntly meant that he wasn't hiding that anymore. The fae were coldly practical. And as I looked at him, I understood the chilly practicality of his words; he would kill for my safety, as I did with the *draugr*. A part of me was warmed at the thought of being held in such regard, but another part of me whispered that the feelings I was so afraid of were already deeper than I'd realized.

I took a deep breath. I couldn't deal with that right now. First, I had to figure out what to do with Odem. Walking away seemed irresponsible, and I wasn't going to take the suddenly sentient *draugr* to my home.

But I really didn't want blood on my hands because of my mistake—which is why I was about to do what might be the stupidest thing I'd done in years.

And that was saying something.

I was as sober as a judge when Eli and I walked to the door where we'd entered the morgue. I guess either I needed more of Eli's touch to stay drunk or my magic had burned the drunk out of me. Either way, I was painfully clear-headed as I said, "I need you to get into the car first."

I escorted him to the driver's side rather than stopping on the passenger side. "Please?"

He unlocked and opened the door, but that was it. "Talk to me."

"I have to tell someone about Odem," I said as I shoved him

backward into the car. "I'm not even sure she'll come, but I need to try."

"Tell who? Tell her *what?*"

"Beatrice. Just give me ten minutes." I smiled, trying to appear reassuring. "It's probably not the best plan."

"I'm shocked," he said drolly.

"If you need to leave, I—"

"Two minutes." Eli reached out to me. "Don't be reckless."

"Who me?" I pushed the door shut and leaned against the car. To get out, Eli would need to slam his door into my back. He cared about me and his very expensive car enough not to do that unless it was truly urgent.

Cautiously, I sent my magic out like a net and thought her name, "Beatrice."

I could hear Eli through the haze that was over me. Too much magic. Too often. I'd resurrected a man tonight. Oh, he was still dead as nails, but he had his mind. That ought not be the case. It had never happened before—and I was damned if I wanted to take all the blame. Maybe it was the injection.

"Beatrice, Beatrice, Beatrice," I chanted.

The *draugr's* name made me wish to be elsewhere. It made me want to be the sort of cold bitch I tried to be, but even if I didn't care about the three men here at the morgue, I knew Odem had grandkids. A widow. Staff. A dozen humans would be there, innocents in most cases, and all I could think of was getting a call because children died.

"Geneviève." Her voice was there before Beatrice was. This time, she was wearing the equivalent of an early Victorian formal dress. Her skirt was full, bodice fitted, and the whole thing seemed to be sewn of some kind of blue shimmering material. Darker blue lace trimmed the edges of the overskirt, the décolletage, and hem. A full dark lace waterfall draped from the sleeve edge and over her wrists and hands. A hat with a feather and a cameo necklace were her only accessories.

I nodded at the scary dead lady. My choice. My idea. Damn, I had some lousy ideas. I'd never met anyone as old or as scary as her, and I wasn't entirely sure I could trust her. My aversion to *draugr* meant that I did not trust her fundamentally, but *someone* needed to know about Odem.

"Thank you for responding." I tried to sound calm, but my sword was in my right hand and my gun was in my left.

"Have you invited me to a beheading?" Beatrice glanced at my weapons. "Perhaps a duel?"

I scowled. "I'm not sure I could behead you, and I'm not intending to try tonight."

Her laughter was musical, and I liked being laughed at about as much as I liked being sucker punched.

"Did you bring me a snack all wrapped up in a pretty box?" Beatrice glanced at the car, raised her brow, and peered inside.

The windows were darkly tinted, but I still prickled at her words. "If you ever—"

"*Yours* are all safe from mine, at least those who obey me. I know your nest's names and faces. They are marked as protected," she said in a tone that reminded me far too much of my mother when she was exasperated with me.

"My *nest*? Protected?" I goggled at the thought. Why would they be protected? And who was Beatrice in their world that people obeyed her that way? I had more questions the more she spoke—although she said everything as if I should already know it.

But Beatrice frowned, and she sniffed delicately. Whatever she sensed about Eli was enough for her to add, "*That* one, however, would be safe either way."

I resisted the urge to look at Eli. I couldn't see through the glass anyhow, but I wanted to stare. I wanted to ask what she smelled and if I smelled it, too, but didn't register it to identify it.

"There are things older than I am," Beatrice said mildly.

"Fae."

"Lovely for other indulgences. Not for snacking, sadly." She stared into the car as if seeing an animal in an enclosure. Her lips parted as if hoping for a kiss, and my irritation increased. Eli might not be my lover, but I wasn't keen on a dead woman trying to get into his bed. "He was at that tavern you frequent. He doesn't carry your scent, but you smell angry now. Is he unattached? Or yours?"

I swallowed my tangle of feelings. Possessive. Protective. Fearful. I had no idea what to do with it other than say, "He's *mine*."

She nodded once. "He is a fitting choice for your status. Beware the consequences, Daughter of Mine."

"Not your daughter." I bit off the words. My mother might be as flighty as a dragonfly, but she was my mother. I would have no other call me theirs. "Not even the monster that impregnated my mother was foolish enough to call me his daughter."

Instead of answering me, Beatrice stared into Eli's car and announced, "I have no quarrel with those who speak to earth and stone."

I rolled my eyes. I was way past whatever mood I'd need to be in to parse the situation, and from the way she'd looked at Eli, even with glass between them, there was a meaning in the words beyond the obvious bit about no quarrel. My theory was that she was offering a ritual statement of some sort or another.

"How old are you?" I asked bluntly. My magic pushed toward her, as if I would pet her and read her with my grave knowledge. It wasn't exactly carbon-dating, but there was a process akin to scientific dating when I let myself lean into it. Tonight, I knew I could read more than I ever had before in my life. Beatrice's attire was Victorian, but there was no way she was younger than four-hundred-years.

Again, she laughed. "I danced with kings whose bones are dust, and watched men burn women like us alive over plagues and cattle."

I revised my stance to five hundred.

"Helpful." I obviously wasn't getting a clear answer tonight, so I pointed at the building with my gun. "Dead guy in there."

Beatrice followed my gaze. "It *is* the morgue, Geneviève. One would hope that the dead were in there."

I nodded. "Usually my preference, as a matter of fact. I'd prefer the dead don't walk."

This time, Beatrice merely smiled. "And yet you have invited me here to speak . . ."

I sighed, looked around the lot, and wondered if this was the worst idea ever. There was no easy way to confess this to a *draugr,* especially this one, but I needed to know the Odem family wasn't going to be dead by dawn.

I met her gaze. "Dead guy who *should* be muttering and rocking. Biting at flies."

"Flies? Truly, Geneviève?" Her voice held all the laughter she didn't show in her expression.

I shrugged. "I was here to investigate him. Saw the venom." I swallowed louder than I meant to and admitted, "And when I saw it in his skin, I did as with rotting corpses. He was going to wake soon, but I pulled and he woke, and now, he speaks like he's been out of the grave at least two or three decades."

"That's not possible. The venom, yes, but such alertness . . . no." Beatrice pressed her pale lips together.

"Maybe it was the venom," I offered hopefully. Please, let it be the venom. Not me.

She opened her mouth, and I expected a question.

Beatrice whipped her head to the side to glance at the building, and I knew without another word when she felt Mr. Odem's presence. As her shock made her energy flash out, I felt echoes of her age and revised my assessment of her age to earlier than the Elizabethan era. I was guessing the early Renaissance, perhaps even earlier. It sent a wave of fear through me.

In a blink, Beatrice *flowed* toward the morgue. I could typically track the motion of a *draugr,* but she moved so swiftly it was as if she'd teleported. She hadn't, obviously. Whatever she'd done, however, meant that the door to the morgue opened in the next moment after she'd arrived at the top of the steps.

Mr. Odem, clad in suit jacket and pair of jeans I assumed the men had stolen from a locker, looked like a spry graduate student rather than wealthy businessman. Dead or not, he moved with a grace that old humans lacked. He *flowed* and was up the steps, staring at Beatrice in an instant.

"Where did you get the venom?" Beatrice demanded. She had a hold of Odem, lifting him to her face as if he weighed nothing. His legs dangled as he was held in front of her like an oversized doll held by a child.

The suits exited the morgue in a run, and behind them was Tres. I wasn't sure what Beatrice intended, but she was the oldest, strongest monster I'd ever met. It didn't give me a lot of hope that this would go well.

"Fuck," I muttered as I *flowed* toward the angry *draugr* lady, the far-too-agile Odem, and three vulnerable humans.

Chapter Nineteen

BEATRICE WAS HOLDING ODEM ALOFT AND STARING AT HIM with the kind of intensity that made me sure that there was a magic to *draugr* that I hadn't known until this moment. Behind her the three human men looked various sorts of shocked. I couldn't blame them. I was betting that not many suits had up-close contact with again-walkers, and even if they had, the two here were the most unusual I'd ever met—unless I counted myself, which I didn't. *Draugr* ancestry or not, I was very much alive.

And I truly did want to stay that way, but I'd clearly underestimated Beatrice's reaction, and since my reason for calling her was to prevent deaths, I felt like I kind of had to intervene. With a sigh, I moved behind her so I could put myself between the humans and the two *draugr*.

"Not his fault. He was injected against his will," I told her in the most soothe-the-predator voice I could muster. "Murdered, just like another man I recently sent back to death."

Odem was silently staring at Beatrice. He did not behave like a sentient man, nor did he rage like a new *draugr*. I realized then that Beatrice was reading him, much as I did with the truly dead and with her kind.

"He's yours," Beatrice said softly.

"What? My what? My problem, my—"

"Yours," Beatrice repeated as she turned to face me. Her eyes had slipped from human to narrow slits as mine often did. It was unsettling to see my eyes in her face. Most *draugr* didn't do that, and as much as I'd thought it was a trait that I'd inherited from the dead jackass who impregnated my mother, I'd not seen it in other *draugr*. Why did Beatrice have snake eyes? Why did I?

"You bound him to you, Geneviève," she added mildly.

"Dick waffles." I tried to think of how I had done that and offered, "Not on purpose."

Beatrice stared at me in silence, and then, she dropped Odem to the ground, where he sat and looked around. Something about Beatrice made him opt to stay there rather than standing. I couldn't blame him. My knees felt weak, but I think that was a mix of shock and terror. Okay, admittedly, that was probably exactly what he felt, too.

Eli joined us. I felt him crossing the lot and stopping behind Beatrice. I wasn't sure whether to move so I was between him and the monsters or stay where I was, so the humans were behind me. My logic said to defend the weak, but my instinct was to protect Eli.

I glanced at him where he stood behind Beatrice. The glittering night sky that he usually hid was shining in every strand of hair. He glimmered. There was no polite way to tell him to tone it down, not without drawing her attention to him. I wanted to ask why, to tell him not here, to get him out of here.

But then Beatrice sighed and folded her arms. It was disconcerting how maternal—or grandmotherly, perhaps—the terrifying dead lady was. Oddly, it made me like her a little bit more. Intense, powerful women made up an easy ninety percent of my idols. Maybe Mama Lauren wasn't the cookie-baking maternal prototype for most people, but she was *my* template, which meant that deadly women made me relax a bit.

"You truly had no idea you could bind," Beatrice said, continuing the weary-mom-who-could-flay-you schtick she had going on.

I shuffled awkwardly. No one really loved being called stupid, and aloud or implied, that was what she was saying. In my defense, I'd been kissing a hot mostly-fae man and dealing with some complicated feelings about my own magic. I wasn't exactly at peak clarity.

"I knew I could with the ones I put together and pull from the soil," I said, my words slipping out in a voice quieter than I meant to be. "The truly dead will obey me. Follow me. That's why I tuck them back into their graves. If not, it's like this combo of surprise army and needy kids all in one."

"I bind my subjects to me," Beatrice said mildly. She stared down at Odem with a strange expression. "The new are unpredictable, and once I bind them, they are not wandering off gnawing on the peasants."

"Peasants?" Eli echoed. He'd taken another step, so he was closer still.

Seriously, I could've smacked him for drawing Beatrice's gaze to him. She looked him up and down, not like he was a food source but like he was a beautiful man. Her gaze was pure predator, but less like the lion looking at the gazelle and more like the lioness picking a lion for a romp.

"*Mine*," I growled, staring at both of them.

"Always," he replied with a smile just for me, and I decided that particular smile of his needed to be patented as a panty-dropping weapon.

Beatrice shot that vaguely amused look at me again and stroked her chin lightly with one hand. "You would fight me over"—she motioned at Eli—"this?"

"Mine," I repeated, moving between them. My back was to

him, defending him. A rational part of my brain screamed not to attack the scary dead lady, but another part saw only that she was looking at someone I could not sacrifice.

My sword was suddenly out and raised.

"Geneviève?" Eli touched my shoulder. "Bonbon, I do not think she means me ill."

"I recognize you now, Son of Stonecroft." Beatrice sighed and then gave a moderately deep bow in Eli's direction, not taking her gaze from us as she did so. When she straightened, she said, "I knew your grandfather. The earth mourned his loss."

Eli looked pained, but I didn't know enough about his family *or* his culture to understand why. "You speak in words that I would not expect to find on this side. *Draugr* are not typically so eloquent."

"Those who walk among the peasants are not," Beatrice corrected. "We are not all the same. Much like your father's kin. Much like humans."

"Do you all eat people?" I asked cheerily. I'd rather be cheerful and fight her than see Eli look wounded. Admittedly, I'd caused that look more than a few times, but I was trying to do better, and I sure as sugar wasn't going to let anyone else cause it if I could help it. "Nosh on the living? Nibble unwilling necks? That sort of thing."

"Yes, we do require living food." Beatrice straightened her very elegant dress. "Not flesh. Merely live blood. The young only take flesh because they are uncontrolled."

"Huh. Good to know," I muttered.

Eli gave a single nod at her. "I, and my blood, belong to Geneviève Crowe. . . and she to me."

Beatrice looked back at me appraisingly while I was trying to figure out what that vow was. Beatrice smiled, and I swore she belonged in a court, not a crumbling asphalt parking lot outside a funky smelling morgue. She looked like there ought to be a

throne, elegant cloak, and simple jeweled circlet. Nothing ostentatious, but definitely not this kind of run down.

Her royal deadness fixed that imperious gaze on me and half-
ordered, half-offered, "Gift Odem to me. I will mind him and ask
the pertinent questions. If his conversion to clarity is temporary, I
shall inform you."

"And you won't release him to his family," I said. The brief
flicker of seeing Beatrice's humanity seemed to vanish at hearing
her admission that even those *draugr* I did not see were killers.
She was a killer.

But then again, so was I.

"Agreed," Beatrice said. "I will safeguard him and take him as
my subject. I will neither murder him nor release him into the
wild."

"Geneviève!" Tres called. "Miss Crowe!"

I ignored him. I knew I was handing his hope of more
answers to a monster. I knew, too, that if there was information
about the injection, Beatrice would learn of it. She might be a
draugr, but on this, we were on the same side. At least, I
thought so.

"Beatrice, I release Mr. Odem to your care."

I watched him, wondering if the transition of the binding to
her would change anything about his grip on reality. Had I accidentally created his sentience by binding him? Or was it the injection? Or was it simply a result of my magic being released?

Beatrice held out her hands, and Odem took them. In that
moment, it looked like the strangest handfasting ceremony I'd
ever seen. Beatrice looked bridal in her Victorian evening gown as
she gazed at Odem in his mismatched suit. No words were
spoken, and we had the necessary witnesses—which left me as
the armed minister. It was an apt, albeit amusing, image in my
head. Beatrice was about to bind him to her until one of them
had a second death.

I felt her magic flare out as she tied the recently revived

draugr to her. It was familiar in a way that answered a question I hadn't thought to ask until now.

"You're a w—"

"Hush, daughter." Beatrice held a finger to her lips.

Maybe it was knowing that she was a witch, too, or maybe it was that she was a more-or-less-dead witch in a Victorian dress. Questions. More of them. She was like a bottomless well of details and clues I didn't understand. There was a *draugr*-witch standing in front of me. Like me, but far more dead—and I truly doubted that she'd been born like this.

When I opened my mouth to comment, she said, "Shush!"

I shuddered at the creepy, *draugr*-witch standing in front of me with a glee-filled grin. Not even the unblinking china-faced Victorian doll at my mother's house looked as eerie as Beatrice did in that moment. I didn't speak her secret, although it was clear to me. Beatrice, who was seemingly whatever the *draugr* called their leader, was a witch before she walked as a dead thing.

"I have questions," I said once she'd released Odem's hands.

She nodded once. "Of course, you do. I would expect no less."

But then she *flowed* with Odem trailing behind her. I had no answers, no corpse, no quarrel or anything else to explain the unsettled feeling rippling over me. I couldn't have left Odem unsupervised, though. If he lost the clarity he seemed to have or even just got too hungry, his family would die.

As would neighbors.

And strangers.

So, I was left standing in the darkened lot with Eli, Tres, and the suits.

"What just happened?" Suit One asked.

The other suit shrugged.

"Miss Crowe sent Mr. Odem away with a *draugr*," Tres said coldly.

"Not just any *draugr*," Eli amended.

Tres glared at me. His adoration of before was tinged with a hostility that was equally unwelcome. I was neither goddess nor demon. I was a woman who had an uncanny gift for ending up in bad situations, and I was over it. "What if he didn't *stay* coherent, Mr. Chaddock? Would you let his entire family die?"

"You healed him," Tres insisted with the obstinance of a man who just couldn't grasp that I wasn't able to be what he wanted me to be—or maybe it was the privileged rich perspective. I had no doubt that Tres was used to getting exactly what he wanted.

"I did not." I pointed at him with the sword that was hanging loose in my hand. "He was injected. I simply bound him to me, and I cannot *draugr*-sit. My neighbors are still pissed about covering the lawn with the 'zombies.'"

I made air quotes with my free hand because, really? Wrong damn word. There wasn't anything Haitian about the dead folks that were scattered on my lawn last year. I didn't *create* them. I simply summoned the dead to life. Basic necromancy.

"But . . . two men have been killed," Tres objected. "At least two more are missing."

He walked closer, and I felt Eli step to my side. I wasn't a bone to be tugged between two men either. Tres was a client, and Eli was my partner. I pushed my rising temper away. It wasn't really about the word, or the anger from Tres, or even needing to summon Beatrice.

"Two more?" Eli asked.

"There are four members of my father's club unaccounted for," Tres said.

"Perhaps they are on trips, yachts, or with mistresses."

"Not every businessman has a mistress," Tres muttered.

As calmly as I could, I explained, "I want answers, too, but I won't risk the Odem family's life to get them. Beatrice—"

"The *draugr*?" Tres asked.

"Yes." I cleared my throat before saying a sentence I'd never really expected to say: "I trust her."

Eli shot a quizzical glance at me.

"On this," I added. "She wants answers, too. She'll get them if he has them. I'll figure it out from there, but I'm not babysitting a corpse—or releasing it to eat people. So"—I shrugged— "I asked her to take him."

I turned and headed to the car. I'd already let Eli see me *flow* twice tonight, so I didn't bother being circumspect. It felt freeing.

In not much more than a blink, not as fast as Beatrice, but a lot faster than most *draugr*, I was beside Eli's car. I thought briefly that in this state, I could flip the thing. Not that I would, but it was a detail to file away for future encounters with monsters. If I thought I could, I was sure some *draugr* could too.

I watched Eli walk toward me, trying to ignore the smile he wore as I stared at him. I refused to look away. I liked looking, and tonight, I wasn't going to pretend otherwise. He'd offered himself up for my use. His kisses left me feeling languid.

"Do you suppose we should discuss your ability to flow, peach pie?" Eli asked as he reached the passenger door.

"As soon as we talk about you telling the dead lady that *your blood* was mine or I was yours, sweetbread."

He raised his brows. "Sweetbread is not a baked food. It's part of a dead animal."

"True."

"Are you threatening me? Or admitting to craving me?" Eli gave me the sort of smile that probably resulted in most women or men hastily shedding clothing. "You should realize that I'm content either way."

"Why would you say I was in possession of your blood?" I asked in a slightly calmer voice.

"Why did you declare me yours? I heard you, Geneviève. You said 'mine' in a way that was far from meaningless." He paused. "And asking me to watch your corpse after you died? We all have secrets, but you can trust me with yours. My body or my blood,

Geneviève. Fighting at your side. Tell me what you want, and I will give it to you."

For a moment, I stared at him. Quietly, I admitted, "That isn't working, is it? I asked for space."

"You did. You also kissed me," he said just as quietly.

Instead of answering, I jerked open the car door. "Either drive me home, or I can *flow* and get there on my own."

Eli motioned for me to get into the car, closed the door, and got into the driver's side. Even when facing my temper, he was a gentleman, and sometimes I wanted to punch him for it.

Chapter Twenty

ELI STAYED SILENT AS HE PUT THE CAR IN MOTION. SOMETIMES, I stared at the dim alleys, the people sliding into the shadows, and I wondered at our world. I realized that New Orleans was seedier than a lot of cities, but there were plenty of places like ours. Someday, I would visit Prague or Amsterdam. I'd see what it was like there. Did they have more police? Was it simply that they let the again-walkers feed on the homeless who were out at night or was the tolerance a tactic, a cheap way to deter criminals? Were there fewer muggings in the large cities with *draugr*?

I knew on some fundamental level that the *draugr* had not suddenly appeared in the world. Were they few and rare at the beginning? Had the *draugr* grown in relation to the food—humans —populating so much of the planet?

I surely didn't buy the "angry god" answers. I didn't see the rise of the dead as a sign that the divine was angry at humanity for this or that, especially when it usually boiled down to folks grumbling over women having opinions, people marrying folks they loved, or the like. But then again, I'd never been a fire and brimstone, hell-is-waiting-for-you, person. Jew and witch by birth didn't lead to *that*. Instead, I wondered about the science of it all. Were the diseases, the plagues of modern life, a divine pay-attention-or-else, or had we created them in our labs? Or, with our destruction of other predators, of the very earth, had these man-shaped killers grown more numerous?

I had no answers.

"Geneviève?" Eli's voice tugged me out of my thoughts.

"Just thinking about *draugr*," I said.

He kept his gaze fixed on the road as he said, "I offered my blood because you have enough *draugr* traits that I've had my suspicions about your humanity. If you need blood, mine is available. I would've offered sooner if I thought you really did need it now." He glanced at me and teased, "But mostly, you appear to need liquor not blood, so I offered that instead."

His smile had me making a rude gesture at him, even as it eased the tension between us. There was only so far we could contain whatever was between us, and my impulsive kiss earlier had eroded some of that peace. Honestly, the fluctuation of my magic had started it months ago.

It hit me that it was related. "My magic . . ." I shook my head, feeling like an idiot. My magic had identified him as my partner, and it was erratic from being unbound, but magic was not some weird thing with no rules. The thing binding me for most of my life was magic, too. It and my own gifts were at odds. I needed to be tethered. "I think I need to have sex."

"I'll offer that, too," he said lightly. "If memory serves, I *have* offered."

I sighed. "And I am considering it, but—"

Eli stopped the car alongside the street, sliding into a narrow parking spot as if he could drive with his eyes closed. He still had one hand on the wheel, but he twisted to stare at me. "Truly?"

I sighed again. "Yes."

"With me?" he clarified.

"I liked kissing you." I shot him my wickedest smile. "The

handcuffs idea wasn't without merit either."

Eli's quiet groan made me need to muffle my own response. Whatever else we were, our chemistry was excellent. It was the "what else" part that complicated my life. Still, I felt like I had to tell him.

"Eli?"

"Cream puff?"

"It's not just that. My magic is weird lately because my mother made a bargain. A faery bargain." I felt like the air itself went still when I said it. I also felt like he deserved to know, since he was a factor. My shift happened because Eli had become my partner, and of course, he was dealing with the fallout. "And that whole 'mine' thing that happened was just my magic being crazyballs."

He made a "continue" gesture.

"I went to see my mother. She made a faery bargain so my beacon to the grave would be tamped down," I said. "And my *draugr* traits tamped down. Until I met 'a true partner, loyal and able to stand at my side.'"

Eli stared at me as if I'd just declared him a frog who ought to kiss me, or maybe since I was the one who'd been restricted, I was the frog in this fairy tale. Either way, I felt like he was hearing sentences I didn't mean to say.

"Geneviève . . . I am honored." His voice was thick with emotion I didn't want to identify.

"Honored?"

"That your magic chose me," he said in that same voice. He took my hand in his and lifted it. "It means more than I can say."

I was running out of fight. "I trust you."

His lips brushed my knuckles. Such a gentle thing ought not make my heart race or my knickers damp. His allure somehow ignored what ought to be and how my body ought to react. I pulled my hand away.

"And you have my back," I said as calmly as I could. "You protect me. Who else would be my partner?"

"Geneviève . . . I have waited for years to hear you admit these things."

Again with the perhaps-we-weren't-in-the-same-conversation. This was why dealing with the fae—and probably the *draugr*—was fraught with misunderstanding. It was like cross-cultural conflicts, but cross-species. A friend of mine had accidentally ended up engaged because she'd accepted a gift that *she* thought was sweet, and the man thought was a statement of intentions.

Carefully, I said, "You're one of my closest friends."

Eli gave me a look with so much heat in it that I was suddenly grateful he'd respected my requests not to seduce me. Then he said, "And I am more than ready to prove that you will never need another person in your bed."

"Somehow, I don't have *any* doubts of your prowess after that kiss," I said quietly. Admittedly, the women at the tavern who stared at him like they would sell their souls for another night with him had already convinced me that I would more than enjoy being naked with Eli.

"Tell me that if you are taking anyone to your bedchamber tomorrow that it will be me?" He leaned forward.

I closed the distance to brush my lips over his. "Can I think about it?"

"You have been." He kissed my throat. "For years. As have I. Why delay? We're here."

"In a tiny car," I said softly. Despite the skills I knew he undoubtedly had, I wasn't going to try to do anything in his little convertible. The gearshift between us, and the lack of a backseat didn't leave too many options. Even if the seat were to recline enough, I wasn't sure there was room for the things I wanted.

"Name the place. I'll bring the handcuffs," Eli tempted.

I shoved the thoughts of Eli at my mercy back and leaned away with a loud sigh.

"I'm just grateful that my mother worded the bargain like that. Can you imagine if she'd said a word other than partner? I'd never be unbound. Fae literalism actually worked in my favor. Put that one in the books. A faery bargain working out on the bargainer's side doesn't happen often."

Eli gave me an incredulous look, but he said nothing as he pulled the car out of the parking spot and rejoined the flow of traffic. I felt a bit unnerved by it.

He kept his silence until he arrived at my building.

When he parked, he looked into my eyes, and said, "Sometimes, my tiramisu, you are an absolute fucking idiot."

My mouth opened, but no words came.

"Faery bargains do not benefit the bargainer. Not truly." He caressed my face. "We play to win, and you, my love, are lying to yourself. The words—and your own magic—know what your infuriatingly obstinate self denies."

I met his gaze for a moment. "You are my business partner and friend, and I . . . care about you a lot . . . and want to fuck you. That's all."

And Eli laughed. It was a joyous sound, but I wasn't in on the same joke, apparently.

"What?"

"That's *all*? My dear, surely you realize that my people marry with far less compatibility. You count me as a friend and a business ally. You *care* for me and want me. Our interests align. Our sexual compatibility is intense enough to make you run from me. And you would fight the mistress of the risen-dead for me. How can you not see that we are perfectly matched?"

Romantic partner? Magic choosing? I mean, I wasn't exactly new to powers-beyond-my-control fucking with my life. . . but I wasn't a picket-fence kind of woman. I really *really* wasn't ever going to be the marrying sort.

And I was dangerous.

This couldn't happen.

Eli caressed my face. "I do not think your magic or the bargain misunderstood *at all*, Geneviève."

Chapter Twenty-One

I STEPPED OUT OF THE CAR AND WAS INSTANTLY FOLDED INTO Eli's embrace. There wasn't anything magical about a hug, but there was a sort of magic to finding someone who felt like home. In my heart of hearts, I admitted that *this* was why I had to push Eli away. Losing him would tear a wound in my heart that couldn't heal.

But there was a perfection to the way I felt as Eli held me that I didn't think existed anywhere else in my past—and I feared it would never exist with anyone else. We simply fit. Dear Goddess, we fit. There was a point at which total denial was impossible, and I was finally there. I closed my eyes, let myself not think, and simply feel.

"I am terrified," I whispered.

"I know."

"I want you," I whispered against his throat.

"And I want you." He leaned back and stared into my eyes.

"So . . . we boink like bunnies? Risk our friendship for some orgasms?" I tried for light, but I sounded panicked even to myself.

"I give you my vow, Geneviève Crowe, that I will not stop being your friend if we ever start and then stop *boinking*."

The air felt thick as he spoke, as the magic that rode in his words floated beside us. I felt the magic press into my skin. "Eli of Stonecroft—"

"You do not need to make a vow," he reminded me. "This is not a bargain."

"I want to. I want you to know that I feel the same, that I want to preserve our friendship," I explained. "Eli of Stonecroft, I will not stop being your friend. No being alive, again-alive, or dead will cause me to abandon you."

The smile he gave me would melt ice on a frigid day. Quietly, he said, "I accept."

We stood there beside his car a few moments. A part of me wanted to shove him against his car and kiss him again. Another part of me wanted to say "I can't" and run.

I leaned back and said, "So, I guess this means we agree that sex is an option . . ."

He grinned. "It appears that way."

I stared at him, waiting. "Well, we had a bargain: One kiss at your choosing. We could start there. I did kiss you earlier."

"Oh, cupcake, you know me better than that." His voice was back to the familiar teasing one that I treasured. "I will not ruin this moment by claiming *that* kiss. . Unless you are finally inviting me into your bed tonight, I will bid you goodnight."

I felt nervous. Being with him made me feel as awkward as a virgin at an orgy. This was real, not one of the fantasies of him I indulged in during quality time with a vibrator.

I chickened out. "Not tonight."

He continued to be silent. When he extended a hand to me, I accepted, and in an instant, I was in his embrace. No kisses. No wandering hands. He simply *hugged* me again. If he'd kissed me, I would have dragged him to my bed. Instead, Eli was making the decision all mine.

"Soon," I said. "But I need a minute. We . . . I . . . I'm nervous."

"I'm nervous, too," he whispered. He released me and walked back to his side of the car. He paused and gave me a smile, and I recalled briefly how many things he'd done to ease my worries. He was good at this.

I walked to my door and jabbed the code into the door. When I stepped into the lobby, I looked back at Eli through the closed heavy glass door and waved. Then I stood and watched him drive away, feeling like a much younger, much less experienced woman. I wasn't sure I knew how to start this after so long avoiding it. Our kiss had been powerful, and . . . now what?

I sighed and turned toward the firedoor to enter my floor of the building. The light above it must have burned out, so I made a mental note to bitch at the manager in the morning. My vision made the lack of light an improvement, but if my friends visited at night, they'd be stumbling into the umbrella stand or the bench. Having done that in a few drunken moments over the years, I wasn't going to wish it on anyone else.

I needed to text Tres and cancel lunch. Whatever was going on there with his vaguely Renfield-like behavior, I wasn't going to be seeing him alone.

I was pulling my phone out of my pocket when a noise drew my attention.

Alice Chaddock stepped out from behind the stairwell. She stood there in an elegant coat and thin heels and stared at me. She took a halting step forward, and I struggled to remain calm.

"Mrs. Chaddock?" I had no idea why—or how—she was in my lobby, but I'd already had at least three more crises than should happen in any month . . . and I was over it. I just needed a long fucking nap. "Whatever this is, can we do this tomorrow?"

She sobbed and threw herself into my arms. I definitely don't cuddle clients as a rule—and I didn't even *like* the widow Chaddock. She was clinging to me, though, arms around me like a determined koala.

"Okay, what happened?" I started, not quite able to detangle her clutching arms. Whatever the damsel-in-distress class was, she took it and aced it. Firmer now, I asked, "Why are you here, Alice?"

I heard footsteps, the unmistakable clack of heels. I looked over Alice's shoulder and saw another woman about my age standing there. "Who are you?"

Before I could say anything more, something jabbed my upper arm. Sharp. Burning. It felt as if my very bone had cracked, and I swayed under the pain. Everything was wrong. I felt my muscles going loose, and icy agony spiraling down from whatever pricked my arm.

"What . . . have you done?" I slurred as I fell to the floor.

The two women looked down at me. The second one, a stranger, said, "Why is she still talking? Alvin and Jimmy were dead by this point. The maid, too."

Alice shrugged. "Maybe it's like a witch thing? She's freaky strong."

I was felled by a hug. If I could stand, I'd kick my own ass.

"Here." The stranger pulled something out of her bag. I couldn't see what she was holding out, but I hoped to hell it wasn't a gun.

I managed to say, "Why?"

"Hold on." Alice crouched beside me and tugged my shirt up.

I could see her hand and a syringe in it. I tried to lift my hand to bat it away, but all I managed to do was flop my hand onto my belly.

I felt and saw the needle inject me again, and the world went sideways.

Chapter Twenty-Two

I WOKE TO VOICES. I LET MY MAGIC SLIDE OUT BEFORE FORCING my eyelids to lift. I felt the spaces in my home, three bodies filling the usually empty air. Another trickle of magic told me that Christy, Sera, and Jesse were here.

Friends. Family. No rich bitches with crocodile tears. I was safe.

Christy and Sera were in my bathroom. Jesse was beside me, sitting on the floor next to my sofa. He was still, but watching me, guarding me. All of this might mean I was recently dead —or not.

I wasn't sure what dying felt like.

I knew I was on my sofa, on top of what I thought was a tarp, and I had an overall chill, a very cold stomach, and general sense of dampness. I had no idea how I got here. I was home. Not in the building lobby, but inside my home. The last thing I knew I was in the lobby. Had I crawled here? Did I get dragged here? My brain was muzzy, and I knew that it was probably from whatever jabbed me—or a result of the throbbing in my head from hitting the lobby floor.

I forced my eyes open and turned my head to stare at Jesse. "Up."

"Keep the ice there. You stopped convulsing when we got ice on you." Jesse helped prop me up. "You were burning up when we found you."

"How long?"

Jesse glanced at the wall clock over the sofa. From this angle, I couldn't see it. "Maybe an hour since we found you. About twenty minutes since you stopped thrashing. Two minutes since you started to wake."

I nodded. "Time now?"

"One-ish. You didn't call or reply to any of our texts, so . . . we're here." He shrugged as if it was no big deal that they had come to check on me and probably saved my life.

"Dead?"

He shook his head. "Not that I'm aware of."

Time would tell if I'd stay alive. I felt the venom in me. What did *draugr* venom do to someone who was a living but genetically-similar *draugr*? It was a question I'd asked myself more than once when something cold, dead, and surly slavered on me in attempts to gnaw on my carotid. The poison was inside me, but I had no idea if it would kill me because, technically, it might not be poison to me. It was like a rattlesnake with a cut in its mouth. Did the venom injure the snake? Or was it different because I hadn't swallowed it, but had it injected in me.

"What do you need?" Jesse prompted as he scooted closer.

"Cold drink. More ice." I swallowed. My whole body felt like it was on fire on the inside. I could trace every vein.

Jesse turned his head and called, "Water. Ice bags. She's awake."

I noticed that he was wearing black disposable gloves, as if we were about to dye my hair. Actually, they looked like they were the ones from my bathroom used just for that. He'd been careful in this, at least. Who knew how much venom had been on my skin?

"Vodka," I corrected, even as I felt the air displaced as one of the women moved from bathroom to kitchen. That was Sera. She was a hummingbird where Christy felt like a jay. Jesse was always more owl in his presence, watchful and strong. Someday, he'd be a great father to children who would be my "nieces" or "nephews." We weren't blood, but sometimes family was what you chose.

Jesse looked at me and said in a low voice, "I can try again to kick them out or you can risk getting all confessional. Asking for vodka after convulsions is going to raise a couple questions. You want to tackle that?"

"Vodka." It was that or call Mama Lauren for one of her weird medicinal concoctions.

"Your call, little sister." Jesse started to push to his feet, probably to fetch my booze.

I felt woozy and started shivering, and I wasn't entirely sure I'd see sunrise.

Amateurs. The women who did this only left me half-murdered. Fucking amateurs. That was why I liked beheadings. No doubts there. Sever the head, and bodies dropped, even *draugr* or whatever the fuck I was. If I healed, I was going to be . . . unpleasant at best. Why would they risk that? What if I woke up a *draugr*? The thought of that particular nightmare made my heart speed. I really, really didn't want to find out that I was a *draugr* now.

I tried to lift my arm to grab him and totally missed.

"Stay for now," I rasped.

Jesse took my hand. "Hey, Gen? Focus on me, yeah?"

My eyes were not sure how to focus. I convulsed on my sofa.

"Panic is going to spread the venom." Jesse was using the calm voice, the one that meant I was legit injured. It was not comforting, but I knew by now that the calm voice meant that I needed to listen to him.

"No panic," I promised.

The venom in my body should have killed me. Was it just slower because of the ice? Where was Eli? Where did all the ice come from? I had the sort of questions that made me worry about twelve things at once. Adrenaline shot with a hemotoxic edge. I glanced down and saw blood oozing around the plastic bag of ice I was currently clutching to my belly.

As carefully as I could, I said, "Where is ice from?"

"Sera called a friend." He made air quotes. "Had it delivered to the building. Bags and bags of it. No one else came in."

Sera and Christy came into my living room then. Christy had a bottle and two plastic ziplocked bags of ice. Sera had icepacks, ointment, and a cleaning cloth.

"Vodka," I said again, staring at Jesse.

He nodded and stood.

I didn't think the women heard me, but Christy raised her brows at me as she handed me a tall, closed metal water bottle. I shrugged, took the bottle, and swung my feet to the floor. I took both ice bags and pressed one of the icepacks to my shoulder, and the awkward angle made the one on my stomach fall to the floor.

"Vodka?" Christy repeated.

I grabbed my fallen ice and plopped it and the new bag of ice on my chest.

"You're bleeding! Why is she bleeding again?" Sera came over with a damp cloth and lifted my shirt. "We pulled the needle out. Why isn't it closing?"

When I saw the watery blood, I grabbed her wrist. "Don't touch it."

I felt my panic swell again. "Did any of you touch it?"

"I did." Jesse held up his gloved hands. "But I was careful. There was a broken needle in your belly. I wasn't going to leave it there. Pulled it out. Tossed it. Iced you."

"Cloth," I said, holding out my hand.

Sera let me have it, and I wiped away the thin watery stuff

seeping out of my skin. Yes, there was blood, but that wasn't all. I looked closer and saw a red mark. Circular. Raised. One tiny puncture in the middle. I could feel a bump in there, like a tiny lump of poison where the widow Chaddock had injected me.

In a calmer than I felt voice, I said, "I need a bag to put contaminates in." I met Sera's glare. "Did *you* touch any of my blood?"

"No."

"Are you sure?" I stared at her, my magic zinging at her, studying her, seeking the green glow of venom in her. She seemed clean.

"Dude! Put the magic away." Sera glared at me in the way of a friend who was used to all of my quirks. "Don't go all mind control or whatever that is."

"I can't control your mind," I said lightly. "I was just—"

"Slapping your magic at me," she finished. "Well, stop. Jesse refused to let us touch you. He put on gloves and got *cleaning rags* to wipe up your blood."

"Good." I nodded at him.

"Toss it in there." Jesse motioned to an industrial paint can I used to store salt and as a base for the training dummies I built. Jesse had co-opted an empty one as a makeshift bin for contaminants. It was a smart plan. Bloody rags and water were piled in a reddish mess in the bottom of the can.

"Not my first time needing to be sure I wasn't going to catch something from a woman," Jesse teased. "I'm very in favor of prophylactics of all sorts."

"TMI," Christy said dryly. "And don't say prophylactics talking about your sister."

I grinned, grateful as ever for the smart asses that were my friends. "I'm glad he's making sure he's safe. Smart man. Good catch even." I shot her a look. "And you ought to be glad. I mean, *I'm* not the one here who's sleeping with him."

"You told her?" Jesse said.

"No, dumbass." Christy shook her head. "You just did."

I laughed, the movement spilling more venom from the injection in my belly. I typically healed faster than this. I sopped it up again with the rag, noting that the ooze was leaving red trails on my skin. I dabbed instead, trying to absorb it.

"Christy? I want to hear more about you two later, and you"— Sera pointed at me— "can stop with distracting or magicking me to forget or whatever else you want to do to avoid discussing this."

"I can't magic you to forget," I muttered. Of all the traits I wished my dad had given me, *that* one had yet to show up. I wasn't sure it was even real. Could *draugr* make people forget? There was speculation, but my father, frat boy of darkness, was dead so I couldn't ask. Sometimes I was livid about that, that my temper slipped so badly, that I was not as in control as I wanted-- but most of the time I thought the decision to murder him was a good one.

Being covered in ice wasn't going to work long-term. Freezing the venom to buy my body time to eject it was a start. What would happen when the rest of it hit my system though? Would I die? Re-wake? Transform without dying? I had no answers.

Christy plopped another bag of ice on me. "Keep it cold."

My brain was zinging in overtime. Colder was making my mind clearer. I wanted to ponder everything except what was happening to me right then. Maybe if I survived, I'd ask Beatrice about what exactly *draugr* could truly do. My accidental mind-reading skills might be either my dead bio-father's genes or the result of being a hybrid. My witchy mother couldn't do it.

"Get your arm. You're bleeding there, too," Sera muttered, pulling my focus back to now before she flounced out of the room again.

I felt my arm. It was oozing, too. Worse yet, it felt icy to the touch without any ice packs. No venom ball there. It was in me. Magic wasn't necessary to see the venom under my skin.

"Going to fill us in?" Christy asked.

"I was injected."

"Obviously. With what?" Jesse prompted, even though he knew. Of course he did. They knew I was at the morgue because someone was injecting people. They still stared at me with hope.

"*Draugr* venom, I think." I dabbed my stomach. It was oozing more than my arm. "My blood isn't coagulating right. Did it feel cold through the glove?"

"Chilly, but not icy." Jesse met my eyes. "Will your bio offset this?"

He didn't say "bio-dead-dad" or even "biology," but I knew exactly what he meant. Would my bio-deadbeat *draugr* and the fucked-up biology from him offset my reaction? I mean, I couldn't really say for sure. I hadn't been injected before now. Obviously, to some degree, there was offset. I wasn't dead.

"So far, I think it helps," I said. "They thought I would be dead after the first dose."

"Why aren't you dead then?" Christy asked.

"Weird biology," I said lightly. I was glad I sounded much calmer than I felt. The widow and her friend had tried to kill me. Lots of dead things had tried to kill me, but having a human woman try it was new.

I'd rarely had such cause to celebrate my mother's bad taste in bedmates. If I were simply human, I'd be dead. Of course, I wouldn't be a target for well-dressed women with poison if I were merely human—or able to stop them if I survived.

That aside, I didn't get it. Why inject people with *draugr* venom? There were much easier ways to kill someone, but draugr venom had killed Chaddock and Odem. I had been guessing the other woman was Odem's widow, but she was young. Odem's wife supposedly wasn't. Daughter? Another dead man's wife? Either way, she was a woman who had tried to murder me. Why me? Why them? Why venom? And where did they get it? Only venom from a century-old draugr was lethal, and none of those would be easy to milk like snakes.

"How did they get to you?" Jesse asked. "Were you distracted? Were there a lot of attackers?"

That was not the question I wanted to answer.

"She hugged me," I said sheepishly. I could face monsters, kill, hunt, and generally bad-ass my way through life. Today, though, I was felled by a hug. It was mortifying.

"The widow was hiding in the lobby when I got home, and she hugged me. I didn't know she had a syringe. Once I was down, the other woman handed her a second dose because I wasn't dead yet." My heart sped in anger, and I stood.

My magic lashed out in a pulse that—based on Jesse's expression—was visible even to my completely mortal friends, and my eyes slipped toward grave vision so quickly that I felt queasy. I knew my eyes had slid into reptilian slits, that my friends could see that I looked more like a *draugr* than I would like them to see. The vision of the grave let me see that they were, all three, healthy. I glanced at my hands. Green glinted under the skin. Venom.

"Talk to me, Gen." Jesse stepped between me and my other two friends. "Are you . . . still you?"

I flipped him off because speaking was outside my grasp. Some measure of venom was processing, blending with my already fucked biochemistry, and the result was that I felt less human than normal.

"Do we call a doctor?" Christy asked.

"Her mother?" Sera added.

Jesse came closer. I saw my gun in his hand. He held it loosely, but he held it. "Any urge to bite people?"

"Love you, brother," I told him finally. My mouth struggled to form the words. The fact that he'd shoot me rather than let me hurt them was enough to make me tear up a little from relief and pride.

I looked at Christy and Sera. "You, too."

My muscles looked like they were moving on their own.

Twitches and ripples. It made me wince as it grew more intense. I could see the darkening green everywhere I could see my skin. I lifted my shirt and looked at the injection site there. Vibrant emerald glittered inside me so brightly that I reached down to touch my skin. It was icy, making me feel more like a corpse than living person.

I swallowed and said as calmly as I could, "My body is processing the venom faster now. It was a hard bump, like you'd frozen it, but it's not staying there."

Then I leaned over and vomited into the industrial paint can they were using as a makeshift trashbin. I was starting to shake violently, and my magic was not content to stay quiet as my body resisted the toxins. I felt my magic reach out, seeking the dead. I tried to keep it, find another way to release the energy because I didn't need corpses crawling through the windows right now.

My magic wanted to release itself, to roll out and find the dead, to be utilized. I wasn't sure I could keep it in check. I closed my eyes and whispered, "Salt the sills and along the walls. Everywhere. Do it now."

My three closest friends went to the vats of salt I kept around the house. They all knew the dead came toward my magic, and no one here wanted that. I wasn't up to standing, much less swinging a sword. I'd developed great control over my grave magic since childhood, but today wasn't a great day for controlling much of anything.

I concentrated on trying to stay focused on my magic behaving properly as my friends poured salt lines for me.

My home was the entire floor of the building, and it was the ground floor, so there was an odd risk that the dead would try to rise through the ground. Concrete was impervious, fortunately, but a good solid salt line should keep the dead from trying to crawl through windows or throw themselves at the door. That had happened once in my childhood. An old man, clad in his burial suit and loafers, kept battering himself against my bedroom window. I woke to bloody, broken glass and an injured dead man reaching into my room.

Such things had taught me to have better control, because even with my mother's faery bargain in place, I had sometimes struggled. Now that I was unbound, I'd struggled more than I had in fifteen years. And, tonight, after the injection, I wasn't sure I was going to find control.

There were too many ways my friends could be in danger, so they needed to get out of here. The most likely case was that the dead would start clustering in the parking lot. I might be able to stop them from coming into my home, but I wasn't swearing to that.

I felt all of them: *draugr,* corpses properly interred, and lost bodies hidden in places the dead ought not be buried. My magic wanted to claim them, animate them, gather them.

"Phone."

With a shaking hand, Christy gave it to me. "Please don't die on us. Please."

"Hoping."

I pressed a button or several. I couldn't actually say, but in a few moments, I heard his voice. "Geneviève," Eli answered. "What a pleasant—"

"I need you." I took a shuddering breath, forcing my heart to stay calm to not spread the toxin throughout my body even faster. "Right now, Eli. I think I might be dying."

And then the convulsions made my whole body feel as if a drunk stranger had me on marionette strings.

Chapter Twenty-Three

I WOKE COVERED IN ICE AGAIN.

Somewhere near me, Sera said, "We're going to run out. Then what?"

Between the convulsions and the puking, my attempts to stay calm were not working as well as I'd like. I'd convinced my small group of determined nursemaids that they could only stay until Eli arrived. I couldn't decide if I was more irritated or awed by their steadfastness. They weren't asking me why the venom hadn't killed me. They weren't worried that I was going to wake up dead and eat their faces.

"I'm not safe for you to be around," I said for the fourth time. I tried to sound rational, even though I felt like screaming at them that they were being irresponsible. Carefully, I explained, "Injected. Could re-awake as *draugr*."

"So what? You'll have a few *draugr* traits. You're still our Gen." Sera folded her arms and glared down at me.

As adventurous as Christy but two hundred times more maternal, Sera was a rock for me. Right now, though, she looked like she was as reasonable as an angry bear.

"I want *you* to be *safe*," I stressed. "After all the times you said that to me, you ought to understand."

"And I want you to have help while you heal." Sera tapped one foot. "You will heal, Gen. You are not allowed to die, and if that means we stay here while you think you are a threat to us, then—"

"I am a threat."

Sera waved my words away. "I'm not going anywhere until Eli gets here, at the least. I could stay then, too." She motioned to her purse. "If I need to, I'll shoot your knees or something if you change into a *draugr*."

"Told you," Jesse said quietly. He kissed the top of my head and helped me to stand. "Come on. You wanted to be in your own bed, so let's get you there."

The room felt blurry, and I realized my eyes were flickering between normal pupils and serpent slits. As my eyes shifted, so did my vision. It was like someone had shoved a broken strobe light inside my head. I swayed and forced down nausea.

"I can carry you," Jesse offered.

"Piss off." My bones were intact. My muscles, too. I was going to walk or I could stay on the damned sofa. I took a stumbling step and grumbled, "Fuck it. *Fine*. I need help."

Sera and Christy swept in to support me. I had one friend on either side, arms around my waist, guiding me across the open room toward my bedroom. It was one of the few times I'd cursed having a large living space. The distance that seemed fine most of the time was too far tonight.

I wanted to let Jesse keep his gun in hand. Just in case.

A few halting steps later, the pain in my low abdomen made me gasp. The venom was changing me. I felt a burning, like a kidney stone and hangover got together for a tango. It was making puking only one of my worries. Walking felt like I might piss myself—or worse. A part of my brain, a calmly rational streak, reminded me that this was what the human body did at death. Organs gave up, muscles released, and things came gushing out. I *really* didn't want that.

"Take his gun, Christy? Swap places, I mean." As soon as they did, I muttered, "Carry me."

Jesse swept me up into his arms, and without a word about me admitting my inability to walk there myself, he carried me toward my bedroom.

"I have money saved," Jesse said as he strode across the hallway to the unit where I slept. "Enough for twelve years in a T-Cell House."

"Seriously?" I managed to say.

"You're exposed to biters all the time. We *all* encounter them in the city. I know the risks living here," Sera said from behind him. "I have enough saved up for fifteen years."

"Eighty here," Christy offered from my left, where she strolled with a gun in hand.

"Over a hundred years in hand, already." Jesse stopped at the foot of my bed. The room was darker than the rest of the floor. I'd walled up the windows when I moved in.

Sera tugged back my rumpled bed linens and fluffed my pillows, as I watched from where I was held in Jesse's arms. "We are a family," Sera stressed. "Families look out for one another."

I felt tears well up and sniffled to stop the sob that went with them.

When Jesse lowered me to the bed and got me situated, they all stepped back and stared at me as I sat on my bed. It felt like a wake, but with the corpse still alert. As far as wakes go, it wasn't awful—but I didn't want to die.

And I sure as fuck didn't want to wake again.

I felt the need to puke, but didn't want to do that either.

As they stood there, gathered around me, I felt like I ought to tell them some sort of deathbed wisdom. I had no insights. No wisdom. Just this ball of terror that whatever happened after this was larger and more overwhelming than I could fathom.

Christy turned to go, and I blurted, "Wait. I'm not ready. I'm not . . ."

"What do you need?" Sera asked softly, and I knew as well as I knew anything about this world that she saw my terror. Her gaze met mine, and I wanted my friends to stay as much as they wanted to do so.

But then a shudder made me lift off the bed, and my magic rolled out with the kind of uncontrolled wave that I hadn't had since I'd murdered my father. I tamped it down as hard as I could and said, "I need more ice, but also a bowl with hot water, as hot as it can be without burning my skin. Rags. Box with sealed suture supplies. Med gloves."

Christy and Sera didn't question me. Not yet at least. I did get a suspicious stare from everyone when I added, "Silver knife. Fire till it's hot. Keep it in the bowl of water so it stays sterile."

Once they'd left the room, I stretched out in bed, eyes closed, while Jesse tucked me in as if I simply had the flu.

"Status?" Jesse asked now that we were alone.

"Chills. Fever. I see the venom inside me with my grave vision." My brain was remarkably clear, even as my ability to convince my tongue to create words at a reasonable pace wasn't. "Going to need to cut part of venom out."

"Cut . . .?"

"Cauterize after if necessary."

Jesse looked as nauseous as I felt. He sat on the edge of my bed. "Ice is what's keeping the shock down. Is heat a good idea?"

"No, but letting it slowly leak into my organs isn't working out either. It needs to come out before it finishes melting or whatever the fuck it's doing." I had the start of a plan, but it was probably a terrible one.

Step One wasn't absolutely awful. That was simply to have Eli here. The other steps were varying degrees of terrible. My brain was processing too many things, but all I really wanted was to call the dead toward me. That had to be a warning sign of some sort.

I had the energy to bring hundreds of dead things to my side. I could feel them, all through the city. With a veritable army of corpses at my side, I would be a terrifying force—but to what end?

I wanted to *do* something with this energy: to summon, to bind, to hunt Alice.

Alice.

Tres.

A flicker of a thought hit me that Tres was in danger.

"Phone," I mumbled.

Jesse gave it to me without question.

I struggled to focus my eyes on the here and now. With shaking hands, I texted Tres: "Alice injected me. Dying maybe."

After I hit send, I realized that there were a lot of other things to add. It wasn't the calmest or most articulate of warnings, and I hoped it wasn't too late. Alice had expected me to be dead. I could picture her designer heels passing me as I stared up at her with eyes and mouth open. My body was in shock as she and her friend stepped away and left me there to die.

I felt my magic dancing through New Orleans, spreading out for miles, and I felt more older *draugr* than I knew were in the city look up as if to find the magic that had grazed them. One of them was Beatrice. I felt as much as saw her say, "Geneviève?"

I jerked back, tried to roll my wandering strands of magic back to me. It reminded me of trying to stuff a fishing net into a sock. This much unfurled magic wasn't going gracefully back into the small space inside of me.

"Geneviève?" It wasn't her voice this time.

When I opened my eyes, Eli stood in my room next to Jesse. He was holding a bag half-filled with ice. At his feet were two tall white buckets of ice, and I realized that several more bags were piled on my stomach, chest, and arms.

"You seized up," Jesse said. "Moving . . . or warming up?"

I nodded.

"Sera texted to bring ice," Eli said, and I wondered if he'd say much more if we were alone. He was very open with me in private, at least compared to the reputation of the fae, but there was a witness here.

"I'm glad you're here." I gave him what I hoped was a convincing smile. I was incredibly cold, but my brain was clearer again.

It was odd seeing Jesse and Eli there at the same moment, especially in my bedroom. The undercurrent between them meant they were typically at odds. Tonight, they were in rare accord. Who knew that all I needed to do was be near death to get them to be at peace?

Even if I wasn't used to reading his emotions, I'd have realized that Eli looked stricken. I must look worse than I thought.

I smiled at him. "Hey."

Eli didn't move. "Jesse filled me in. I should've walked you inside or—"

"Nah. . . but I do have a terrible plan," I murmured. "Just need your strength to make it work."

Seeing the same anxious look on both faces was like a punch to the stomach. I stared at them, and then only at Jesse. I felt like there were a million things to say, and I couldn't make myself say any of them. He was my brother. My rock. My family. I didn't want to leave him alone, and I sure as hell wasn't willing to wake up without remembering everything. My greatest fear was becoming like my father.

"Try not to die," Jesse said in a rough voice. "I'm going to need you here when I screw up with Christy again."

I nodded and held out my hand to him. I wasn't going to die on purpose. I had things to do yet. "Take care of them if—"

"Yes," he said. "And I'll manage Mama Lauren if . . ." His words faded, as if saying it would make it real. "Love you, little sister."

"Love you, too."

After a few moments, Sera and Christy were standing in the doorway behind Jesse. They all looked like I felt, as if none of us was certain we'd meet again. "I'm planning on not dying," I said forcefully. "I need you all to go first, though. I can't do this with you here. I need to focus."

"Hot water," Sera announced. "I brought the suture supplies." She held up a needle and tweezers and scissors. "You'll have to swab it to disinfect before you—"

"I know how to sew her up," Eli said softly. "I've had practice."

Sera continued, "And sterile gloves."

I tried to keep my eyes human, but I was losing the fight there. My pupils reshaped into something monstrous. I said, "Eli stays. You all go. Now."

"We aren't g—"

"My father was a *draugr*," I blurted out, as much as it horrified me to admit those words. "My mother gave birth to the child of a dead thing. I'm not sure what will happen to me if the venom keeps changing things. I feel it inside, guys. My kidneys. My heart. My vision. I don't know, and Eli is . . . Eli is strong enough to. . ."

"We can help you, too," Sera insisted.

"Ven-om." I broke the word in two and glared at her. "If I change . . ." My voice fractured then, and I sobbed. "I could hurt you. Eli's strong enough to stop me. He works with me because of it. He could . . . he could stop me from hurting him."

I felt like something in me was breaking. They ought to fear me, hate me, be disgusted. Instead they were standing here. They'd offered money for a T-Cell House. Who *did* that? I wanted to explain that it wasn't that I thought I was dying, but that if I did die, I'd wake again, and I would not, absolutely could not, be like that. To the best of my knowledge the only person on any record of bringing a recently perverted corpse to instant clarity was me, and that was something I'd managed exactly once.

If I was dead, I had no idea what I'd be like. Would I be even stronger since I already had a *draugr*'s strength while living?

"I suspected you were bitten years ago," Sera said. "This explains it better, though. You almost *flow* sometimes. Not totally, but it's like you're here and then you're there."

"Told you." Jesse grinned, despite everything. "We all still love you. And if you end up in a T-Cell house, we'll still be—"

"Please? I can't do this and worry about hurting you. I need you all to leave."

Christy nodded. "Still love you. Still want to stay . . . *but* we'll go so you can do whatever." She looked at Eli. "Keep her alive. If not, we wait for her to come back. If she changes, we have money for a T-Cell."

She took Jesse and Sera's hands, and they left.

"Geneviève," Eli began.

I stared at him, daring him to argue with the inevitable next request. In a low whisper, I said, "I won't go to a T-Cell House, Eli. I need someone strong enough to stop me if I . . ." I swallowed and shoved the ice aside. "They had to leave in case you need to kill me."

I pushed to my feet and tried to stand. Eli helped. I lifted one of my swords from the wall rack in my room and put it on the bed.

"Geneviève . . ."

I sat down, hand on the hilt, and looked up at him. He was staring at the sword. "If you wrap your hands in something before you lift this, it won't hurt you that much to—"

"Killing you would more than *hurt*." Eli tore his gaze away from the sword between us. "It would destroy me."

"You understand then. I cannot be something that kills people. I can't become like that, Eli, and no one else I know is strong enough to stop me." I'd begun to shake. The few moments without ice was too long. I couldn't live in bed under ice for the rest of my however-many-decades-or-centuries of life, and I couldn't become a worse perversion of life than I already was. I grabbed the ice and piled it on my skin again, and with shaky hands, he helped.

"Geneviève . . . what you ask . . ."

I hated the way Eli was looking at me. If this got worse, there weren't many choices left. I needed him to agree before we tried to cut the venom out.

"I guess the guillotine purchase wasn't as bad of an idea as I'd thought. If my plan fails . . . don't warehouse me. I don't want to be *that*."

Eli met my gaze.

"If I turn, will you kill me? Please, Eli, I know it's a lot to ask, but . . .?"

The moments dragged, but finally, Eli gave one nod, took a steadying breath, and shifted to a businesslike demeanor. I was grateful for it, for him. The familiar light tone in his voice was a total lie, but I was still glad to hear it when he asked, "What is your plan to avoid changing?"

"It's a terrible plan," I warned Eli as I lifted the heated knife.

"I would expect no less of you." He was clearly trying to continue to sound light hearted, but he watched me warily. I guess asking someone to kill you is awkward.

"Sanitize that?" I nodded at my belly as I took the bag of ice off my skin.

The skin was red with splotches of white. I wasn't sure what was from the ice and what was from the poison. All I knew for sure was that the venom wouldn't stay in this knot. Whether the broken needle or the ice had bought me this much time, I didn't know. The amount in the first injection was more than enough to scare me. More wasn't an option. It had to come out.

"I'm going to cut it out."

"You're going to . . ." He stopped himself and tried to match my calm. "Would you like me to . . . do that?"

"Not really." I braced myself for the pain. "I will need you to stitch me after I do this. For now, put your hands here and pull the skin taut."

I directed his hands to my bare skin. It was not how I wanted him to touch me the first time we were in my bedroom, but I couldn't imagine trusting anyone else to be at my side for this. I loved my friends, but only Eli could be here. His strength. His willingness to let me control my fate. I asked a hard thing of him —I knew that. My job was to accept that very request: behead people's loved ones. It was different when it was someone *you* loved, and while I didn't think he loved me, he certainly had feelings.

I couldn't say all of that. I simply said, "Thank you."

Then I let my eyes slide toward grave sight, so I could see better. I had to find the edges of the poison so I could excise it like a cancer. I couldn't carve away what I couldn't see.

"Geneviève . . .?"

"I'm here. Need different vision." I stared at my skin and the pulsing emerald under the surface.

It was wider than before. Something—whether the failed injection, my body, or the ice—had enclosed it a capsule. I could see it writhing, though. The venom was fleeing in little trickles.

"The venom they injected is more than even I can process. The shot in my arm might still change me. If this was injected carefully, I'd be—" I shook my head, stopping my own words, not wanting to think about the certain death I'd narrowly missed. If it was properly injected. If my friends hadn't come. If they hadn't thought to use ice. If this home surgery of mine didn't work. . .

I had to cut it out.

I had to succeed.

Or Eli would have to behead me.

I let myself think about what to do next. I'd either give up or I'd be too late. I took a deep breath, and then I jabbed the knife into my skin. Despite best efforts, I made a noise. I might be okay with pain and have more experience with it than anyone should need, but I was not impervious to it.

In my anxiety over getting it done, the tip of the knife went in a bit further than I wanted. I wasn't exactly skilled in self-surgery. I twisted the blade so it slid under the ball of venom that we'd effectively frozen. A whimper escaped my lips, and I felt more than saw Eli glance at me.

He didn't speak.

I couldn't speak.

Parting my lips would let out cries of pain, rage, and fear.

My hand wasn't unsteady in a dangerous way yet, so I tried diligently not to think about the fact that this was my body I was stabbing. Okay, it was a *little* unsteady. I gouged out a bit more flesh than maybe I needed—but I wasn't sure I could stab myself twice.

I pulled the blade out, trying not to look at the blobby thing I'd cut out. It looked like a clutch of frozen frog eggs. My hand hovered in the air, not sure what exactly to do with the lump I'd carved out of my body.

Then I felt Eli's hand on my wrist. "I am here, Geneviève. Let me stitch this."

I let him take my knife, watched it drop onto a rag on the floor, and closed my eyes. I felt tears slip through my closed eyes as Eli cleaned blood away, stitched, cleaned, stitched. There was something soothing about it. I sucked at letting people take care of me most of the time, but over the last year, I'd let more than Jesse, Sera, and Christy in. I'd let Eli in.

"Still with me?"

"Thinking," I said. I counted stitches, seven so far, and concentrated on the rhythmic tying together of my flesh. Another wipe, another stitch. The needle pierced my skin. I hated when he had to do this. I knew that Eli could manage steel in the way that true fae couldn't, but it wasn't exactly pleasant for him.

"Thinking about?" he prompted.

"You," I admitted.

He paused for a flicker of a moment, but then he wiped my skin again and stitched again. "Oh?"

"I trust you."

"Good . . ."

"No, I mean, I *really* trust you. When I was hurt, my thought was that I needed you, and when I think about keeping my friends safe, I need you to protect them. And when I think about being put down—"

"'Put down?' You are not a rabid animal, Geneviève." Eli wiped again and looked at his work. "And I thought I was counted among your friends."

"Fair." I scooted up slightly. "My *point*, Eli, was that I don't trust easily. I've known Jesse my whole life, Sera and Christy for almost a decade. It's a short list."

He gave one of those half-shrugs that shouldn't be charming but was and said, "I waited you out."

Then he grinned at me.

My tension slipped away as I watched him look less calm, more agitated, more emotional. It was a peculiar thing to know that his calm visage was probably the most obvious signal that he was upset. Seeing him less reserved, less controlled was how I knew that we were both thinking that things were probably going to be fine.

I opened my mouth to reply and felt elongated teeth drop down from my gums. I reached up with one finger and felt them. *Fangs.* I had fangs.

Eli reached out to me. "Geneviève?"

"Fangs!" I clamped a hand over my mouth and grasped my sword with the other. I had failed. There wasn't any way to stay safe, to keep my family or friends safe. I jumbled with the sword until I had the point under my chin. I held it there with one hand, and then I took the one that was over my mouth and made a slamming gesture at Eli.

"No," he said in the calmest voice ever. "I will not shove you onto the sword blade. You're panicking. Are you still coherent?"

I gave a slight nod.

He pushed the sword away from my throat. "Do you want to bite me?"

I tilted my head, and then shook it. I didn't. Maybe I just wasn't hungry. Although I could feel my heart thudding in my ears, I still reached down and checked my pulse.

"Alive?"

Live people didn't have fangs. I had a pulse—and fangs. I had not had them before, though, and I really didn't want them now. Passing for human was hard enough with often reptilian eyes and the ability to *flow*. If people knew I was inhuman . . . I blinked tears. I wasn't sure what was going on, and I stared at Eli and wondered if he had answers. Ideas. Something.

He took my hand in his, unfolding my fingers so I released the sword. He shoved it away and sat close beside me on the bed. He pulled me against him, holding me, trusting me, and stroked my back and arm. "We need answers, love."

I waited. It was that or uncover my mouth, and that sounded like a lousy plan.

"The only solution I see is to seek the ones who might know," he murmured. "Beatrice seems to like you—or at the least, want you to like her. Could you reach out to her?"

I watched him warily. This was turning into an awful day, or maybe it was way past that. I'd figured out who the murderer was by accident, been left for dead, and now I had fangs.

"She is the last idea I have," Eli said. "But if the alternative is losing you, bring the dead, crème brûlée. Call for her because there must be a solution that doesn't involve your death."

Chapter Twenty-Four

ELI'S SUGGESTION WAS NOT ONE I LIKED, BUT MY MAGIC FELT like it was choking me. There was a ball in my throat, like I had the physical need to vomit but the will to stop it. I wanted to release my call to the dead. My magic pushed out, no longer able to be held back.

"Can you call Beatrice specifically?" Eli urged.

"Maybe . . .?"

I closed my eyes and . . . let go of my restraints. It was a relief to let my magic free, as if too-tight trousers, pinching shoes, underwire bra, and a bitchy neighbor were all removed in one glorious moment. Although I was trying to concentrate on Beatrice, on the unique traits that were her, my magic rolled from New Orleans to the Outs. I could see fields, trees, and for a split moment, I could smell the scents that were home to me. Beatrice wasn't there. Instead, I could see home and my mother.

"Darius?" Mama Lauren's voice had a thread of girlish hope. She looked up from her herb-strewn table and seemed to see me. She smiled beatifically. "Baby girl?"

I watched my mother, who was staring into the darkness of

194

her work room and smiling. At me. She was smiling at me, and I had zero idea how.

"Look at you," she said in a teary voice. "I knew you'd become something sacred. I *knew* it. Just look at you."

Beatrice.

I jerked away, followed the flow of the land, let myself ripple across the air as if the land was too limiting. Air. I was a creature of air *and* land, of water, of fire. I was *Witch*. The fire of life and death was in my veins, and I could end a life or create one from the ashes of death. Small dead creatures rested in the soil. The bones of a wolf scattered on the ground as flowers pushed their blossoms between dried remnants of its ribs. The hunter had become the food. His meat had fed the soil, and seeds had sprouted. I could bring wolf and prey to life again.

I jerked away. My magic usually only sought humanity's dead. Not creatures. I didn't want to uproot bone or flowers that grew there.

Beatrice.

My attention slid to a river, and my magic rolled over current and stone. This was not where death was. The dead did not belong in water that gave life to land and animal. I pulled away again. I felt my magic seeking the dead, and the dead that looked back at me were waiting for the spark of life I carried.

Eli's voice carried all around me, an echo over land and water as he urged, "Geneviève, focus. I need you."

Eli. Eli was a shelter, a strong rock under which I could find rest and peace. If I found the dead creature I sought, I could return to Eli. My partner. My tether. Peace to my violence. Balance. A thread of truth there called me. Balance was my source. Life and death. My nature-bound mother and the dead thing that fathered me.

I needed a specific dead, not one I called to speak from ash-made lips. I needed one who was dead, but again-walking.

Draugr.

Beatrice.

The thought of her name again, the third call to her, was enough to send me hurtling toward her. She stood in a room I couldn't see, surrounded by people. Seven. Eight. There were others watching her. These seven were the ones I should see. Another time I would ask, study, understand. Today, I simply wanted to live.

"Leave me." Beatrice pressed her lips together.

I knew she didn't mean me. She was sending them away. She offered me privacy.

The bodies left. Doors closed.

"Stop trying to see beyond me, Geneviève." Even without being beside her, I could tell she was exasperated again.

"You are beside me."

My magic surged. She was here. In my home. With Eli. Was Eli safe?

I felt her sigh echo in the chambers of my mind, a warm strong breeze. It rushed around, battering at the fog that seemed to be filling my mind. I didn't like the fog.

"You're not in my home, nor am I in yours. Yet. I gather you are grievously injured then?" Beatrice was moving, footsteps on marble. Her floor was marble. I saw a glimpse of heavy drapes as she passed them. Red brocade.

"Burgundy," she corrected as she left the building.

I stayed next to her as she walked. I could smell grass, wet earth. This was not within the city of New Orleans. The Outs? My mother—

"Lauren is fine." Beatrice sighed again. "I would never harm your mother. None of mine would unless they'd like to find their second death."

I shook my head, and I felt Eli there next to me. He was in the room where I was in physical space. The part of me that was drifting along on magic was far away, but my body was with Eli.

He was stroking my face. "Geneviève? Come back to me, love.

Find the woman and return. I can't get your fever down this time. Geneviève? Please, I could not bear to lose you." He was weeping. Tears sizzled on my flesh. "Please."

At that, I felt myself return to my body. I stared up at him, but I could not speak. I could not move. My body was motionless, but I heard my pulse.

Come, I called, with every sliver of my magic.

I could not untie myself from this form or place. I'd never projected before, at least not that I was aware of doing. I'd send my magic out in waves, but not my very *self*. Somehow, tonight, I'd sought out my mother, and I'd found Beatrice. My astral body was tied to my physical self, but I was able to explore. A trickle of fear suggested that this was a result of my impending death. Apparently, it wasn't only feats of great strength that were possible in times of peril, but feats of new magic.

I'd pulled myself away from where I was in the world to seek help. I had no idea if it would work. Did Beatrice know where I was? Could she hear my summons and find me?

If not, there was no time left to give her that information. I shivered in the cold I felt but could not see. Eli must have added more ice, covering me, and as my temperature lowered again, I felt caught, like some sticky fibrous mass was wrapped around my body, melding me to the flesh, the space, the moment where I was. I could not leave my building to find Beatrice, and I wasn't entirely convinced that her aid was something I wanted.

But I didn't want to die.

Again, I sent the word out on the pulse of my magic: *Come.* Then for good measure, I added, *Beatrice, please come.*

She didn't answer, and I was unable to untether myself from my body again. When I heard the pounding on the door, I wanted to tell Eli it wasn't her. They were human. I could feel them, but I could neither move nor speak.

"Let me see if that is our knight in an elegant gown," he murmured as he kissed my forehead. Only then did he release my wrist. Eli wasn't beheading me, despite my requests to him, but in his defense, I wasn't technically dead either.

"I need to see Miss Crowe," an angry voice insisted.

"She is unwell," Eli rebutted.

"Well, the whole fucking lawn and the parking lot are filling up with zombies again. That's her doing." The man's voice grew louder as he yelled, "Crowe! Stop whatever hocus pocus you're doing. I ordered take-away, and the delivery man is quivering in his car."

"Could you walk to his car?" another voice asked.

"Sure, right. I'll just march through a herd of zombies. Great idea, Martha."

And then, no one spoke.

I felt Beatrice arrive. The air and the space that had been vibrating with anger was suddenly still. Terror rippled through the air. No one would have doubt as to what she was.

"Lady Beatrice," Eli said warmly.

"I come for Geneviève. Do I need to kill these people to reach the door?" Beatrice's voice was loud enough to carry.

"No," Eli said drolly. "They noticed that Geneviève was dying and came to speak to her."

"Indeed." Beatrice sounded amused. "Shall I disperse those worrying in the lot?"

"If you wouldn't mind," my neighbor, Rosemary, said cheerily. I'd always liked her. No nonsense. No fear. If I lived long enough to grow old, I wanted to be like her.

If I could laugh, I might.

"It's a temporary solution, unless Geneviève dies or recovers. Currently, her magic is...summoning the dead," Beatrice said lightly. "Including *draugr*."

My neighbors' replies were too muffled to hear, but whatever their opinions, they weren't arguing with the scary dead woman in the doorway to my home.

I heard the others leave, as well as a cheerful voice from Rose-mary, "Well, she seems nice, doesn't she?"

Nice? I doubted that Beatrice was nice by anyone's standards, but she was efficient. Right now, I was grateful for it. If I recov-ered, I suspected I'd need to figure out why she was so interested in me, but not today.

I can hear you, Beatrice whispered in my mind. She sounded like she was amused.

Really?

Did you think you were the only one who can read minds? she asked.

I swear she sounded like she was laughing. *No . . .?* I replied. *Is it a* draugr *thing?*

After a long pause, she said, *No.*

Then I heard Beatrice and Eli come into my room, but I was still silent and motionless as he filled her in on my situation. I could not move or speak. My body had entered some sort of stasis.

"Paralysis," she said, meeting my eyes. "She hears us. Sees us. The venom paralyzes as it starts to liquify her organs and muscles. It should have been painful before this stage."

"It was." Eli stroked my face. "Can you . . . is there something we can do? I'll do anything. I'd really rather not have to kill her."

At that, the old *draugr* looked appalled. "Why ever would you do that?"

"Her wishes."

Beatrice shook her head. "If you stay this way, between living and dying, the dead will continue to gather. Do you understand me?"

Help. HELP. I wasn't sure what I needed, but this, this weird vegetative state, wasn't it. I'd rather die. *Someone help me!*

She looked at me. "Don't yell, daughter. That's why they are all gathered. If you stay like this, they will drain you. We could fix this, but the paralysis will last for days. If there are bones, you will find them." She paused. "When you sleep, Geneviève, you will have no control. Would it not be better to be like me?"

No. Not ever. No. Please no.

"What if she went where there were no bones?" Eli's tone scared me. I knew that one. It was mine, the one I had when I was about to embark on a terrible plan. "Would she heal?"

"If there was no venom left in her," Beatrice said mildly.

"How?"

I drew in a sharp breath because I knew this answer, felt the inevitability of it before she parted her lips and said, "Well, I would remove it, of course." She stared at me as she asked, "Do I have your consent to remove the venom from Geneviève?"

"It's that or death?"

"Yes. Or this suspended state, summoning the bones of the dead to rebuild them, calling *draugr* to her until she expires." Beatrice met my gaze. "What will it be?"

Not this. I couldn't answer. Whatever was happening to me, I couldn't reply with my magic—or she was ignoring me. I couldn't tell.

She glanced at Eli.

"I don't know if you'd choose this or death," he said quietly. "I know you would not like to revive after death." He glanced at Beatrice. "This won't—"

"I am removing the venom, not adding to it," she said in a voice that wouldn't be out of place in a classroom.

"Save her," he said. "You have my consent."

Beatrice leaned closer, and in my paralysis, I could not pull away. I was helpless as something older than Shakespeare drove teeth into my arm, right over the injection. I felt her magic drawing the venom, separating it from blood and organ, calling it to her. My gums clenched. My stomach and kidneys did. My lungs. The places the venom had been already processed wanted to obey her summons, but in those cases, some venom was already absorbed.

Beatrice was a witch and a *draugr.* Like me. I had more questions than before, but I also had what I thought was an answer. She was the closest thing to what I was that I'd ever heard of. How long had she lived as the only one like her? Were there other witches that were again-walkers?

I couldn't ask, but from the way she smiled at me with my blood on her lips, I had suspicions that she knew my questions.

"Rest," she whispered as she stood and accepted a tissue Eli extended.

"In time she will wake and move, but until then, she'll summon the dead. They'll tear down the walls to reach her." Beatrice brushed my hair back. "You will live, Geneviève. Not exactly as before, but not dead. Not wholly *draugr.*"

Then she motioned to the doorway. "May I escort you to the door?"

"To . . .?" Eli asked.

"*Elphame,*" Beatrice said quietly. "There is no other place without bones in the soil. I know who you are. I know where you take her. . . and the cost you will pay for doing so. I have heard whispers, Son of Stonecroft."

What cost? Beatrice, answer me. Stop this!

Beatrice only met my eyes and smiled, and I knew then that she'd heard me—and that she was ignoring me.

Chapter Twenty-Five

I WOKE IN A ROOM WITH ONLY TWO WALLS. IN FRONT OF ME—
and likely behind me—was a meadow. I heard birds, a waterfall,
trees dancing in the wind. That sound, more than the rest, was
one I missed. The music of wind through nature was one of the
things that was lacking in New Orleans. Rain fell. River rolled.
Birds sang. Those were as present in the city as in the country,
but the city didn't give me the rustling of thousands of leaves as if
they were instruments that the wind had called to song.

"Can you stand? Speak? Sit?" Eli's voice came from my left.

I turned my head toward him. "What have you done?"

"Brought you to safety." He motioned around the room. "To
my *other* home."

My gaze slid over the walls; natural rock with trickling water
to one side and what appeared to be tightly woven trees on the
other. The roots extended into the living space and formed the
frames of chairs, a table, and a lounging sofa. It was more magical
than I'd expected, but it was as welcoming as Eli's home in New
Orleans. I felt peace here, but I felt like a part of me was missing.

I sent out a pulse of magic. I felt dizzy with how easily the energy flowed outward, but there were no gaps in the canvas. Nothing dead. My own essence wanted to follow the magic, see where it would lead, but I clung to my physical form. I was afraid to project. It was only a thing I'd done during my near-death.

"The bones of the dead aren't here," Eli said softly. He moved to sit next to me on the bed of soil where I was resting.

I was in soil, and it took no magic to know where it was from. I felt *home* through the dirt and rocks. I slid my fingers through it. "How?"

Eli offered that half-shrug, as if to dismiss the inexplicable feat of gathering so much earth for me in *Elphame*. "I called in favors, and it was brought to me. You were ill, and I was . . . determined." He cleared his throat. "Jesse helped."

I couldn't decide whether to be more stunned that Jesse and Eli worked together or that there was soil-of-my-home here for me. I started to reach into his mind for answers, but stopped myself. Leaving him with a migraine because I was trying to rummage around in his mind was wrong.

"You can look at my memories, Geneviève."

"What?" I stared at him.

"I know you can do it." He smiled at me in that vaguely amused way. "I felt you a few times."

"It wasn't on purpose," I blurted. "I mean, just now was, but—"

"I tried to project," he interrupted. "Images of us, naked. Of me, thinking of you in my home. Of—"

"I missed most of that."

He nodded. "It was worth a try. Go ahead and look. We couldn't stay where we were."

"It hurts if I do it on purpose," I warned him.

He shrugged.

I wasn't entirely sure I knew how to glance into a mind without harm, but with an invitation, maybe the walls that protected the mind were lowered—or maybe it was because he wasn't human. My rooting around in the treasure troves of some-one's consciousness was allowed—and safe for him—because he'd invited me.

The dead were gathered like a soil-caked army. As Eli carried my unconscious body in his arms, bridal-style, the mass of semi-healed corpses surged. It was as if ripples slid over them.

"Do not pause," Beatrice ordered. "I can give you a few meters of space at best, so you need to keep moving."

I could see the wave of animated corpses, clad in magically-restored clothes from eras past, older than I ought to be able to call from graves. They moved around us as if they were a ghastly escort. Lights from windows in the buildings we passed illuminated terrified faces.

"To me," Beatrice murmured.

Draugr pushed through the walking dead, clustering between us and the revived corpses. They were clawed and battered, shoved and trampled. They were Beatrice's to command, and she was clearly commanding them to aid her in her protection of Eli and me.

"Near?" she asked, voice strained.

"Yes."

And then we were in Elphame where we were greeted by guards with silver swords. A man stepped forward—

I was thrust out of Eli's memory.

"If we had stayed in the city, they'd have torn you limb from limb in their eagerness to be near you, Geneviève."

"You could've beheaded me."

He gave me a look of utter heartbreak. "If you had died, I would've. If you'd changed into a *draugr*. . . I would've. I agreed to your request." He took my hand in his. "You are alive, Geneviève, and I would pay near anything to have it so."

"What will it cost you? I heard Beatrice. Who was that man? Why—"

"I will pay the cost if I must." Eli stared at me, as if this was a declaration, and maybe it was. I had no idea because he wouldn't tell me anything substantive.

"Did that hurt? Letting me in?" I asked. He seemed fine, but I needed to know.

"Not at all," he said.

I nodded, relieved. "How long have I been out?"

"A month, but—"

"A *month*?" I shoved to my feet, somehow transitioning from prone to standing far faster than I'd intended. "Have you contacted my friends? Tres?"

"Geneviève. . ."

"They all probably think I died." I was pacing, seeking boots and weapons, noticing that I appeared to be wearing some sort of vaguely medieval-looking nightdress. "What about Alice's crime? How many more people are dead?"

"Geneviève!"

I paused and glanced at him. "Where are my weapons?"

"In their world, it's been three hours."

"Oh." I stood in his home in this fairy tale place and simply stared at him. I suspected I was panicking. It was easier to focus on my friends, my clients, and the safe things than to ask myself about the changes I could feel in my body.

I ran my tongue over my teeth. The fangs were gone, or at least, retracted. I could feel the hard edges of my new unwanted teeth under the skin. I wondered if they'd retracted permanently or—

Fangs slid out, extending into my mouth.

Eli, uncharacteristically, approached and wrapped his arms around me. "They retract and extend, bonbon."

"How . . .?"

"You make faces when your teeth extend," he said with that small shrug of his.

"Do you owe Beatrice?" I stood there, staring at him with the gorgeous meadow just outside the missing wall of the building. "Do I?"

"No."

A chime echoed through the house. Eli's expression shifted to the restrained one that I often thought of as his fae face. Sometimes I forgot how much he revealed to me until that expression appeared.

"Gun? Sword?" I asked quietly.

Eli shook his head. "Not that kind of threat, cupcake."

There before us was the same man from Eli's memory. He was handsome in the way of feral animals, sharp lines and prominent muscles. If not for the grandeur of his fur-lined cloak and wealth of jewels glittering on his hands and wrists, I'd suspect him to be a warrior. He did not look any older than Eli, but determining age with the fae was a skill few possessed.

"Your majesty," Eli said with a brief bow.

"I see the girl is awake," he said with a cursory glance at me.

"Woman," I corrected. "Witch if you prefer."

The apparent king of *Elphame* stared at us. He did not address me, but instead spoke to Eli. "You entered the land of your grandfather with death at your side."

"Geneviève is not death," Eli said mildly. "She is a witch. A human."

"She smells of death," the king said.

I sniffed. "I smell just fine. Maybe a little flowery, but—"

"Your blood." The king gave me a sad look. "I know the scent of death."

"I told you she was injected," Eli began.

"And I offer my condolences," the king said, meeting my eyes briefly. He shook his head then. "Now that she is awake, however, we must address the things left unresolved as she healed. She cannot be here as your guest, son of my brother, prince of my throne."

My head swiveled to Eli. "What did he say?"

Eli sighed and stepped between me and his uncle, the king. He glanced over his shoulder and whispered, "I am sorry, sugar cream."

Eli had effectively blocked the king from my view. That did nothing to muffle the roar of laughter.

When the king's laughter subsided, he said, "You didn't tell her?" He motioned to Eli. "He fled from home when it was time to choose his bride. He's been in your world for years, hiding from his duty. The prince knew that when he returned home, he would be staying here permanently. You, dead witch, can return to your world of steel and violence. The heir to my throne will be right here where he belongs. Finally."

I stared at Eli's uncle with a mix of rage and fear. I was fairly sure that attacking the king of *Elphame* was a terrible idea. Even if he wasn't Eli's uncle, he was a powerful creature, and I was in his domain—and unarmed. I felt a ball of fury squirming in my gut. Magic drew together, urged me to strike.

Apparently, my temper was not improved by my increase in *draugr* nature.

"You cannot demand that he stay, punish him because he was being a decent person." I reached for the sword that was not there and fisted my hand in irritation. No hilt. No gun butt, either. My hands had only air to grasp—or the absurd nightdress I was wearing. I was *not* a skirt person and definitely not a medieval nightdress person. I was jeans and steel swords, boots and bullets. I could go with barefoot or even naked. Unarmed always seemed stupid.

At least I wasn't truly defenseless, thanks to my magic, but I would rather have my gun or sword. Sometimes the threat of violence was enough. I would love to be able to make a few threats and leave. I didn't think the consequences of attacking the king would be great.

"The half-dead and the dead are not welcome in *Elphame*," the king pronounced. "You must leave."

"Pulse. I have one," I said mildly, my hand touching my throat. I may have been injected with venom from the *draugr*, but I was, in fact, alive.

"My nephew has returned due to your murder, but you must go back to your world, Geneviève of Crowe." The king smiled as if he was being kind. "And Eli must take the next step in his journey."

"So, I go, and he stays?"

"Yes."

"You're going to punish him for saving my life?" I asked in an increasingly agitated voice.

"Being in *Elphame*, in your view, is a punishment?" The king gave me a look of disdain. "No unnatural creatures, save you. No need to work. A devoted, beautiful wife to fulfill his every need. How is this a punishment?"

Despite everything, the king of *Elphame* sounded genuinely confused. He motioned to the glorious landscape outside the house. "Our land is fertile, healthy, free of invaders."

"Uncle. . . the world *there* suits me. Our land is beautiful, but I want to know my mother's world as well."

I reached out and squeezed Eli's hand.

The king's gaze dropped to our clasped hands. "I see."

"Uncle . . ."

The king pivoted and left with no ceremony, no further word, and I felt like I'd just fucked up. I tried to pull my hand away from Eli, but he stopped me. He laced his fingers with mine. "I knew the price, Geneviève. I could not endure losing you to death."

"You don't need to stay here," I whispered. "What will they do?"

"Burn my ancestry from the land. I will not do that to my mother or father," Eli said as he folded me into his embrace. "My father's soul rests in my hands. My mother was human, one of those humans my people once stole. Traditionally, when we saw a mortal we wanted, we left a bag of twigs and rocks behind as a 'changeling.' My mother was such a stolen mortal. My father's memory, his honors, will be vanished. Never spoken. My family's tree will be razed."

"Oh." I felt awed that he was telling me such things and horrified that he carried such a weight.

"My grandfather went to your world and chose a bride. My father did, too." Eli continued to explain as he led me out of his house and into the meadow beyond. "They found their true loves, and they stole them."

"So you would? You'd *steal* someone? I'm sorry. Never mind." I squirmed away, as much for asking as for the look he gave me.

Eli's expression was implacable. That never boded well.

"Geneviève, in fae-human marriage, the human is bound to the fae lifespan. My mother lived much, much longer than any human could, but when my father died, she expired simultaneously." He stared at me as if there were layers of meaning I ought to understand, but all I could think was that I was grateful that my mother outlived my bio father—although technically he was already dead prior to conception.

"What if they aren't married?" I plopped down on the ground. My parents weren't wed, and I was grateful for it. "What happens to the kids? Do they stay here no matter what?"

"Any child of such union, carries the fae ancestry almost entirely. A fae child is fae."

"So, the quarter-fae in our world—"

"Lying," Eli said coldly, as if lying were the most heinous crime ever. "You are fae, or you are not-fae."

Flowers seemed to surge toward me. My magic was life-affirming. That was *why* I called the dead so easily. A carpet of wildflowers surrounded me, and in my glee, fangs extended. I felt weirdly like some sort of fanged fairy tale maiden—neither sleeping beauty nor the wall of briars, neither the hungry wolf nor the hooded maiden. I was always stuck between two options.

My voice was lisping because of the fangs as I asked, "What if they're just . . . burning through a bit of tension? Are they doomed to togetherness because of an oops baby?"

"Conception requires *true love*. It is why so few children are born to us. We arrange marriages based on compatibility, but love is necessary for conception."

"But what if it's just a moment? Fleeting?" My voice rose in outrage, and I cut the edge of my tongue on the spare teeth now protruding into my mouth. "Or what if the human doesn't know? What if they grow apart? Or . . . the fae spouse wrecks a car? The human just *dies* at home as a result."

He offered that suddenly-infuriating half-shrug and stroked his hand through the carpet of wildflowers. "There are no cars in *Elphame*. No wars. No diseases."

"But if the human spouse leaves to go visit—"

"They cannot. No one but the fae can open the world door," Eli said carefully, as if he expected me to lash out. He glanced up from the blossoms. "Mother never saw the world of her birth again. Gran didn't either."

"So, you could trap me here." The pit in my stomach was deep enough to bury bodies.

Another shrug. "Perhaps if I explained what you truly are capable of, but my uncle forbade it." Eli plucked a purple flower and handed it to me. "To the fae, you are 'half-dead,' Geneviève. If you were human, you'd be kept here in hopes that you would select a husband from the eligible men. He thinks you are of the grave."

I stared at Eli in growing horror as the weight of his mother's —and grandmother's and countless other women's—fates came clear to me. My teeth retracted. Apparently, sorrow worked the opposite of rage. I tried to stay calm, to stop my rage at these women's fates. Carefully, I said, "To be brought here, to be trapped, married in order to breed. . . Forced marriage is a legalized rape."

"No," Eli said sharply. "Relations must be consensual. If

brought here, a woman can build a life, and she can stay unwed. Marriage requires a naturally forming love bond or *explicit* consent."

"But if they don't fall in love or have sex, they're still trapped in your world. They can *never* leave." I had never felt grateful for my dead-side, but that heritage was saving me. "If I was just human . . ."

He nodded.

"I can't decide if I'm grateful not to be welcome in this world," I whispered. I leaned back so I was stretched out under perfect, cloudless skies and resting in a mound of flowers. "I'm not keen on the speciesism. Xenophobia is shitty. . . but being trapped *anywhere* would suck, too."

Eli stared at me, and I realized then that there were things I'd missed that he was expecting me to understand. I rolled it all over in my mind. I suspected it was the "sex could result in marriage" part. Maybe he thought I'd be angry at that?

"Were you going to tell me about the love-bonded-insta-marriage thing?" I asked.

"Why? You are so certain that we are merely business part-ners, that you want no relationship, so what risk is there to you?" Eli leaned down and kissed my cheek, my forehead, the tip of my nose ever-so-softly. "Or are you lying to both of us, Geneviève? Is there a risk that we will be wed if we make love?"

"No," I answered quickly.

He laughed. "As you say." He remained half-propped up over me. "Shall we stay like this, or should I carry you to your bed? You look tired again."

"I am, but I could walk."

"Easily?" he asked.

"No." I closed my eyes to better enjoy the feel of the sun sliding over me, the soil under me, and the man next to me. "Can we do something?"

"Of course, bonbon. What would you have of me?"

"Can we just . . . not *deal* with any of it for a moment? No injections. No faery kings. No hard questions. No thinking about how close I was to death."

Eli's hand stroked my cheek. "I would be fine never again thinking of how close to death you were." He paused. "I was afraid in a way I've never been."

My answering half-laugh was equal part sob. "Yeah. Me, too."

"Shall I leave you here to rest in the sun while we avoid everything?" he asked softly.

I opened my eyes finally, needing to see the face hovering so close to mine. I reached up with one arm and languidly pulled him closer. It was a gentle kiss, nothing like the one we'd shared outside the morgue. It felt more dangerous in the context of what we'd said, though. When I released him, he was still close enough to feel my words as I said, "I won't admit to saying this later, but . . . would you hold me?"

Eli stretched out beside me and pulled me closer, so my cheek rested on his chest. "I shall never speak of it," he promised.

Eli had saved my life. He'd brought me here to heal—and in doing so, he'd condemned himself and given me time to heal without the clock moving in my world. It wasn't a proclamation of love, but it was damn close to it.

And as much as I didn't want to think about forever, in the right now, I was grateful for Eli's love. Without him, I'd have died —not once but twice, because the venom that had been injected into my body would've killed and converted me.

Chapter Twenty-Six

BY THE NEXT DAY, I WAS FEELING CLOSER TO NORMAL—AS long as I didn't think about the question Eli had asked. Would I end up accidentally married if I spent some naked time with him? I didn't love him. I couldn't. I'd woken in his arms on the ground, and he'd carried me back to the soil where I continued to revive. If I had the choice, I'd appreciate a few more days to restore my strength, but that was not an option.

Today, we had been summoned to see the king of *Elphame*. A human woman arrived with a dress for me and orders that we attend the king's meeting in an hour.

"I'll wear my own clothes." I glared at the diaphanous mass draped over her arm. "I'm not really a dress person." That was a lie. I was fine with them, but not that one and not today. I smothered a sigh and was more truthful. "What I mean is *that* dress is not my style."

Eli reached out to pull me to his side, and I flinched. I didn't intend to do so. It was a reasonable gesture after saving my life— and holding me while I slept. However, showing weakness in front of Eli alone was different. There was a stranger present, assessing me, sent here by a faery king who disliked me. That changed everything.

"You can't wear blood-stained clothing," the woman insisted. "Or a nightdress."

"I have trousers and a tunic she can wear," Eli replied before I could.

She scrunched her face up into an unpleasant expression. "I'll leave it here. I was instructed to deliver the dress to the dead woman."

"I am—"

"We have it from here," Eli said loudly, as if to drown my protests and explanation. I wasn't dead, though. Not converted to *draugr.* Not bleeding out on a floor. I felt like someone ought to be able to grasp that rather significant detail.

"Not dead," I muttered.

The woman left without another glance my way, and I was left with the choice of the dress she had brought or Eli's clothes.

"You are alive, sugar-drop." Eli's gaze swept me. "So, would you like to wear the delicate gown or would you like to get into my trousers?"

He delivered his offer with a perfectly sincere expression, and I couldn't help the snort of laughter. I did try to sound serious, though. "I suspect I'd be much happier if I could get into your trousers."

He nodded sagely. "I've thought so for years."

Then he led me to his bedroom. Surprisingly, it was utterly devoid of interesting details. The room was plain wooden-walls and neutral-colored tile floors. Inside was an oversized-king bed with a plush down-filled quilt. If I knew quilts I might be able to read hints of a story or meaning in the pattern, but all I could say for sure was that it was geometric and bold. To the left of the bed was an immense wardrobe.

Eli went to the wardrobe and opened it. Silently, he withdrew several pairs of trousers in various fabrics, assorted tunics, a few pairs of what looked like leggings, and a heavy capelet.

I lifted a green pair of the leggings. "Yoga?"

"Formal events." He smiled. "Nothing athletic, but definitely exhausting."

"Well, yoga pants for formal events is a bonus in your world."

"Women still wear gowns," Eli said. "And the remaining attire for men is far from comfortable." He held up what looked like a misshapen, jeweled turtle shell. "Codpiece."

I smothered a grin and shook my head. "You can keep your crotch-armor, but I will borrow your yoga pants and a tunic."

Eli paused awkwardly. "Are you able to . . ." He made vague gestures between me and the clothing I'd picked. "Or do you need help?"

"Just privacy."

He nodded and, after grabbing several items, left me there to dress myself in his clothing.

———

WE WERE LED INTO A NEARLY-EMPTY ROOM, AND ELI WAS directed to the center of the room. The king entered, took his throne, and glanced at us. I wasn't sure if he was studying me or what he wanted of us. He was exceptionally fae and thoroughly implacable. If I didn't know he found me objectionable, I'd be warmed by his bemused look at my make-shift court attire. I looked a bit foolish in emerald green leggings and a deep brown tunic. If I had my weapons, I'd feel like a fairy tale character who'd spent too long in the forest.

"Be welcome tonight, nephew." The king met my gaze. "Death maiden."

"*Not* dead," I muttered. Louder, I said, "Faery king."

Eli winced, but the king laughed. "You are not without charm."

I wasn't sure if it was a compliment or not, and I had no idea if words of thanks were acceptable. So, I nodded. I *was* capable of some caution.

Then the king made a gesture, and a long line of faeries filed into the room. Women specifically. Rows of beautiful women lined the throne room. Feet bare, arms bare, and bosoms nearly so. With hair loosened, and in some cases nearly to their knees, the fae women were lovely. I had no idea why they were in the room, though.

"What's happening here?" I whispered. My brain was connecting the dots from what the king had said and the women. Hopefully, I was wrong. The act of choosing a partner, a lover, surely wasn't this shallow. What was Eli to do? Check their teeth? Their bra sizes? Ask a few questions? Waltz?

"Pick one. Kiss your intended, and we'll be done with this stand-off." The king made a gesture, and somewhere in the shadows beyond the room, a band began to play.

The women started walking up to us, curtsied, and slowing circled so he could see the full view. They smiled. They met his gaze as best they could while he stood beside me in a state that seemed somewhere between resignation and polite disinterest.

"If you don't want to stay here, we'll fight our way out," I told Eli quietly.

Eli glanced at me with a kind of regret in his eyes that made me question everything I'd felt. He stepped closer to me and took my hand. "They'd cut you down if you tried. You are unarmed, cupcake."

I shook my head. "For now."

My gaze slid over the room, seeking options. The throne room was filled with several dozen faery women who were all available and eligible. Guards now stood around the perimeter— not to keep the women in, but to keep Eli in.

"I knew the cost when I brought you here," Eli reminded me. "I expected this."

My mouth opened, but no words came. I realized that he made decisions while I was unconscious. I realized that taking me here to heal was what he thought was necessary, and maybe it was. I just didn't like the thought of leaving him here. I felt guilty. If he left against the king's wishes, I would cost him his home and family history. If he stayed, he lost the world where he'd been living for at least six years.

And me. I couldn't pretend that I wasn't a loss. Whether or not he loved me, Eli certainly had high regard for me. He'd basically torched his life to save me—and now we would be separated.

"You *knew* there were consequences for me if I came home. I do not regret any cost if it means you are alive." He held my hand tightly, as if I was the sort of woman to charge an armed faery guard to try to steal a weapon.

He knew me well.

But the odds of success in such an endeavor weren't high, but I really and truly hated feeling trapped. And the guard two over from the king wasn't as attentive as the rest. Maybe I could—

"My nephew will be in *Elphame* until he has filled his duty," the king pronounced. He stared at us from the throne, and I wondered if he was as much of a warrior as he looked. I could *flow,* reach the inattentive guard, and draw that blade against the king and . . . Eli would lose his family. Fighting wouldn't undo this mess.

"I'm sorry," I said quietly. "I don't know how to fix this, and I just want us to go home."

"I do not want to leave you alone in New Orleans either," Eli said softly. "But attacking my uncle will not help." His gaze drifted to the guard I'd been eying. "Please don't do that."

I sighed.

"I could . . . I *understand*." I felt tears in my eyes. "It would be wrong to just pick one of them, right? Get engaged, and then leave."

My voice sounded hopeful, and I felt like a terrible woman. A kiss from Eli would turn any of them into his future bride. If he didn't select a bride, he was trapped here. They were strangers to me, but that didn't mean I ought to throw any of them under the proverbial bus. So many beautiful faery women, willing to love him and give him children. I hated each of them.

"Could you select one? Choose the woman to be in my bed one day, Geneviève?" Eli leaned his forehead against mine. "Tell me whose body am I to touch wishing she could be you?"

"No."

His hands cradled my face. "Then how can I?"

The king's voice cut through the moment. "Tell her goodbye and pick a bride."

Instead of releasing me, Eli said, "There is another option."

"Fight?" I asked hopefully.

Eli smiled. "No. There is another choice. One that would mean I could leave with you and still come home. A choice that would mean *you* would have a haven here."

We stood in silence as if he was trying to will me to understand. What would allow me to be here? The only way to do that would be if I was . . . his.

I started to shake my head, but he had my face in the cradle of his hands. "This is not what the king wants."

"And you? Do you want me to forsake you?" Eli asked.

"I am not marriage material," I reminded him. "You know what I am. You knew that when you—"

"I will take my kiss now," Eli said softly. "I am owed one by the terms of our bargain."

I stared at him, feeling more betrayed than I could even attempt to explain. "Eli . . ."

"Geneviève, did you or did you not make a bargain with me?" Eli asked quietly. "One kiss at the time of my choosing."

"Don't do this." I tried to think of another answer, one that would not mean losing Eli or being his betrothed. There had to be one. "Maybe you can ask your uncle for more time?"

"You know that answer." He gave me a look, one I admittedly deserved. He'd had time. He'd spent it running a bar, indulging in the same frivolous one-night-stands I did, and working with me.

My mind raced, trying to sort out other plans. "Maybe you stay briefly. Break the engagement, and—"

"You entered a bargain with a faery, knowing full well that we are skilled in negotiations," Eli said in that same unreadable tone he would adopt when I was panicking. "A kiss."

I glanced around the room. Could I walk away and leave him? These were my choices. I stay and deal with the consequences of this kiss—or I flee. I was free to leave. Eli was not.

"I will not forgive this," I warned him. "I am a warrior, a witch, not a . . ." I couldn't even make my mouth say such nonsense as "queen" or "wife." Those words weren't for me.

"Faery marriages have been built on less than what we have," he said lightly. "Your sword at the side of a king. Your needs met. A safe place to be. I won't ask you to be less than you are, Geneviève."

"Please?"

Eli sighed and said loudly, "I claim my kiss, Geneviève Crowe. Here. Now."

"So mote it be," I whispered.

And Eli's mouth slanted over mine, sealing my fate to his. I wanted to pull away, but he'd bought this kiss and I was bound to accept it. Like every other time he'd touched me, it was perfect. My lips parted, invited him in, and I resisted the urge to take control. My arms had found their way around him, and his hands were splayed on my back.

My magic was no longer willing to stay quiet as my entire body was filled with the need to touch and be touched. I let go of the restraints I'd built, and I flooded him with my magic. I saw Eli as a child mourning his mother and father, as a young man arguing with his uncle, as a man in New Orleans watching me. I felt his fascination. I felt his determination to know me.

I released more magic. Calling it from the soil under the floor, seeking the bones that were lost somewhere in earth, and when no dead answered, I felt the land answer. I lowered myself to the ground, feeling the life of the land respond.

Eli was still kissing me. He was pressed to my body, and through the magic and the fabric between us, I could feel Eli's need for me. I arched my hips, seeking more, seeking the connection we'd yet to reach.

I flipped him over. I wasn't the sort of woman who handed over control. I was astride him, staring down at him. He smiled with kiss-stung lips, and I felt a surge of possessive hunger. I reached for his belt.

"Geneviève, my love," he murmured. His hand stopped mine, covered my hand and held it. "I've waited this long, but . . . not *here.*"

And it hit me then: We were in a room in the palace of his people, and he was under me. We had been kissing as if we were alone. The reality of the situation washed over me like a sudden unplanned dip in icy water. I pushed away from Eli and stood.

The room was empty, save for the faery king and a few guards. That at least was a comfort.

"Nephew," the king said. "You are a credit to your mother's cleverness."

Even in my lust-soaked mind, I could hear the king's anger. Whatever history they had was hidden between words that sounded kind on the surface. They weren't, though.

Eli bowed. When he straightened, he said, "I shall return to meet with you, Uncle. We will begin the work of learning how to transition our people should disaster strike." He met the faery king's gaze. "But I would ask you to strive to be hale and hardy, to employ the poison testers to full advantage, to do all that you can."

"Indeed."

"And I wish you fertility, uncle, so that this *gift* can be bestowed upon a worthier son," Eli added.

"So mote it be," I whispered.

Both men glanced at me and gave me impenetrable stares. I shrugged. What else could I do? I wasn't marrying Eli. I wasn't popping out a baby. And I certainly wasn't interested in an eternity in *Elphame*. I wasn't abandoning my family, my mother, or my responsibility to New Orleans.

I had no idea before what I'd evolve into, but I was even less prepared for what would happen now that I'd been injected.

No marriage.

No kids.

No trying to build a family I'd destroy the next time my magic decided to call a graveyard over for tea. I kept my expression passive, hoping to hide my emotional turmoil.

The king stood and bowed. He sounded more impressed than angry when he said, "Welcome to our family, Geneviève of Crowe. May you find haven and happiness among the shelter of our trees."

Despite everything, he sounded sincere, and all I could do was bow back. I knew I was to curtsy, but dammit, I wasn't going to pretend to be dainty. Let them all grit their teeth. When I figured out how to safely break my engagement, they'd be glad to see me go.

I straightened and walked out. The dead still needed my attention in New Orleans, and fiancé or not, I was going to go home and handle the problems I'd had to put on hold while my body processed the near-toxic dose of venom the grieving widow jabbed into my body.

Chapter Twenty-Seven

I LEFT ELI WITH HIS UNCLE AND WALKED IN THE GENERAL direction of *away* from them. The ground was thick with greens, browns, and whites. In the forest undergrowth, trails twisted in a dozen directions, and dark gnarled branches bent like doorways. I had no idea where any of them went, and setting off into a fairy tale wood in the actual home of the fae seemed like a terrible plan.

Instead I walked slowly in a general "away from them" route. Not exactly precise, but it was as close as I had to an actual direction. Eli had said he'd "return" so that meant he was intending on coming home to New Orleans with me. I might not be able to deal with my accidental engagement, but I could still do my job. I had to—and not just because the widow Chaddock decided to inject me with venom, ruin my life, and oh, yeah, now I was fucking *engaged*. Nope, not because I was furious, and definitely not because it was complicating the absolute hell out of my already bonkers life.

Okay, maaaaybe that was a factor. Stopping her was also the right thing to do. I mean, I wasn't going to go all shock and "why,

I never" over murdering her husband. I'd killed my father. Sometimes families were complicated. Injecting Mr. Odem? Me? That was two so far. She was looking a lot like a well-dressed serial killer.

Also, I was engaged because of it.

I took several calming breaths, wishing I could recall that "inhale peace" stuff they did in my one and only attempt at yoga. Witch or not, I wasn't good at meditating. I was more likely to be one with my surliness than peace.

Focus.

Concentrate.

Details. Details always helped. The root of the problem was the person or people who had been injecting businessmen. Widow Chaddock and her friend. Why? I forced myself to weigh more facts. There were two dead businessmen so far. I didn't know how many others there were, but the grumpy-venom-injecting-women were fucking with people's lives, including mine, and it was pissing me off.

"Geneviève?"

Eli was finally at my side, and he didn't even have the grace to look guilty about the mess we were in now. He was hesitant, at least, but it wasn't enough. A part of me wanted to tear into him.

The rest of me was all in on compartmentalizing this mess and fucking with him. "I can't believe he fell for that," I said lightly.

"Fell for. . . what?" He reached out to touch a thick tree, as if petting it.

"You've bought time, so you get to come home." I stared at Eli, trying not to think about the fact that this accidental engagement meant we absolutely, positively wouldn't be getting naked. My libido had some strong opinions on *that* decision. With an internal whisper of "down, girl," I schooled my expression well enough that I might have been fae, and added, "It's not as if we're *actually engaged.*"

"Geneviève. . ."

"Am I a citizen of *Elphame?*" I prompt.

"No." Eli's expression tightened.

I smiled sweetly. "Then why would you or he think I am bound by this?"

Eli stopped mid-step. "We had a bargain. I claimed my kiss and chose you—"

"And *you*, Eli of Stonecroft, may be bound by that kiss and that king's dictates. I, citizen of New Orleans and witch-draugr, am not." I crossed my arms. "You claimed your kiss. End of the deal. Resolved. There is no further significance to it."

I paused.

"Except the obvious," I added. "I like you. A *lot*."

He grinned. "You are remarkably infuriating." Eli leaned in and kissed my cheek. "Shall we return to our fair city, my crème brûlee?"

"Why do you do that?" I stared past him to a glimmering doorway in the copse of trees that hadn't been there when we walked to our meeting with the king.

"What?"

"The dessert thing." The doorway glowed brighter. He had to see it. "Why do you call me dessert names?"

Eli laughed. "My people crave the taste of rich desserts, cream, decadent tastes. And you, my love, I cra—"

"Got it," I interrupted. I blushed, and then I sighed at the realization that the sex I thought was on the horizon was now out of reach. Engaged *and* intimate? I wasn't about to risk that. "Is that our exit? The glowing thing."

"It is."

The tree he'd been petting unfurled a twist of branches that seemed woven. Inside were my weapons. Eli handed me my holster, gun, longsword, and short sword. They'd been held inside the arms of a tree. I didn't ask why or how or any of it. I accepted my gear, motioned to the blindingly bright doorway and asked, "Will you open that? Or am I stuck here?"

"After you, Geneviève," he said gallantly, and the door slid open. "Let us go to New Orleans."

We stepped into the city midday. I remembered that a month of days in *Elphame* was only hours in my world. So, it was the same day I'd left, but a few hours later.

We were at Eli's house, and while I had questions on how here was connected to there—and thinking of how hard that must've been like knowing his world was passing by that close to him— now was not the time. I started to follow Eli to the house, but that felt like wasting time.

"Tres."

Eli glanced at me.

"She'll kill him." I motioned in the direction of Eli's car. "Can we—"

"I need the keys, bonbon." He gave me a smile. "I knew where we needed to go, too, but I cannot *flow*. . . and you choose not to."

I nodded. He did know me, and know what needed to be done, so I stood there awkwardly in my fae-woven yoga pants and tunic. I was barefoot still. That seemed perfectly fine in *Elphame*, but not so much in New Orleans. My city might be wet, but I'd seen everything in our streets from Mardi Gras beads to chicken bones, syringes to vomit. I needed to attempt to wear his over-sized-for-me shoes or swing by my place.

I started up the stairs, to tell him, only to see Eli descending with keys and a pair of boots. Boots that looked suspiciously small for him. Quality leather boots.

"What size are . . ." My words dwindled at his expression. I accepted the boots.

"Your size, Geneviève," he said drily. "Why do you continually find these things confusing?"

"Because no one else I know randomly keeps things in my size in their house," I said tightly.

"They are not your fiancé, though, are they?"

"That *just* happened, Eli."

He smirked. "So, you acknowledge that it happened? We are engaged."

I sighed and walked toward the car. "Piss off."

His laughter made me glad he couldn't see my smile. I would cede this point. Arguing, debating, with a fae took a level of alertness I currently lacked.

As Eli opened my door, he smiled at me as if we were both in on a secret.

I said nothing, merely put my boots on and stared out at my city. I was grateful that I'd been able to return to it. I mean, it wasn't the pristine, safe, natural escape that was *Elphame*. It was home, though. I felt a tie to it, not the same one to the soil where I was born, but one wrought of choice and blood. I protected the city. It was mine.

As Eli drove us to the Chaddock house, I could feel death in pockets of space. Graves. *Draugr*. No magic needed—or at least no conscious choice to extend my magic. My sense of the dead was simply there, like hearing or sight.

When we arrived at the Chaddock house, Eli stared at me a moment too long, and I knew that my eyes had shifted. My vision was unsettling; both my grave sight and normal sight were layered together.

We approached the gate to be buzzed into the Chaddock Estate. This time, no one replied.

I could feel a *draugr*-sized pocket inside the house, so I zapped the gate with a pulse of magic. I never did such things if I could avoid it. Leaving a gate broken was a special sort of wrong when you knew it was there to keep out things that wanted to gnaw your face. Today, the face-gnawer was inside.

"Biter," I explained, jerking my head toward the house.

I pushed open the gate.

At the door to the Chaddock House, Eli twisted the knob. It

was unlocked. Inside the house was seemingly empty, but I felt the presence of death. Gun in hand, I crept up the stairs. There was a possibility of life in the house, too, but the pulse of the dead was too strong to ignore. I had to reach the dead, and if I was intercepted, I'd deal with it.

At the top of the beautiful curving wooden staircase, I turned left.

Eli followed behind me. The carpet was so indulgently thick that our steps made no sound. The house was the sort of posh that seemed to need to announce wealth with art and high-end everything. We'd sought again-walkers often enough that it felt familiar. What was new was how much the dead called. Typically, my magic found them, and I could call them to me. This time, it felt as if I was the one being summoned.

Using one booted foot, I carefully nudged open the door to the room. My gun was drawn, and my sword was held at my side. Call it paranoid, but the lady of the house had damn near killed me the last time I saw her.

Inside the room was a massive wooden-four-poster bed, not just a king but embarrassingly large in a way that screamed custom-made and possibly orgy-time. The dead body of Tres Chaddock was in the bed, and at his feet, holding a pistol, was the widow Chaddock.

"You came!" Alice Chaddock looked so relieved I almost questioned my memories. "I wasn't sure if you got my messages, and I was so worried and Tres said you saved Jimmy Odem and—"

"You tried to kill me," I pointed out, cutting off her verbal vomit.

"Well, not really." She pressed her lips into a pout that had exactly no effect on me. Okay, it pissed me off, but I was fairly sure *that* wasn't the result she was seeking. "I tried to misfire the second injection. I couldn't stop Lydia, but I figured you were still alive so. . ." She waved her hands as if a gesture would substitute for filling in the sentences. "And you're here. It turned out fine!"

I raised my gun. Fine? Excruciating pain. Angry neighbors. Worried friends. Summoning Beatrice. Accidental engagement. So very not fine.

She stood and put herself between us and Tres' body, as if that would stop anyone intent on reaching him. She had a gun, and she held it like she knew how to use it, but I beheaded face-gnawers for a living and had just overcome dying. I was fairly sure a woman who was sobbing wasn't going to be my demise—although she had come near to killing me once already, so I could be wrong.

Either way, I couldn't shoot Alice. I didn't shoot for vengeance or in anger. She wasn't an imminent threat. If not for the venom glowing vibrant green all through Tres' body, I'd be tempted to call the police and leave.

Well, the venom *and* the need to be sure the murder of businessmen was at an end. Both Tres and Beatrice had paid me to find answers, and Alice had some of them. Walking out wasn't going to help.

Alice Chaddock was a sobbing mess, and from the looks of her reddened, swollen eyes, she'd been crying for a while.

"It wasn't me, Geneviève," she said. "I didn't want you dead. Lydia was going to call the police about having you take care of Alvin. She wanted him to wake, you know? And I ruined her plan, and she found out and—"

"She killed your husband?" Eli asked, interrupting her with a calm I didn't have. "Lydia killed Chaddock?"

"Lydia Alberti." Alice nodded. "She wanted to kill her husband. He was going to divorce her and there was a prenup, you know?"

She leaned down and brushed Tres' face with the hand not holding the gun. "He looks like his father." She glanced at us. "You must believe me. I had no other choice. I was trying to do right by Alvin, and things just got out of hand."

"I have trust issues with those who try to murder me, Alice," I said dryly. "Move away from Tres."

"I didn't kill Tres *or* Alvin!"

As I stepped forward, Alice threw herself over his corpse. Sobbing and clutching him, she was still somehow holding a gun. I was at the end of my patience.

I glanced at Eli. He was so much better at delicacy than I was ever going to be. "Help?"

"Mrs. Chaddock? Alice?" Eli walked over and took the pistol from her hand. She didn't resist.

That alone eased my anxiety. Murderess with a gun? It wasn't a comforting look on anyone. *My* attempted murderess? That made it emotional in ways I hadn't expected to confront.

After Eli had the gun, he glanced at me inquiringly.

I shrugged.

"Alice!" I raised my voice. "Get off Tres. You're embarrassing yourself."

"Promise you won't chop off his head. Swear it!" Alice was wrapped around the dead man like a violently possessive monkey. "I want you to *wake* him. Like you did with Jimmy Odem. I can't figure this out on my own. I don't want Tres *and* Alvin dead. I need someone to look after me!"

I rolled my eyes so hard it hurt. "I am not going to 'chop off his head.' Move now. I have questions."

Alice hopped up and launched herself at me, hugging me. "Thank you!"

I froze. "The last time you hugged me, you tried to kill me. Let go of me."

She jumped back. "Bad idea, huh?"

"Terrible plan," I said.

Eli stared at her, dumbfounded, and I started to laugh. Honestly, I think I'd just lost the trophy for "worst ideas ever."

I realized that both Alice and Eli were staring at me, but more importantly, Tres' dead body called out for resurrection in increasingly loud summons. Did I let him revive? Did I revive him? Putting him in a T-Cell was the expected next step, but we all knew what I could do.

Nothing about my life had gone according to plan the last month—and the month was only half over.

I motioned for Alice to leave the room. I had questions, and I couldn't focus with Tres' corpse beside me. He was transforming internally, and I could practically hear each shift. He would be a *draugr* when he woke, and I'd need to either behead him or subdue him so he could be taken to a T-Cell House.

Or wake him myself.

Chapter Twenty-Eight

SOMEHOW, AFTER WE LEFT TRES IN THE ROOM, ALICE HAD reverted to wifely diligence when we walked out of the room with her dead step-son. We followed her into the hallway and descended to the main floor.

"Tea? Coffee?" Alice led us to the kitchen. "Tres sent the staff home before he . . ." She shook her head and smiled. "I can make tea or coffee, though."

The clip of her steps was even as she marched toward the stainless steel and stone kitchen. She paused and glanced at us. "Both?"

"Who killed Tres? Who is Lydia?" I asked.

The polite façade that the widow Chaddock had suddenly evaporated. "Promise not to be mad?"

Eli and I exchanged a look.

"Of course," he murmured quietly.

I tried not to think ill of people as a rule, but Alice—aside from the whole trying to murder me thing—was pushing so many of my buttons that I had the fleeting urge to pivot and leave. I could get answers later. If not for Tres' corpse, I may have done just that.

Alice motioned for us to follow her through a doorway to a closed door across from what looked like a formal living room— not the one where we'd waited previously. This was more elegant, from silk drapes to elegant period reproduction furnishings. A gleaming marble hearth and fireplace dominated the far wall. The rug in the middle of the room was obviously missing. Brighter hardwood in a rectangular area showed that there had been a rug.

"Where is the rug?"

"Garage." She paused and glanced at us. "I'm not a bad person. I was just so angry."

She turned the knob and opened the door a crack.

"She wasn't thinking clearly," Alice added. Her hand tightened on the doorknob. "Lydia had killed my Alvin, and then tried to kill you and I needed your *help*. Then we came home, and she was arguing with Tres." Alice started to sniffle again. "I warned him, and she shoved me, and Tres fell against the fireplace."

"He fell?" Eli prompted. "So, he's truly dead?"

"No." I'd felt him, seen venom under his skin. "He was injected when he was alive. Multiple times, right?"

Alice sobbed, but she nodded. "Little bits. I just kept jabbing at him when he wasn't looking. I was afraid of him dying and leaving me alone. So I just . . . put the venom in him in little itty bitty pokes."

Alice's confession made me realized that Tres' odd regard for me was because of the venom he'd received in micro-doses before we met at the morgue. It wasn't *grief* that made him act so odd, and the dead that I sensed when I was at the morgue wasn't *just* because of Odem. It was Tres, too. The venom in him made me feel a pull to him.

I glanced at Alice. "So Tres had the venom in him, and then he fell."

"Mmm-hmm. His head made a *thunk* sound. He wasn't

moving. So, I injected him again and called you. Then I injected him a few more times. I used all of it I had left. You can fix him. He wasn't dead at first, but he wasn't moving. I didn't think you could fix brain damage, but if he was dead . . ."

I reached around her and shoved the door open.

"And then I shot Lydia," Alice whispered. "A lot."

The woman who'd been with Alice, the one who'd injected me the first time, was more or less in the tub. A pile of clothing was in there, too.

"I didn't want to call the housekeeper, so I figured I should just get rid of my bloody clothes," Alice explained in a tone that was more pride than sorrow. "I cleaned the floor. Bleach. Like the internet says. I washed all the blood off Tres, too. His hair. Gave him a clean shirt. And I tucked him in. It's what Alvin would've wanted if he knew Tres could survive."

I thought about the fact that the senior Mr. Chaddock belonged to SAFARI, a hate group, and I had more than a few doubts about Alice's theory.

"I was wrong about *draugr*," Alice said calmly. "I mean, my Alvin wouldn't want to be dead and biting, but after Tres said what you did for Jimmy Odem—I mean, *mostly* Tres yelled that if I had waited, you could have healed his dad. I still don't think he would want to be a . . . walker."

"You can't heal death."

Alice waved her hand in the air. "I should've just trapped her, so Tres had something to eat when he woke. I've been worrying you wouldn't come because of that misunderstand—"

"My attempted murder?" I turned to walk away.

"I never wanted you dead. I *cried*." Alice grabbed my arm, and I lost my temper. I jerked free and shoved her. She stumbled against the wall.

My voice was anything but calm. "You killed a woman, poisoned your stepson, stored the woman you shot in your bathroom, and—"

"It's a guest bathroom."

I shoved into Alice's mind.

Do you want to go to jail, Allie? The woman, Lydia, sat at a table. *Low lights. Tasteful music. Privacy. Cocktails sat in front of them on a white linen tablecloth.*

"N-no."

"Do you want me to kill Tres? Let him come back and kill you?" Lydia withdrew a syringe from a box inside her undoubtedly expensive designer handbag. She put it out beside the drinks. "I answered an ad for a research project."

"What is that?"

Lydia leaned back in her chair and smiled. "That is what killed your husband, Jimmy, and my Edward. Among others. They wanted a few influential men, SAFARI members, injected. It's a clinical trial."

"It's murder."

"It's a way to get around the prenups, so I picked people I liked. I freed you. You should all be grateful." Lydia wasn't even pretending to whisper.

"Patty Odem wasn't a second wife. They were together for longer than we were alive." Alice sobbed. "And I loved Alvin. I wanted to be together forever."

"If only Edward died, it would look suspicious." Lydia sounded as irritated as I often felt as she stared at Alice. After a moment, she downed her martini. "I need four more. Your little draugr-killer *is one or Tres. Your choice. Or I call the police and tell them all about your murder spree."*

With more force than I meant, I jerked myself out of Alice's memories. I hated her a little extra for being honest. She really wasn't lying. Lydia had blackmailed and threatened her.

Eli stepped between us. "Geneviève."

I closed my eyes, counted to ten, and resisted the urge to point out that she was a grown-ass woman. Her failure to adult was remarkable. She was roughly my age. The same age as Tres. How was she like this?

I let my magic flow toward Lydia.

Wake and speak to me, Lydia Alberti.

She was so newly dead that it took but a moment to open her eyes. The animated corpse of Lydia Alberti sat up, the bullets in her body pushed out as her wounds sealed. They fell with a series of *plinks* onto the tile floor and tub. When she resumed death, the wounds would reappear, but the bullets were no longer in her body.

"Bitch." Lydia looked past me to the shrieking widow Chaddock.

Answer me, Lydia Alberti. Who hired you? Where did you see the ad? What do you know about the source of the venom?

The corpse looked at me and said, "Fuck you."

It took a lot of emotion to resist my questions. A side effect of necromancy--one that I sometimes felt guilty about—was that it compelled most corpses to tell me the truth. It wasn't a guarantee, but necromancy created a compulsion in *most* corpses. Lydia was a bucket of rage in a blood-stained, ripped dress, but I had a lot less guilt since she was the one who was actually trying to kill me for unknown reasons.

Answer me.

"You matter to Beatrice," she said, words blurted as if she was trying to stop them from escaping. "And you need to die. Abomination."

Then she ran.

As she did, I looked into her memories. A corpse's mind wasn't as clear as the living.

I saw an email to Lydia. The sender's name was a series of letters and digits in seemingly random order. The message simply said, I CAN HELP YOU FIND FREEDOM. CALL ME IF INTERESTED.

She called.

A second email arrived. It listed an address to a post-office box on Magazine Street with the instructions: YOU WILL FIND A KEY UNDER YOUR DOORMAT TOMORROW. EIGHT. YOUR CHOICE.

In the post office box were ten syringes, my name, a stack of bills, and nothing else.

There were no other memories. It was not enough. Lydia was murdering SAFARI members because she wanted out of her marriage—without breaking the prenup. Whoever gave her the means knew it, and knew how to get venom, and had a grudge against Beatrice, me, or both of us. I hadn't stopped the possibility of murder-by-venom, but Alice had stopped *this* murderer.

I withdrew my magic, and the corpse of Lydia Alberti crumpled. I wasn't an investigator, but I had an answer for both Tres and Beatrice.

Tres.

Who was an innocent bystander, like most of the victims. The only intended victim was Lydia Alberti's husband. And me.

I had no idea what the right next step was, but I felt Tres growing closer and closer to waking. Sentencing him to a T-Cell wasn't any fairer than beheading him. I was here as he was about to wake. I could spare him years of being a danger, of muttering incoherence, of trying to bite people.

"Keep her here," I said.

And then, without another word, I turned and walked upstairs. I left the slumped corpse and the sobbing widow and my accidental fiancé behind. I could help Tres. That much was in my reach.

I paused and put a few tranquilizer rounds in my gun just in case Tres wasn't like Odem. I'd rather have Eli there to shoot Tres with tranqs, but I couldn't trust Alice to stay out of the room—and as obnoxious as she was, I couldn't let her near Tres in case he woke up like every *draugr* other than Odem.

Inside the room, I let tears fall. There was no right answer. If I'd been in his place, I'd hope to be beheaded. Hell, I'd asked for it.

But if I could be awakened and still be me?

No, I'd still opt for death. Biting people was horrible. How could I exist knowing that I needed to cause pain every meal? I couldn't even eat a hamburger or a fish.

I wasn't Tres, though. I knew enough to know he'd rather exist even in a T-Cell than be permanently dead. So, I locked my disgust away, and I let my magic flow through him as I had with Jimmy Odem. I saw the venom sliding under the skin, but it wasn't the injections that killed him. Alice was not his murderer. The head injury from Lydia would have killed him without medical intervention. Alice sped up the process by injecting Tres with venom.

Wake up, Tres, I urged, hoping that the Odem situation hadn't been a fluke.

And hoping it had.

I stood beside the bed and pushed grave magic into him, filling him from the soles of his feet to the top of his head. I drew him from wherever he was waiting. Mind. Heart. Clarity. It took very little effort, and that terrified me. No one, not even me, should have the power to raise *draugr* to life.

Tres opened his eyes. "Geneviève?"

He smiled, and his first instinct was, apparently, either to bite or to kiss me. He sat up and reached for me, and I didn't wait to see which it was. I jerked away, letting myself flow faster than I realized I could.

But Tres was *draugr*. He was out of the bed, fortunately still dressed under the bedcovers, and beside me a fraction of a moment after I reached the door. This time he reached out with both arms as if to embrace me.

I was faster. My gun was against his forehead at almost the same moment. "Speak to me, Tres Chaddock."

"I'm missing a few hours," he said, stepping back. "You called. I argued with Allie and Lydia Alberti. Then . . . why are you in my bedroom?" He frowned. "And why are you . . ."

He reached up to his throat, seeking a pulse he wouldn't find. "Geneviève . . .?"

"You're dead." I felt tears start to fall. "I can either behead you or call Beatrice."

"Like Jimmy Odem," Tres murmured. "You saved me."

I shook my head, swallowed hard, but my voice was still shaky. "You're *dead*."

"I feel fine. Fabulous actually." Tres grinned. "You are a goddess, Geneviève. My goddess. Anything you need. Anything I can do to make you happy. Any . . ."

His expression shifted, and in the next instant, he was kneeling at my feet. He looked up at me, and the sheer raw lust in his gaze was a frightening thing.

"Let me please you, mistress," he whispered. "I am yours to command."

"Whoa." I stumbled backwards and jerked the door open and ran.

It might not have been the bravest moment of my life, but I was at my wit's end. I went directly to the kitchen, grabbed Eli's hand, and continued right out the front door.

"Beatrice!" I yelled as loud as I could.

Beatrice! I repeated in whatever internal thought-speak I had.

"Beatrice, please," I said again. "I need you."

And then I let myself be drawn into Eli's embrace again. He murmured words I didn't understand in a language I didn't know, and I rested my head against him. That's how we were still standing a few moments later when Beatrice arrived.

"Geneviève."

I stayed in Eli's embrace, but turned so I was facing Beatrice. Instead of something Victorian, this time she was wearing a burgundy medieval-looking gown and fur capelet. Instead of seeming regal, she appeared more like a warrior.

"You are still alive," she said in greeting.

"And you're still dead." I smiled, though, despite my innate animosity toward her. She'd helped me twice now, once with

Odem and once with the venom Alice had injected into me. Softer, I added, "Thank you."

She nodded.

"I have information and a problem," I said levelly. Then I looked at her and offered, "You can have the memories of the injections."

Beatrice smoothed down the sleeves of her medieval-looking gown.

"Are you testing to see if your skill is of your mother or father's line?" she asked in that almost-laughing voice of hers.

I borrowed Eli's half-shrug in lieu of an answer.

Beatrice leaned close enough that I felt Eli tense behind me. She whispered, "But if I am of both lines, the question is unanswered."

Before I could reply or puzzle out what that meant, she was in my mind. I felt her there, an already familiar presence, as she sought the information on the source of the *draugr* venom, the injections, and my reason for calling her again.

A scant few moments later, she touched my face with icy hands. "You have done well. I will send your payment." She kissed my forehead. "Shall I kill the widow? Or do you want the honor?"

I blinked at her. "I don't know who hired Lydia. She'd dead. Alice is . . . not culpable."

Beatrice laughed. "You are tender-hearted."

"I am not." I scowled. After a brief pause, I asked, "Could you take Tres, like with Odem?"

"No."

I looked over to where Tres and Alice both stood.

"He's your responsibility," Beatrice said with a shooing gesture. "He was bound to you before he died."

"But—"

"Take your subjects for now and leave. I will remove the corpse. By morning, you may return."

"My what? They are not—"

"The boy is bonded to you. You wouldn't let me kill the murderess." Beatrice ticked them off on her fingers. "And you already made yourself clear about the faery. They are yours."

I followed her as she *flowed* to the front porch. "At least keep Tres—"

"You do realize I can hear you?" Tres said.

Beatrice walked deeper into the shadows of the house and said, "I'm not ready to answer anything else tonight. I have companies to oversee. Inquiries. Go home, daughter."

"Not your daughter."

Beatrice's laughter echoed around the room. It wasn't a complex bit of magic, but it was one that left me shivering.

Be careful, her voice slid into my mind. *There are those in this world and in* Elphame *not kind to abominations like us. Go, now. I will handle the corpse and evidence. If you want any of their lives ended, leave them here. Odem is fine. Your new* draugr *is as safe as any in your command. More so than a human or fae.*

I looked up and met her gaze.

"Will you take your subjects and leave?" Beatrice asked. I heard the alternative echoing in my head, her offer to rid me of any of them.

"Come," I said, looking at Tres, Alice, and Eli in turn. This was my life now; I had the responsibility of three lives. The alternative was their deaths, and I wasn't that much of an abomination.

I hadn't answered all of my questions, but I was alive.

We stepped outside, and I texted Jesse, Sera, and Christy, "Meet at bar? Alive. Could use a drink. Tres, Eli, and Alice C with me. Will explain there."

Honestly, I wasn't sure how to explain, but my friends still loved me despite my ancestry, Eli was at my side more-or-less contently, and I was about to have a drink with a *draugr* and my almost-murderess. It wasn't the worst plan I'd had that month.

Hopefully.

"I loved The Wicked and The Dead! A sassy, ass-kicking heroine, a deliciously mysterious fae hero, and a wonderful mix of action and romance. Add that to Melissa's usual great world-building, and I'm already looking forward to book 2!"

Jeaniene Frost, NYT Bestselling Author

———

"A characteristic of the draugr...or rather animated corpses...is that they frequently come out of their barrows, and walk, or even ride abroad, which is thought by the living to be an undesirable habit. This occurs most frequently in the evening; but it sometimes happens that a mist or temporary darkness heralds their approach even by day. "

N. K. Chadwick
"Norse Ghosts (A Study in the Draugr and the Haugbúi)"
FOLKLORE MAGAZINE June 1946

Excerpt of Blood Martinis and Mistletoe

Blood Martinis and Mistletoe:
A Wicked & Dead Novella
AVAILABLE:
Under a Winter Sky (November 2020)
and
ebook stand-alone (June 2021)

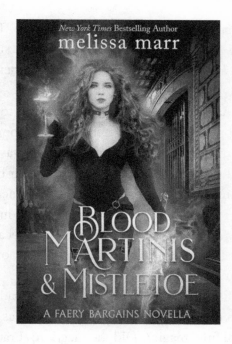

Chapter 1

Giant aluminum balls hung around me even though I was standing in the cemetery not long before dawn. I didn't know who hung the balls, but I wasn't too bothered. Winter in New Orleans. We might have *draugr* and a higher than reasonable crime rate, but damn it, we had festivities for every possible occasion. Gold, silver, red, blue, purple, and green balls hung from the tree. Samhain had passed, and it was time to ramp up for the winter holidays.

November--the period after Samhain--was uncommonly active for necromancy calls. Unfortunately, a certain sort of person thought it was festive to summon the body and spirit of Dear Uncle Phil or Aunt Marie. Sometimes the relatives were maudlin, and sometimes they were thinking about the afterlife.

Now, the dead don't tell tale tales about the things after death.

They can't. I warn folks, but they don't believe me. They pay me a fair amount to summon their dead, so I always stress that the "what happens after we die" questions are forbidden. Few people believe me.

Tonight, I had summoned Alphard Cormier to speak to his widow and assorted relatives or friends who accompanied her. I didn't ask who they were. One proven relation was all I needed. Family wasn't always just the folks who shared your blood.

Case in point, the faery beside me. Eli of Stonecroft was one of the people I trusted most in this world—or in any other. I closed my eyes for a moment, which I could do because he was at my side. I was tired constantly, so much so that only willpower kept me upright.

"Bonbon," Eli whispered. His worried tone made clear that a question or three hid in that absurd pet name. Was I going to be able to control my magic? Did he need to brace for *draugr* inbound? Were we good on time?

"It's good." I opened my eyes, muffled a yawn, and met his gaze. "I'm still fine."

Eli nodded, but he still scanned the graves. He was increasingly cautious since my near-brush-with-death a couple months ago. My partner stood at my side as we waited in the cemetery while the widow, her daughter, and two men spoke to their reanimated relative. Mr. Alphard Cormier was wearing a suit that was in fashion sometime in the last thirty years.

Why rouse him now? I don't know and wasn't asking.

"Twenty minutes," I called out. I could feel the sun coming; I'd always been able to do so—call it in an internal sundial, or call it bad genes. Either way, my body was attuned to the rising and falling of the sun.

"When he is entombed, we could--"

"No." I couldn't force myself to glance at him again. I was bone-tired, which made me more affectionate, and Eli was my weakness. Cut-glass features, bee-stung lips, and enough strength to fight at my side, even against *draugar*, Eli was built for fantasy. His ability to destroy my self-control was remarkable—and no, it wasn't because he was fae.

That part *was* why I wasn't going home with him. Trusting him, wanting him, caring for him, none of that was enough to overcome the complications of falling into his bed.

"Are you sure that's a good idea?" Mr. Cormier asked, voice carrying over the soft sobbing women.

The man with them handed Cormier something metallic.

I felt as much as saw the dead man look my way, and then his arm raised. Gun in hand. The relatives parted, and there was a dead man with a gun aimed at me.

"Fuck a duck." I darted to the side.

Eli was already beside me, hand holding his pretty bronze-coated sword that I hadn't even known he owned until the last month. "Geneviève?"

I jerked the magic away from Mr. Comier. It was my magic that made him stand, so I wasn't going to let him stand and shoot me.

REST, I ordered the dead man.

"I'm sorry, ma'am. They made me. Threatened my Suzette if I didn't . . ." His words faded as my shove of magic sent him back to his tomb.

I could hear the widow, presumably Suzette, sobbing.

"I do not believe those gentlemen are Mr. Cormier's relations." Eli glared in the direction of the men who had hired me to raise a dead man to kill me. They'd grabbed the two women and ducked behind mausoleums.

"Why?"

"They seem to want you dead, buttercream," Eli said. "If they were his family, that's an odd response."

A bullet hit the stone across from me. Shards of gravestone

pelted me. Oddly the adrenaline surge was welcome, even if the bullets weren't. Nothing like a shot of rage to get the sleepiness out.

"Not why *that*." I nodded toward the men who were staying crouched behind graves. "Why go through the hassle? Why not simply shoot me themselves?"

"Dearest, can we ponder that *after* they are not shooting at you?"

I felt my eyes change. As my rage boiled over, my eyes reflected it. They were my father's reptilian eyes, *draugr* eyes. The only useful thing he'd ever done was accidentally augment the magic I inherited from my mother. Unfortunately, the extra juice came with a foul temper—one that was even worse the last few weeks. After I'd been injected by venom, my moods were increasingly intense.

I wanted to rip limbs off.

I wanted to shove my thumbs into eye sockets and keep going until I felt brain matter.

Before the urges were more than images, I was moving from one spot to the next. I could *flow* like a *draugr*. I could move quickly enough that to the mortal eye it looked like teleportation. I *flowed* to the side of the shooter and grabbed his wrist.

Eli was not far behind. He didn't *flow*, but he was used to my movements and impulses. He had his sword to the shooter's throat a moment after I jerked the gun away from the man.

"Dearest?"

I concentrated on his voice, his calm, and I punched the other shooter rather than removing his eyes. Then I let out a scream of frustration and shoved my magic into the soil like a seismic force. With rage searing me, I felt a brief moment of alertness.

The dead answered. Dozens of voices answered my call. Hands reknitted. Flesh was regrown from the magic that flowed from my body into the graves. Mouths reformed, as if I was a sculptor of man.

"You do *not* wake the dead without reason," I growled at the now-unarmed man who dared to try to shoot me. *Here*, of all places. I stepped over the man I'd punched. I ignored the cringing, sobbing widow and the other woman who was trying to convince her mother to leave.

And I stalked toward the shooter in Eli's grip.

"Bonbon, you have a scratch." Eli nodded toward my throat.

"Shit." I felt my neck where Eli had indicated. I stepped closer to the shooter. "What were you thinking, Weasel Nuts?"

"Would you mind covering the wound?" Eli asked, forcing me to focus.

His voice was calm, but we both knew that I could not shed blood in a space where graves were so plentiful. I'd accidentally bound two *draugr* so far, and blood was a binding agent in necromancy. Unless I wanted to bring home a few reanimated servants, my blood couldn't spill here. I had to focus. And I didn't need an army of undead soldiers.

"Take this." Eli pulled off his shirt with one hand, using the other hand to keep the sword to Weasel Nuts' throat. He pressed the blade just a bit. "And, I believe you need to answer my lady."

I shot Eli a look--his *lady*? What year did he think this was?-- but I pressed his shirt against my throat. I did not, absolutely did *not*, take a deep breath because the shirt smelled like Eli or struggle to keep my gaze off his chest. Eli's body could make statues of Grecian gods scurry off in shame.

Eli smiled as I took another quick extra breath.

"Thou shalt not suffer a witch to live." Weasel Nuts spat in my direction. "Foul thing."

I opened my mouth to reply, but Eli removed his sword blade and in a blink turned it so he could bash the pommel into the man's mouth.

Weasel Nuts dropped to his knees, and this time when he spat, he spat out his own teeth and blood.

"Geneviève, would you be so kind as to call the police?" Eli motioned toward the women. "And escort the ladies away from this unpleasant man?"

It sounded chivalrous—or chauvinistic—but it was an excuse. I needed to get my ass outside the cemetery before I dripped blood. I needed to be focused and away from here. Eli had provided a way to do so gracefully.

"Ladies?" Eli said, louder now. "Ms. Crowe will walk you toward the street."

The women came over, and the widow flinched when my gaze met hers. My *draugr* eyes unnerved people.

But then she straightened her shoulders and stared right into my reptilian eyes as if they were normal. "I do apologize, Ms. Crowe. They have an accomplice who is holding my grandson as a hostage. We had to cooperate."

My simmering temper spiked, keeping my exhaustion away and my focus sharp.

I stared at the women. With my grave sight, I saw trails of energy, the whispers of deaths, and the auras of anything living. These women were afraid, but not evil. They were worried.

The older woman grabbed the fallen gun and ordered, "Walk."

For a moment, I thought I'd been wrong, but she pointed the barrel at the man who had shot at me. "You. Get up."

Her daughter smiled. "Would you mind helping us, Ms. Crowe?"

Eli and I exchanged a look. We were in accord, as usual. He bowed his head at them, and then scooped the unconscious man up.

In a strange group, we walked toward the exit.

As we were putting the unconscious attacker in the trunk of the Cadillac the women had arrived in, the sun rose, tinting the sky as if it was a watercolor painting. I paused, wincing. Sunlight wasn't my friend. It might trap young *draugr*, but it made my head throb if I was out in too much of it. I slid on the dark sunglasses I carried for emergencies.

"It was nice to see Daddy," the younger woman said quietly to her mother. "I wish it had been closer to Christmas, but still . . . it was nice."

The widow motioned for the other prisoner to get into the trunk. Once he did, Eli slammed the trunk, and the widow squeezed her daughter's hand. "It was."

The daughter handed Eli the keys. She was shaken by the shooting, and I was bleeding from the shattering stone from the shooting. Neither of us were in great shape to drive. However, it wasn't great for Eli to be trapped in a hulking steel machine. Faeries and steel weren't a good mix.

"I'll drive my car," he said, popping the trunk and grabbing a clean shirt. Working with me meant carrying an assortment of practical goods—clean clothes, duct tape, a sword, zip ties, and first aid supplies.

I tried not to sigh that he was now dressed fully again. Don't get me wrong. I respect him, but that didn't mean I wasn't prone to lustful gazes in his direction. If he minded, I'd stop.

He walked to the passenger door and opened it. "Come on, my peach pie."

The widow drove her Caddy away as I slid into the luxurious little convertible that had been fae-modified for Eli.

"Are you well enough to do this?" Eli asked as he steered us into the morning light.

"One human." I kept my eyes closed behind my sunglasses, grateful for the extra dark tint of his windows. I rarely needed sleep for most of my life, but lately I was always ready for a nap. Not yet, though. I assured Eli, "I'm fine to deal with this."

So we set out to retrieve the young hostage. We didn't discuss my near constant exhaustion. We didn't talk about the fear that my near-death event had left lingering issues for my health. We would have to, but . . . not now.

We arrived at a townhouse, and I *flowed* to where the captor held a smallish boy. *Flowing* wasn't a thing I typically did around regular folk, but there were exceptions.

The boy was duct taped to a chair by his ankles.

The captor, another man about the age of the two in the trunk, was laughing at something on the television. If not for the gun in his lap and the duct tape on the boy's ankles, the whole thing wouldn't seem peculiar.

When the man saw us, he scrambled for his gun.

So, I punched the captor and broke the wrist of his gun-holding arm.

Eli freed the boy, who ran to his family as soon as they came into the house.

"Best not to mention Ms. Crowe's speed," Eli said to the women as we were leaving.

The younger one nodded, but she was mostly caught up in holding her son. The widow looked at me.

"Not all witches are wicked, dear." She patted my cheek, opened her handbag and pulled out a stack of folded bills. "For your time."

"The raising was already paid," I protested.

"I took it from them," she said proudly. She shook it at me insistently. "Might as well go to you. Here."

Eli accepted a portion of the money on my behalf. He understood when it was an insult not to and when to refuse because the client couldn't afford my fees.

Honestly, I felt guilty getting paid sometimes. Shouldn't I work for my city? Shouldn't I help people with these skills? But good intentions didn't buy groceries or pay for my medical supplies. That's as much what Eli handled as having my back when bullets or unwelcome dead things started to pop up.

After we walked out and shoved the third prisoner in the trunk of the Cadillac, Mrs. Cormier said, "I'll call the police to retrieve them. Do you mind waiting?"

"I will wait," Eli agreed, not lying by saying we "didn't mind" because of course we minded. I was leaning on the car for support, and Eli never wanted me to be injured. If he had his way, he'd have me at his home, resting and cared for, but I was lousy at that.

So rather head than home, I stood in the street with Eli. If he was waiting for the police, so was I. I leaned on the side of the Cadillac, partly because it was that or sway in exhaustion. "I'll stay with you, too."

Once the widow went inside, Eli walked away and grabbed a first aid kit from his car. I swear he bought them in bulk lately. "Let me see your throat."

"I'm fine." Dried blood made me look a little garish, but I could feel that it wasn't oozing much now. "Just tired. Sunlight." I gestured at the bright ball of pain in the sky. Midwinter might be coming, but the sun was still too bright for my comfort.

Eli opened the kit, tore open a pouch of sani-wipes, and stared at me.

I sighed and took off my jacket. "You're being foolish."

He used sani-wipes to clean blood as I leaned on the Cadillac, ignoring the looks we were getting from pedestrians. Maybe it was that he was cleaning up my blood, or that he was fae, or that there were people yelling out from the trunk.

It, obviously, should not be arousing to have him clean a cut in my neck from grave shards because someone was firing bullets at me, but . . . having his hands on me at all made my heart speed.

"Would you like to take the car?" Eli was closer than he needed to be, hips close enough that it would be easier to pull him closer than push him away.

"And go where?"

He brushed my hair back, checking for more injuries. The result was that I could feel his breath on my neck. "Drive home, and draw a bath or shower. I'll stay here and . . ."

"Tempting," I admitted with a laugh. He had both a marble rainfall shower and the largest tub I'd ever seen. It came complete with a small waterfall. "I've had fantasies about that waterfall."

"As have I."

I pressed myself against him, kissed his throat, and asked, "Ready to call off the engagement?"

He kissed me, hand tangled in my hair, holding me as if I would run.

I'd sell my own soul for an eternity of Eli's kisses if I believed in such bargains, but I wouldn't destroy him. Being with me wasn't what was best for him.

When he pulled back from our kiss, he stated, "Geneviève . . ."

I kissed him softly. I could say more with my touch than with words. I paused and whispered, "You can have my body *or* this engagement. Not both."

He sighed, but he stepped back. "You are impossible, Geneviève Crowe."

I caught his hand. "It doesn't have to be impossible. We're safely out of *Elphame* now. We could just end the enga--"

"I am fae, love. I don't lie. I don't break my word." He squeezed my hand gently. "I gave you my promise to wed. In front of my king and family. I cannot end this engagement."

We stood in silence for several moments. Then he held out his keys, and I took them.

"Meet me at my place. Maybe we can spar," I offered.

Eli pulled me in closer, kissed both of my cheeks, and said, "I will accept any excuse to get sweaty with you."

"Same." I hated that this was where we were, but I wasn't able to change who or what I was. Neither was Eli. He had a future that I wanted no part of, and I felt a duty to my city and friends. We had no future option that would suit both of us. I'd be here, beheading *draugr* and trying not to become more of a monster, and he would return to his homeland. There was no good compromise.

———

GET YOUR COPY IN NOVEMBER IN THE *UNDER A WINTER SKY* anthology with Grace Draven, Jeff Kennedy, and L. Penelope

or

Get a copy in JUNE 2021 as a single-story standalone.

HOW FAR WOULD YOU GO TO ESCAPE FATE?

In this prequel to the international bestselling WICKED LOVELY series, the Faery Courts collide a century before the mortals in *Wicked Lovely* are born.

Thelma Foy, a jeweler with the Second Sight in iron-bedecked 1890s New Orleans, wasn't expecting to be caught in a faery conflict. Tam can see through the glamours faeries wear to hide themselves from mortals, but if her secret were revealed, the fey would steal her eyes, her life, or her freedom. So, Tam doesn't respond when they trail thorn-crusted fingertips through her hair at the French Market or when the Dark King sings along with her in the bayou.

But when the Dark King, Irial, rescues her, Tam must confront everything she thought she knew about faeries, men, and love.

Too soon, New Orleans is filling with faeries who are looking for her, and Irial is the only one who can keep her safe.

Unbeknownst to Tam, she is the prize in a centuries-old fight between Summer Court and Winter Court. To protect her, Irial must risk a war he can't win--or surrender the first mortal woman he's loved.

Recent Work:

Cold Iron Heart (2020)

Pretty Broken Things (2020)

Unruly (2020)

Collections:

Tales of Folk & Fey (2019)

Dark Court Faery Tales (2019)

Bullets for the Dead (2019)

This Fond Madness (2017)

All Ages Fantasy Novel:

The Faery Queen's Daughter (2019)

Young Adult Novels with HarperTeen

Wicked Lovely (2007)

Ink Exchange (2008)

Fragile Eternity (2009)

Radiant Shadows (2010)

Darkest Mercy (2011)

Wicked Lovely: Desert Tales (2012)

Carnival of Secrets (2012)

Made For You (2013)

Seven Black Diamonds (2015)

One Blood Ruby (2016)

Faery Tales & Nightmares (short story collection)

Adult Fantasy for HarperCollins/Wm Morrow

Graveminder (2011)

The Arrivals (2012)

Picturebooks for Penguin

Bunny Roo, I Love You (2015)

Baby Dragon, Baby Dragon! (2019)

Bunny Roo and Duckling Too (2021)

All Ages Fantasy for Penguin

The Hidden Knife (2021)

Coauthored with K. L. Armstrong (with Little, Brown)

Loki's Wolves (2012)

Odin's Ravens (2013)

Thor's Serpents (2014)

Co-Edited with Kelley Armstrong (with HarperTeen)

Enthralled

Shards & Ashes

Co-Edited with Tim Pratt (with Little, Brown)

Rags & Bones

About the Author

Melissa Marr is a former university literature instructor who writes fiction for adults, teens, and children. Her books have been translated into twenty-eight languages and have been bestsellers internationally (Germany, France, Sweden, Australia, et. al.) as well as domestically. She is best known for the Wicked Lovely series for teens, *Graveminder* for adults, and her debut picture book *Bunny Roo, I Love You*.

In her free time, she practices medieval swordfighting, kayaks, hikes, and raises kids in the Arizona desert.

f facebook.com/MelissaMarrBooks
🐦 twitter.com/melissa_marr
g goodreads.com/melissa_marr

Praise for Melissa Marr's books:

PRAISE FOR THE WICKED LOVELY SERIES:

"Marr offers readers a fully imagined faery world that runs along-side an everyday world, which even non-fantasy (or faerie) lovers will want to delve into" --*Publisher's Weekly* (starred review)

"This is a magical novel... the first book in a trilogy that will guarantee to have you itching for the next installment." *Bliss*

"Fans of the fey world will devour this sequel to Wicked Lovely. Marr has created a world both harsh and lush, at once urban and natural." --*School Library Journal*

"Complex and involving." -*New York Times Book Review*

PRAISE FOR GRAVEMINDER:

"If anyone can put the goth in Southern Gothic, it's Melissa Marr. . . . She's also careful to ensure that the book's wider themes —how and if we accept the roles life assigns us, and what happens to us when we refuse them—matter to us as much as the multiple cases of heebie-jeebies she doles out..." —NPR.org

"Spooky enough to please but not too disturbing to read in bed."—*Washington Post*

"Dark and dreamy. . . . Rod Serling would have loved *Graveminder.* . . . Marr is not tapping into the latest horde of zombie novels, she's created a new kind of undead creature. . . . A creatively creepy gothic tale for grown-ups."—*USA Today*

"Plan ahead to read this one, because you won't be able to put it down! Haunting, captivating, brilliant!" —*Library Journal* (starred review)

"Marr serves up a quirky dark fantasy fashioned around themes of fate, free will—and zombies. . . . Well-drawn characters and their dramatic interactions keep the tale loose and lively." —*Publishers Weekly*

"The emotional dance between Rebekkah and Byron will captivate female readers. . . . Fantasy-horror fans will demand more." —*Kirkus Reviews*

"No one builds worlds like Melissa Marr." —Charlaine Harris, *New York Times* bestselling author of the Sookie Stackhouse series

"Welcome to the return of the great American gothic." —Del Howison, Bram Stoker Award-winning editor of *Dark Delicacies*

Acknowledgments

Thank you to the rattlesnake. No, really. If that snake hadn't rolled under my kayak with me, the book wouldn't exist. Realizing you have a snake in your hair? Bad. Realizing it was a rattlesnake? Worse. Getting bitten when you shove it away from your face? *No. Words. Left.*

The resulting insomnia led me to cope as I always do: writing. So, this book is dedicated to "Darius" the Diamondback Rattlesnake. (And no, of course, he didn't tell me his name. Ours was but a brief encounter, and the resulting "child" is this book.)

I rarely write with this side of my voice in a book. So, thank you to Molly Harper & Jeanette Battista for telling me it was okay to sound more smart-assed than normal. It took four years since that conversation when we were all jet-lagged in France headed to a writing colony with a disco ball shower, exploding faucets, and a nearly naked guy in a robe—but I let my smart-assed voice out finally.

Thank you to Kelley Armstrong, Jeaniene Frost, Jeanette Battista, Jennifer Windrow, and Sera Lewis for reading. (Yes, Sera is named after her. Sera, you & your family are and will always be dear to me.)

Thank you to my daughter, Asia, and my partner, Amber, for reading, edit notes, feeding me, and dawn "pandemic exercise" adventures to hike or kayak when I wasn't exposed to any other humans.

Thank also to Yasmine Galenorn, Anthea Sharp, Kate Danley, Diana Pharaoh Francis. Kasey Mckenzie, Dannika Dark, Debra Dunbar, Annie Bellet, and Jeffe Kennedy. So much wisdom you've shared! And books to keep me sane-is during quarantine.

Thank you to everyone who beta read, especially Janae Chapman, Kismet Scott, Cassie Christensen, Amanda Gibson, Brooke Brennan, and Shannon Johnson!

CPSIA information can be obtained
at www.ICGtesting.com
Printed in the USA
JSHW051104200722
27940JS00002BA/12/J